PHOTOGRAPHS AND SOUVENIRS

Patrick T. Leahy

Copyright © 2016 Patrick T. Leahy
All rights reserved.

ISBN: 1539859983
ISBN 13: 9781539859987

*In memory of Arthur and Stella Leahy; and for my brother, Don,
And my children Dan, Tom and Maureen –
And Aggie.*

SEPTEMBER, 1946

1

Stella's feet burned in her new high heels, she'd been standing in them so long in rehearsals. The Governing Board would want to be the first to know what happened, but right now Stella couldn't get home fast enough to break the news to Art. She hurried up the aisle under the dim houselights, then just off the foyer ducked into the ladies' room to check for blood blisters. There weren't any to speak of, so she freshened up her lipstick, dabbed on a little rouge, and left her nylons off. Funny how one moment you're wondering how you'll make it through just one more scene without screaming, the next how much better your legs look without stockings. She knew just how to make Art notice, too. She had so much to tell him, it was eating her alive. Her eyes came up in the mirror like he was coming home to her the way he used to in the old days, before she'd learned to pray that he would walk in sober enough to give a damn.

That morning, just going out the door, Art had told the boys that he would definitely be home before dark, leaving time enough to hit a few and play some catch before it got too dark to see the ball, as though he hadn't sworn the same thing to them yesterday. Last night they'd waited for him clear through dinner, and were about to get up from the table when he stumbled in half-stiff, cursing at whatever made him falter in the kitchen doorway - that goddamn hinge on his leg, gone haywire again. Neither Lou nor Joe said anything like,

'Where've you been, Dad?' They never had any censure for him, no matter what. At school they would brag, any chance they got, that their dad walked every bit as good on his artificial leg as Herbert Marshall in the movies.

Stella hurried across the street to where she'd left the top down on the car, and got in slipping on her new dark glasses. It was that hour when she knew she'd have to plough through choking traffic up on Colorado Boulevard. She swung off El Molino just as the light blinked red and left her stalled behind two other cars caught in the crosswalk. When at last the green flashed, nobody moved, and she sat there in that smell like bleach the smog brought out on her skin while the warm breeze, with its scent of acorns, brushed her shoulders. There up ahead a young soldier came out from under the *Academy's* marquee. He looked up and down the street, then stepped out smartly toward the curb. Suddenly he began to wave, and Stella looked around for the cab he must be trying to flag down, but then saw he was staring straight at her. Behind her in the rear-view mirror a woman in a sunburned little Plymouth sat rigidly with a death-grip on the wheel. Cars ahead began to move, and as Stella ground gears, shifting into first, she saw the eyes of the boy in uniform still glued to her and she thought, why me? Pretty soon he'd see she wasn't really all that young. She telegraphed a helpless face to him with eyes that pleaded no, you've got the wrong gal, soldier. But he was waving now to beat the band, and gee, he wasn't that bad looking, either. Who did he think she was? The blonde in the convertible that made him somebody she could get away with pulling over to the curb for, saying, 'Hi, Joe! Goin' my way?' She saw herself again with Betty in the ladies' room at Ciro's, flushed with her success in *I Wake Up Screaming*. There at the next washbowl Betty said, 'You ever want to take the plunge, honey, all I can say is Stanwyck, Garson – eat your hearts out.' Stella felt so giddy, now, she couldn't bear to leave that young guy high and dry, and twiddled fingers at him as she passed. He gawked and slapped his knees and then he was behind her. She felt a swelling in her heart and took a breath, hearing herself tell Art: 'Guess what,

Art! This GI on the street mistook me for – oh, I don't know . . .' No, they were beyond that kind of kid stuff. If that was what she had to do to make him jealous, no thanks.

Here came her turnoff onto Allen Avenue, and she began to take it slow, now, passing Luther Burbank Elementary, and the lonely, dusty desert shade that fell upon the columns like a touch of Egypt stolen from the fading evening light.

A choking tightness came into her throat as she swung onto Morslay, then geared down under the pepper tree to get a good run up the hill. Way up there you could see the broad relentless shadow climbing past the firebreaks toward the dull glint on the dome atop Mt. Wilson. She turned between the two old lofty palms into the driveway with a pounding heart.

Art's car wasn't there. She parked and tried to make herself believe he'd be along, then shut the motor off and listened for the boys – their voices in the house, Coy's barking to get out. The pink and pale yellow light across the lawn crept into the quiet of her Camellias under the last bright gasp of the sun against the patio wall. Now she could hear the lumbering trombone footfalls of The Fat Man on the radio. They must be in there listening to the last of their serials, she thought.

She sat there slumped and sinking into Art's excuses. Why was it that she never thought he'd gone off the road, slammed into some pileup on the freeway, was being loaded into an ambulance all banged up? She only saw him on a stool in the Black Cat, pushing his glass across to the bartender's tired prescription, 'One more for the road, Art?' She yanked up on the brake, got out and marched up the walk toward the patio gate.

The French doors to the boys' room stood ajar. She heard the Fat Man talking to somebody on the radio, pulled the door wide open and stepped in.

"Hey, you guys're letting in the -"

There was an air of being laughed at by the deserted room. The Fat Man's dulcet voice purred, 'Don't touch that purse, Madame. It wouldn't be at all wise. If you have anything to say, be kind enough to say it from the distance of that chair behind you.'

Stella went over to the radio, switched it off and called out, "Lou! Joe!" The refrigerator hummed and rattled back around the corner in the pantry. She tried to put the boys both in a safe place in her mind: they'd left in such a hurry, dropping everything. That door left open, forgetting to shut off the radio. Where in the world . . .?

She walked around the corner into the hallway, went down as far as the telephone alcove where she'd told them, once, to leave a note if they ever had to. There wasn't any note. But then why would they leave one if they didn't expect to be out after dark?

She thought a moment. That was it! They must have gone up the street to Toby and Roberta's. By five o'clock this afternoon Toby was supposed to blow himself up with his new Chemistry Set. His big sister, Roberta, wanted to prove that he was too little to have one: 'Can you believe a chemistry set in the hands of that little twerp? Wait'll Mom and Dad come home and see all the windows blasted clean out of our whole house! He'll get it good if he's still alive! Come on up after school tomorrow and see!'

Stella looked at her watch: 5:39. Suddenly she remembered what she'd told herself last night she had to do today, or else. That call she had to put in to her father, preferably without Art listening in.

For days she'd tried to get through, but nobody ever answered. Her father had to know what he'd be in for if he went through with his plans to drive down tomorrow. Aunt Ellen had flat refused to come another time: 'It's on my calendar, dear. Stanley's got the car all tuned up and greased, and I won't hear of canceling.' Now at the eleventh hour Stella could hear her father backstabbing his old enemy: 'But honey, I'm your father! I won't be put on hold by that cantankerous old sodbuster.'

Stella picked up the phone and asked the operator for long distance to Lompoc. The bell rang and rang. She was about to hang up when the fussy contralto she knew so well clucked breathlessly, "Hel-looo!"

"Toots?"

"Clara MacPherson speaking. Who's calling, please?"

"It's me, Stella. I've been trying for days to –"

"Could you hold the line a moment, dear? I smell my cobbler spilling over in the oven!"

Stella listened to the clanking and the screeching of the oven grates while Toots took her own sweet time away from the phone. Finally:

"There! We picked so many berries yesterday along the road back from the mission, I said to your father, this is too good to be true! So plump and ripe and it's almost October, no less! I had to use *two* tins, not the one I'd thought we could get away with. Now what can I do for you, dear? How've you been getting along? How're the boys?"

"We're all fine. Is Daddy home?"

"He left for the Bar Z quite early this morning."

"Well, what time do you expect him home?"

"I don't. Not tonight, dear."

"You mean . . .? But he'll be checking in with you, won't he?"

"Whatever for? He doesn't do that sort of thing – go out of his way to make unnecessary telephone calls."

Stella wished she was there to stare the lie off Toots' smug face.

"Well, if he does call and it's not too late, tell him to ring me right away. There's no use his coming down tomorrow. He's got to postpone."

"Postpone? Why?"

"I won't have time to be with him the way we'd planned. We're in very important rehearsals with *King Lear*. I've got a new girl in the role of Cordelia. She's marvelous."

"Rehearsals? You know you might have warned your father about this earlier. He's going to have his feelings hurt."

"I doubt it. I'm sure we can work around that," Stella said.

Toots vented a sigh like she was looking for her breath on the mouthpiece.

"I suppose you know your own mind, dear."

Stella thought suddenly of Toots and her father in bed together, the night they made Eddie. How much her father must have had to set aside for the dead girl who would never return to hear him say that he had loved her so much better.

"Toots, listen. Don't you think Dad will have to stop by the house before he starts out for my place in the morning?"

"I have no idea. I seriously doubt it. In fact no, that's out of the question. Your father made a point of telling me before he left, I'm going straight on from the ranch to Stella's. The reason I remember is I reminded him to pack those two pairs of cowboy boots for the boys. What's more I sent along some of my peach preserves that the boys just couldn't get enough of last summer."

"If I remember right, there's a telephone up at the Bar Z. Could you let me have that number, Toots?"

"That phone is out of order," Toots stated.

"Yes, but Toots – Dad and I have some serious matters to talk over. I don't want to be pressed for time and have to divide my attention between him and other things. It's really just a simple matter of getting through to him, so he can put off this trip until some other time."

"Ah, yes – other things. Would one of them be Ellen Havercroft?"

"Aunt Ellen?"

"Don't be coy with me, dear. I know what's going on. Those two haven't set eyes on one another other since our steak feed in '43, when nobody but Louis Calderon ate any mutton. Poor Louis was so sure the young folks would follow suit. Nobody ever cares for mutton when there's so much beef to be had."

Stella played a hunch and said, "What's Dad doing up at the Bar Z, anyway?"

"We're getting ready for this year's picnic, you know. Your father's contributing a whole steer. God only knows how many sheep the Bradley people will slaughter. Too many, if your Aunt Ellen has her way."

"Listen, Toots – I really have to talk to Dad. Tell him to call me as soon as he comes in, okay? Or if he happens to call you, pass along my message. Will you do that for me?"

"You know when you were little, Stella, I was Clara to you. Don't you remember? I liked that - your calling me Clara."

"I wasn't aware of that," Stella lied.

"Thanks to your Aunt Ellen, your father's term of endearment for me caught on, quite inappropriately. You may not know that Ellen was the one who *insisted* on taking charge of your upbringing. I had nothing to say about it. Just like now, she's lobbying against your father on the matter of this deed for the acreage your mother left you. I daresay Ellen was the one who advised your mother to set aside, quite unnecessarily and *uselessly* in my opinion, a plot of grazing land for a girl who'd never in a million years have any use for it."

"It's a little more than a plot, Toots."

"Of course it is. That's what I mean - as if there was going to be anything in your Mills education to prepare you for a life of punching cattle. You may think I'm speaking out of turn, here, but I'm of the opinion it's high time your father and Ellen had it out. Let them do battle in the open, fair and square. Clear the air once and for all."

"Not in my house," Stella said.

Stella thought she heard Toots swallow.

"Have you been drinking, Stella?"

"You won't tell Daddy on me, will you?"

There was a muted choking sound. Back on the line Toots' voice rose shrilly.

"I understand Arthur has taken Ellen's side. He'd like to see you cling to that land you never will do one blessed thing with. His motives? Well, that's not for me to say. Ellen is the one who's stirring the pot, here. Gathering allies for her plotting against your father, with no regard whatever for the effect that may have on your marriage. Here we go again - the sodbusters and the cowpunchers shooting it out."

"I never said, exactly, that I was against Dad's –"

"You might just as well prepare for the worst, dear. I can't possibly get in touch with him tonight."

"You could give me that telephone number."

"Didn't I *tell* you that phone is out of order? I'd hate to think you're trying to make me out a liar, dear. Me, who's always had your best interests at heart. Now I'd better get my cobblers out of the oven. You be sure and pass along my love to the boys now, won't you? Give them each a kiss and tell them where it came from."

"They'll be thrilled with your peach preserves."

"I never do a batch that I haven't got those boys in mind."

"Goodbye, Clara," Stella said with a strange pang of feeling for Toots' clumsy escape from the child who hadn't really liked her from the start, and she lowered the phone into the cradle slowly, drifting in her mind toward how it was going to be tomorrow, as if she herself had arranged for the collision course between her father and Aunt Ellen, and wouldn't that make Art's day.

A dog began to bark at the back door. Coy wanted to come in. The boys might be with her, coming home. She hurried back through the kitchen and the pantry to the back door.

2

Lou was fed up trying to talk Joe into dying. He'd got him dead to rights, but Joe kept right on running clear across to Mr. Crutchley's lawn and then behind the hedge, yelling, "Too bad, GI! Better luck next time! Come and get me!"

Lou huddled in the trench with his useless, empty .45 that suddenly looked like what it was – a water pistol. Joe had no respect. You couldn't tell him when he made his break for it across the field, slowed down by their mother's riding boots, that he made a sitting duck. The smart-aleck Kraut was bullet-proof. The gopher hole he'd stumbled into didn't go off like the mine it was supposed to be. There was no use telling Joe he couldn't run around like Captain Marvel on a real battlefield, which this was.

From behind the hedge Joe taunted, "Whatsa matter, GI! Haven't got the guts?"

Lou looked up at the dusky sky, then at the copper glint of the late sun on Mr. Crutchley's second story window. Pretty soon, now, they'd have to call it quits. He poked his head up over the top of the parapet, eyes skimming the foxtails. All at once it came to him. He reached for a clump of foxtails, pulled and out came the Bangalore Torpedo, trickling clods and dirt. He quickly stuffed the weed end into his back pocket.

"Okay, Kraut, I'm all out of ammo! I'm gonna surrender! Don't shoot!"

Lou could see the movements of Joe's freckled face and sheep-dog's bangs through the holes in the hedge.

"Don't try any fast ones!" Joe warned. "Start walkin' toward me, real slow – and get rid of the gun!"

Lou dropped his .45, held up both empty hands and started walking. Joe swung his Tommy-gun around the hedge into the open.

"Where's your gun?"

"In the trench! I'm unarmed!"

"Okay, turn around and keep those hands up in the air!"

"Darn it, Joe, are you gonna take me prisoner, or what?"

"Don't call me Joe! I'm Sergeant – y'know – Heinie! Just shut up and keep on walkin'! One false move . . .!"

Lou stopped to look up, squinting, as if there was a bogey screaming down from 12 o'clock to level out at strafing altitude.

"Sorry, Joe, but somebody's lookin' down at you from Mr. Crutchley's window!"

Joe whirled, searching crazily for the face in the window. Lou tore the grenade out of his back pocket, and the movement cranked Joe's head around and then his eyes bugged out and he took off running straight up onto Mr. Crutchley's front walk. Lou didn't wait. He cocked his arm and flung the grenade with all his might. It sailed over Joe's head, shot between two hanging plants in Mr. Crutchley's porch and slammed into the big bay window with a loud thump.

Joe gaped at the dusty smudge on the glass.

"God almighty, Lou! Let's get out of here!"

Lou ran up beside Joe, they stood together in this sudden wreck made of their skirmish among the hedgerows of Normandy.

"No, we've gotta tell them it was us."

"But why?" Joe pleaded. "It could of been a bird."

"A bird with dirt for guts?"

"We're gonna get it, Lou. Mom's gonna kill us."

"Are you coming with me, or aren't you?"
"Where?"
"Up there! I'll knock to see if anybody's home."
"But Lou – we never did it on purpose."
"So what? You want them to look out the window and see us running away?"

Joe searched his brother's face.

"Okay," he said miserably, "go ahead."
"What're you gonna do?"
"I'll stay down here and keep a lookout."
"Lookout for what?"
"I don't know! I'm stayin' here!"

Lou left Joe there at the foot of the steps and climbed up onto to the Crutchleys' cool, shady porch, where ivy clung to the sides of the adobe wall and Mexican planters hung, weeping with Sweet Peas and Begonias. He reached up for the heavy brass knocker and banged it, hard, four times, then listened for noises inside - the creaking of footfalls, a thump or anything that sounded like a person in there. Joe said in a voice that wished his brother deaf:

"You hear anybody coming, Lou?"
"Not yet. They might be upstairs."
"Nobody's home. I say we get out of here right now. Look how dark it's getting. Dad's gonna wonder where we are?"

Lou looked back into the street, saw that the streetlights hadn't yet come on.

"Lemme try the doorbell."

Joe rolled his eyes, moaning, "Jeez, what are we? A couple of Fuller Brush men?"

Lou pressed the button. Inside the muted chimes ding-donged musically. They stood there, listening. Lou shuffled his shoes around on the mat. Finally Joe pressed his clenched fists down along his pockets, stomped one foot and pleaded, "Nobody's home, Lou! I'm tellin' you, the longer we stay here, the worse it's gonna be! We're just askin' for it!"

"Okay, okay." Lou stepped back off the mat. "If only we had a pencil and a piece of paper."

"You mean sign our names to that gosh darn window?"

"Never mind, it doesn't sound like anybody's home." Lou started down the steps.

Behind him a latch clunked, the big ornately carved front door swung open and Lou turned to see a tall, good-looking young man standing in the doorway, staring out at them inquisitively. He looked to be about six feet two or so, with arms bulging in his white T-shirt that showed off more muscles across his big, broad chest. His blond hair, spiked on top, was cut short.

"Hello there," he said. "Sorry, I was upstairs reading."

The quiet of his smile drew Lou into his limpid blue eyes, oddly familiar for a man they'd never set eyes on before, as if he'd been expecting them. Lou started slowly back up the steps. Joe made a move to go up, too, but then withdrew his foot and stayed there on the walk.

"Yes, sir," Lou said. "We're sorry to disturb you, but - well, there's been an accident."

The young man's eyes came up sharply, grew suddenly alert as he peered out on the street.

"Out there?"

"Oh, no," Lou said. "What happened was - me and my brother, here, we were playing on your lot. I mean I don't know if it's yours, but –"

"The lot?"

"Yes, sir." Lou pointed. "The vacant lot, there."

The young man glanced out across the hedge, nodding as if his comprehension of the lot was just as vacant as Lou said it was.

"Oh, yeah. I used to play out there myself. You'd think somebody would've put a house up on it by now."

Lou stared at the young man, wondering when he would begin to care about all this mess out on his porch, the print of exploded dust right there on his window.

"Well, anyway, sir - I ran out of ammunition, so I pulled up a grenade. I meant to hit my brother with it, but it went wild and hit your window, there." Lou pointed at the marred glass.

The young man stepped out onto the porch. He came around and stood back a little from the window, examining the dirt stuck to the glass and the clods spilled onto the sill, as if the work of a renowned painter hung there in which, for the life of him, he couldn't find the slightest merit.

"I see what you mean." The reserve in the young man's voice sounded like he was holding out for somebody else's opinion before he could form one of his own. Lou said hurriedly:

"If you could let us use your broom, we'll clean up all this mess right now, sir."

The young man looked down at him and said, "No need to call me sir."

Lou nodded, feeling his smile strangely out of control. He didn't know exactly who this young man was. He had a pretty fair idea, and his presence, all flesh and blood at last, was not disfigured by the war.

"Well, anyway," Lou said, "if you could let us use your broom –"

The young man shrugged.

"Oh, I wouldn't get too exercised about this. Heck, the birds around here do a lot worse damage to that window all the time."

Lou smiled at the young man's grin and said, "You're Tank, aren't you? My brother and me, here, we heard you were in the war."

"Is that so?" the young man said. "Word gets around, doesn't it?"

Down on the walk Joe said, "We heard you've got a real neat motorcycle, too."

They'd heard it from Dorothy next door, that Tank Crutchley was twenty-some years old, had been a football star in high school, and rode around on a red and silver Indian motorcycle that his father had kept polished up for him during the three years he had been away in the South Pacific. So this was Tank, Lou thought.

Joe lifted a foot up onto the first step.

"The lady we live next to said you got a Purple Heart, too."

"Well, a lot of us guys did who, you know . . ." Tank trailed off, leaving the rest for them to fill in. Probably he didn't want to brag, Lou thought. He didn't look at all like the kind of a person who showed off.

"Did you bring back any flags or guns or – you know, anything like that back from the war?" Joe pursued.

Tank pursed his lips as if considering how to phrase a reply.

"No flags, but a couple swords, some guns –"

"Wow! Swords?" Joe reared up straight. "You mean those real wicked ones the Japs used to – those?"

"That's right, Samurai." Tank nodded, glancing at his watch. He gave the band a twist, "If you guys've got a couple minutes, I'll let you see them and some of the other stuff I brought back. I mean if you haven't got anything else to do."

Joe's eyes lit with excitement. Glancing at Lou he said, "We've got time enough, don't we, Lou?"

Trying to contain his own excitement, Lou said, "Do you think your father would mind if we – well, maybe sometime – played with your guns?"

"Yeah!" Joe exulted. "What kind are they, Tank? You mean real Jap guns?"

"Yes, but playing with them – that's something we'd have to –" Tank didn't have a chance to get the rest out, for just then tires licked the driveway, a car bounced off the street bringing Victor Crutchley's heavy two-tone Packard to a stop, inches from the garage door. Lou stared at the car as if a couple of policemen sat grimly inside. One would get out, dangling handcuffs and demanding, 'All right, which one of you did it?'

"Oh, shoot," Tank said, "Here's Dad. I haven't even gone out to the store for those doggone pork chops."

The car door swung open, and Lou watched Mr. Crutchley get out as if from a safe distance, through binoculars. He'd never seen him this close up before - the piercing dark blue eyes and pencil-line mustache of the redoubtable Editor-in-Chief of the Pasadena Star-News, who'd just as soon glare a hole through your head as pat you on the back pretending kids were anything but disturbers of the peace. He was so small, too, you wouldn't think that he could be the father of a man as big as Tank. Bald to boot, with just a band of closely cropped dark hair around his ears. The two big things that stood out about him were that, one, he always left his porch light off on Halloween; and two, he didn't care one bit for General Douglas MacArthur, who'd gone way too far, he thought, helping the Japs back onto their feet after what they'd done to us in the war.

Mr. Crutchley came around his bumper and shuffled up onto the grass, the cuffs of his trousers flopping across immaculately shined wing-tips. A bad dream, Lou thought. Just as it looked like Mr. Crutchley was about to run right into Joe, he raised his face and gave him a blistering look, then turned the same scowl on Tank who now stood at the balustrade and was leaning over it lazily, with a faintly sheepish smile, ready-made to widen when his father got around to looking at him.

"Okay, Tank," Mr. Crutchley snarled, "why don't you tell me what the hell is going on, here?"

"Nothing much, Dad," Tank said breezily. "There's been a little accident. You see, these boys –"

"I know who they are. As a matter of fact I'm good friends with their parents." He said it, Lou thought, like they were a couple of dogs he'd petted once.

"Yes, Dad - but what I'm trying to say is –"

Mr. Crutchley blinked as if he was so tired, he had to shut his eyes, and he did, then the eyes came open with a start. He roughly brushed past Joe, stabbed his wing-tips onto the steps climbing up, then at the top he took a stance in the midst of the desecration of his porch. Tank said:

"You have to give the boys some credit, Dad. They came right to the door and told me all about what happened."

"Did they? Now *they* can tell me. Who wants to be first?"

Joe's mouth fell slack. Lou spoke up:

"We came over after school to play in the vacant lot, sir. After that—"

"D'you have permission to play in that lot?"

"Oh, we didn't really know if you owned it, sir."

"I *don't* own it. Nevertheless, do you think you can just take over a lot without getting permission from the real owner first?"

"We don't know who the real owner is, sir." Lou felt at a disadvantage with this hostile man. Still something made him want to stand up to the uneven odds.

"Somebody does, I would imagine," Mr. Crutchley said with wicked satisfaction.

Tank broke in, "Hey, don't you remember, Dad? We used to wonder that same thing when we'd go out there to toss the football around, and we thought maybe we could mow it so a couple of the guys and me could use it for a practice field. Who the heck does this darn field belong to? Remember how we used to think that?"

Mr. Crutchley gave Tank a long, suspicious look.

"I must have told you mowing it was out of the question. You don't go mowing a field like it's your own if it belongs to somebody else."

Tank shrugged.

"Maybe nobody owns it," he said.

"Now that's a fairly cockamamie idea, son. Nothing in this country belongs to nobody. Not since we settled all that business with the Indians." Mr. Crutchley strutted over to the window, smeared his hand down through the dust. He looked at his fingers, then reached down and daintily lifted from the windowsill a limp foxtail dangling the few small clods that still clung to the roots. "How did this thing get up here?"

Tank moved toward his father, took a stance between him and Lou.

"You know how boys get carried away, Dad. So they tossed a grenade a little wild and it landed up here. They never did it on purpose, *and*—they offered to sweep the porch and clean the glass. I took them up on that."

Mr. Crutchley surveyed the mess incredulously.

"I'm getting pretty tired of your doing all the talking here, Tank. These boys don't look deaf and dumb to me." Mr. Crutchley faced Lou. "How old are you now, anyway, young man?"

Lou didn't like Mr. Crutchley's tone, getting away with it because he was old. He liked less the expectation that, being a kid, he was supposed to take it.

"I'm twelve, sir."

"That would make your brother roughly ten. Am I correct on that, Joe?"

"Going on eleven," Joe said.

Mr. Crutchley took his time lighting a smirk.

"That hole you boys have been digging out there - trench or whatever you want to call it. What do you suppose the owner is going to think when he comes around to find his property riddled with trenches?"

"We only dug one, sir," Joe said.

Mr. Crutchley waved his hand and was about to speak when Tank said gently, "Dad, the whole time I was growing up, nobody ever came around to claim that lot. How come you've gotta be its caretaker?"

"Now that's very interesting, son. There is such a thing as helping thy neighbor. Ever hear of that? You can look it up in the Holy Bible if you need a reference."

"Shoot, Dad - you haven't cracked a Bible since before Mom died."

Turning red, Mr. Crutchley said flintily, "Don't you boys have something to do? Someplace to go?"

"Well, yes, sir," Lou said. "We're supposed to meet our dad to play a little ball before the sun goes down."

"Well, then – you better get a move on. I don't see much light left in the sky out here."

Tank raised one hand and said:

"I was about to take the boys up to the workshop when you rolled in, Dad. They wanted to see some of the souvenirs I brought home from Saipan."

For a moment Mr. Crutchley looked weighed down by some last straw, then all at once he said explosively, "You've got to be kidding! These boys just said they have to be home before dark. Plus they've got work to do before they leave."

"Listen, Dad – I can take care of this in two shakes. No skin off my teeth."

Mr. Crutchley tilted his head back in a hopeless swoon.

"I see. Doing these boys' work *for* them, is that it?"

"It's not like they came up here and emptied out a bag of dirt, Dad. If it's the principle of the thing, well heck, then –"

"Is that the way they taught you how to talk in the army? Sassing back?"

Tank glared at his father, he took a breath and sighed.

"Okay, you're right. It's getting late. I'll get the broom and the Windex. They can walk home in the dark."

Lou could hear in Tank's voice the anxiety to get away from his father; how cruelly the hulking, shining freshness of him got crushed by his father's prickling words. Words he didn't think the old man had a right to say to his own son who had paid dearly for his manhood out there in the mosquito-infested heat of terrible battles with a sneaky, ruthless enemy that never gave up; and with a wound to show for it, somewhere on his body. Tank didn't have to take it, Lou thought, and wondered why he didn't talk back even harder. He was so soft-spoken for a big, strong man who'd starred on the football team in high school, then gone away to war. But then why couldn't you be big and strong and gentle, too?

There was a trembling around Mr. Crutchley's lips. He shook his finger at Lou and Joe.

"From now on you boys keep your distance when you want to get into a hand grenade fight out on that lot. If this glass would've broken, believe you me, I wouldn't be going so easy on you." Mr. Crutchley leveled a scathing look on Tank. "Now excuse me while I go in and search the fridge for those pork chops you were supposed to bring home."

With a helpless gesture Tank looked at his father. Mr. Crutchley turned and marched toward the open doorway, muttering, "Just as I thought."

Watching his father quick-step into the house, Tank said confidentially, "Don't mind Dad. He's tired."

"We're sorry," Lou said.

"You guys better skedaddle, then. You don't want to be late."

Lou said, "Yeah," but he didn't want to go, yet. It felt like something had been left undone. "Maybe we could see your souvenirs some other time," he said.

"Well, let's see –" Tank laid a finger on his lower lip. "There's tomorrow, but boy - I've gotta get out looking for a job here pretty soon "

"We get out of school at two o'clock," Lou said.

Tank fingered his chin a while, glancing up and then back down again.

"Two o'clock. Dad doesn't get home until around five-thirty. Yeah, two sounds okay to me."

"Tomorrow or the next day?" Lou said.

Tank blinked and reached for his chin again.

"I don't see anything wrong with tomorrow. In fact I'll tell you what. I'll pick you guys up on my motorcycle. How does that sound? Have you guys ever ridden on a motorcycle?"

"No, sir!" Joe said excitedly.

"Well, then - d'you think it'd be okay with your folks?"

Lou and Joe searched each other's faces.

"I guess so," Lou said at last. "Yeah, I'm pretty sure."

"Okay," Tank said, clapping his hands together. "Tomorrow afternoon, then. Two on the nose, school parking lot."

"Yes, sir," said Joe, suddenly looking grave, as if he was the older for remembering to be respectful. Getting even for not dying when he should have, Lou thought.

Out on the street, halfway home, they kept on walking in silence. All at once Lou slowed down as if he meant to stop.

"What's the matter?" Joe said.

Lou picked up his pace again.

"We never shoulda' let Tank clean up after us. Mr. Crutchley's gonna get around to telling Mom. We'll be in real Dutch, then. *I* will, I mean."

"Heck, I'll tell Mom I did it if you want, Lou. I don't mind."

Lou felt a searing like a hot iron on the comfort of the way he almost always felt about his brother.

"Listen, we don't have to say anything to Mom, unless she asks us where we've been. Then you better not lie to her. You got it? I threw the darn thing, not you." Lou took off running at a loping gait for home.

"Wait up, Lou!"

Just as they made their yard and started down the walk to the back door, the streetlights behind them came on.

"We made it!" Joe cried.

Coy must have heard their voices. She came bounding around from the back by the fish pond, barking into the quiet of the coming night.

3

The boys were both asleep in bed when Stella heard the car. Light from the lamp beside her, by which she had been trying to keep her mind on *See here, Private Hargrove*, warmed her bare left shoulder, and she remembered now she hadn't turned on the patio light to make it easier for Art to see his way. She reached for the lamp, took back her hand and listened to him coming maybe in some besotted fear that he was in for it, this time.

The gate creaked, and in her mind she saw him planting his right shoe, swinging the artificial left leg. There was a loud screech on the flagstones. All at once Coy barked. Stella flung the covers back and trotted down the hall until she came into the doorway to the boys' room where the milky blue glow of a moon shone through the French doors and she could see Art feeling his way out there along the picnic table. With every reeling step he took she wanted to blend more into the concealing darkness. Joe in his bed moaned, "What's the matter, Mom?"

She went over and sat beside him, stroked his hair back from his forehead. "It's okay, honey. Your dad's home, that's all."

Across the room on the other bed where Lou lay fast asleep, Coy wagged her stubby tail. "Good girl," Stella whispered. She pulled the door shut softly and hurried back up the hallway to the bedroom.

Art came into the doorway, clearing his throat loudly.

"Still awake, eh, darlin'?"

"I guess so."

There was that crabbed attempt to keep his solemn mask on while his eyes crawled down the length of the black silk of her nightgown to her bare ankles crossed at the end of the bed. She said flintily:

"So how was the crowd out at the Black Cat?"

Art slumped heavily onto the bed beside her, lifting under the stump socket of the leg made by the company he worked for - Milikan's Miracle Plastic.

"You're not gonna believe this, but I got stuck with a client out in La Crescenta. I should've known I'd be in for trouble when he called his new leg a white man's contraption."

"He was a colored man?"

"No, no. Ogalala Sioux. Played football with the Carlyle Indians, '26 to '29. You could tell he'd been a damn fine athlete, too – at one time."

Art's voice fell back into the alibi, and she saw him in some distance, leaving all this behind. Walking along on two live legs, handsome as all get-out. She called to him, but he couldn't hear her for the future he was trying to reach before it pulled out. She would have to tell him later, just at the right moment, how much she had loved him as if, by then, the past was a reliable witness. She said:

"Yes, but – if he'd already paid for the leg –"

Art flung up one hand dismissively.

"He didn't want any part of all my demonstration crap. Forget the barbells and the football and the standing on one leg routine. Just leave the leg and the instruction booklet, he'd write me a check and I could take a powder."

"What took so long, then?"

"Well, I said now listen, pal - as soon as you're alone with the leg you might fall down and want your money back. Then who's the company gonna blame? He said tough shit, he'd take his chances. I told him now, how far do you think you're gonna drive on those white man's crutches, there? That shut him up a minute. Then he agrees to put on the leg if I'll take him out and teach him how to drive. So we go out to the garage and he climbs into his old Studie, and I proceed to show him how to plunge the weight of the leg down on the clutch, then help it back up while he's pressing on the gas. He backs out, and the motor doesn't die. Now he wants no part of my help on the way back into the house, like I'd just told him to go long for a touchdown. Inside he grabs a bottle of Ancient Age and starts to pour us both a snort. I tried to back out, but he says, now wait a minute, Art – are we on a first-name basis, here, or aren't we? You wouldn't want your boss to think you had something against drinking with a redskin, now would you?"

Stella saw the light in Art's bloodshot blue eyes, his waiting for her laughter. She said:

"You *know* what you just proved, don't you? You can still coach!"

"Stell, for Christ's sakes. What did I do but talk a guy into a leg who didn't want one?"

"That's win thinking, Art. The same as what you used to instill in young men on a football field. Still could, if you wanted to."

"I'm forty-four years old and haven't coached in fifteen years. Who'd hire me on a goddamn peg leg?"

Stella turned her book face down on the bed.

"Who'd guess an Indian behind the wheel of a car was wearing one?"

Art grinned, like a stranger who'd mistaken her for his best girl. It came up into her throat – the taste of bourbon, misspent on the shot she'd grabbed while she was fixing dinner. Before he could say anything she said:

"I've got something to tell you, honey."

He looked up sharply. So sharply he almost looked sober.

"Uh-oh. You wouldn't hit a guy while he's down."

She tossed her head with a one-sided playful smile.

"You know me a lot better than that. Get this, Art. This afternoon Louise just upped and quit! Peggy's got Cordelia back, and she's so tickled, I just – well . . ."

"What?" He looked at her darkly, on edge in the murky sightless pools of his bloodshot eyes.

"Oh, I don't know. I kind of felt like hell about it. I never tried too hard to make Louise feel welcome."

"Were you supposed to?"

"Morrie wanted her so bad to play Cordelia, he said we'd bill her like she still had star-power, then let her looks take it from there."

"She hasn't been Miss Glendale Bathing Beauty since 1938. Starlets don't last much past the night some charitable producer tells them they can act."

"Morrie assured Louise that Cordelia's total stage time didn't hardly amount to six or eight minutes, so she shouldn't sweat it. Most of her presence would be symbolic, offstage. Then when she did come on, heck, with a body like that, who's gonna care if she's old enough to be Cordelia's mother?"

"Try Monroe Lathrop in the *Express*, or Edith Isaacs for her *Theatre Arts Monthly*. She's been known to break the careers of titillating ingénues like dry twigs. And Morrie's willing to let you take the heat? Shit, when did he get to be such a big man? All those DA, flatfoot, judge and sheriff roles he's got sewed up at MGM must have gone to his big head."

It's not that, Art. We've been friends for so darn long, and after all – he did agree to take on Lear for free. You said yourself that Morrie's *Lear* gives Barrymore a run for his money."

"Yeah, but darlin' - who's the director here? You or Morrie?"

Stella fell back, sighing. There was a feel of being in the ring with him, but they were shadow boxing, sparring. He pulled every punch he threw, and it wasn't just because she was a woman.

"I know, I know. I should've stood up to him that first day he waltzed in with Louise. For Peggy's sake, if not the play. She ran off covering her face, and Morrie sloughed it off, like what's her problem if she gets to stick around as Louise's understudy? I don't know why I didn't tell him off, right then and there."

Art laid his hand lightly on her knee.

"He's had the hots for Louise ever since she handed Dennis O'Keefe his hat in '*Hold that Kiss.*'"

She looked at his hand. She was afraid of lifting her eyes up into his.

"I guess he counted on my backing down," she said. "What're friends for?"

"Don't beat yourself up, darlin'. It'll all come out in the wash. I mean hell – you're not dancing on Louise's grave."

It was as if he'd said 'You know how much I love you, don't you?' And a wave swelled in her heart, carrying him from somewhere long ago where she had lost him. She knew him, crashing at her feet, and felt the dangerous waters churning up around them. She said lightheartedly:

"Well anyway, poor Louise is gone. You should see Peggy, now. I'm telling you, that girl was just *born* to play Cordelia."

"Like I was born to play Carlotta?"

"You did fool the whole darn student body back then, didn't you?"

"Almost got away with it, until this little prick in my fraternity blew the whistle."

"That was a blessing in disguise. Howard Troutman said he'll see your name in lights on Broadway."

"D'you think I would have made it?"

Stella smiled wistfully.

"You know for a while there, I thought about giving Cordelia's role a whirl myself."

"*You* play Cordelia?"

"I know – me and Louise both. But there's just something about Cordelia, like she's me when I was a girl around that age. She'd let me do things and say things I always wanted to, but never did."

"Like give your good ol' dad a piece of your mind?"

"Oh, I tried to get ahold of Daddy today. He wasn't home. Toots played his mouthpiece to the hilt."

"You're not gonna sign that deed, I hope."

"Probably not."

"He's tryna pull a fast one on you, darlin'. Like you don't love him if you won't sign. What's gonna happen tomorrow when Harry comes down here spoiling for a fight with Aunt Ellen?"

"I made it clear to Toots he's not to come."

"Well shit, if that doesn't fix his wagon – which doesn't hurt my feelings any."

"Of course you've never had anything like murder in yourheart."

Art's eyes grew smoky, searching her.

"Are we gonna have that nightcap, or aren't we?"

She knew she was getting back at him when she said, "No, thanks. It's way past midnight."

He got up laboriously and started toward the closet. Stella waited until he was almost there.

"So are you too tight to tell me I look pretty, Art? Or is it that I don't?"

He turned and his eyes moved onto her legs, and he swallowed. Through the dirty glass of his smoldering red face she saw his love trapped there, trying to look out, not wanting to be seen. That night long ago, to save his life, the doctors had to amputate his shattered leg. They took it out to the incinerator to burn. There in his bed he must have begun to burn, too, like something radioactive, eating from the inside out.

"What the hell are you talking about? Of course you –"

He came back to the bed but turned his face away, sighing like she'd never understand. She understood, all right, and said, "Well, I suppose the tighter you are, right now, the better."

"What's that supposed to mean?"

"I seem to remember you promised the boys you'd be home before dark."

"Stell, you said *you* were prob'ly gonna be late."

"I know. And I *was* late, wasn't I?" She heard the shrillness of her dudgeon crack. Hatred came up wasted in some fire burned down long ago. His eyes shot down at her and brushed her legs as if they were too hot to handle.

"Were they very disappointed?"

She heard the note of sorrow in his voice.

"Oh, not too much. They'd been playing up around the Crutchleys' house. Vic's son was home. You know he just got back from the South Pacific. The boys can't wait for us to meet him. Dorothy says he's quite a guy - knockout good-looking, won a Purple Heart and all. She says the girls are just gonna eat him alive."

Art nodded solemnly, shrugging out of his suspender straps.

"We'll have to have him over some night for spare ribs and your world-famous spaghetti."

Somewhere in her heart love moved, and she almost reached for his hand. Or was it merely pity – that butterfly in a jar, still with all those colors life had painted on its wings? She looked down at her hands clasped in her lap and saw his shining face across the table from her, there in the Avalon Casino Ballroom, their first date. What made him look at her that way? She'd never been the Lana Turner type. She didn't have cat eyes, couldn't get a tan. She'd never had that thing about her that most men want. All she had was, well – the funny thing was, she'd never once caught Art looking at her breasts. Only knew he wouldn't want to do without them in the dark. 'Stella by Starlight,' his brave words to her on the sloop that night on their way across from Catalina. Her father on the telephone had said, 'How can you be in love with a man who smokes that much?' As if the first thing a Mills education should have given her was a cold enough shoulder to keep a reckless high school football coach from getting through the servants' entrance to her heart. She said:

"It's late, Art. You'd better get undressed and come to bed."

He looked at her as if she'd meant in bed with her. Hope was like a habit that hung on and on, long after it had expired. His hands began to fumble with the strap that held his leg on. He pulled his stump out of the socket it had spent all day in, and the smell she never used to mind now made her almost retch. She turned her face away. The moist warmth of Art's hand came down on her leg.

"Art, No!" She yanked his wrist away and flung it off.

"What's the matter? Afraid I'll get you pregnant?"

"Stop it, Art. I –"

"You know I've always respected what the doctors said. That's it, isn't it? Too much respect."

"No, and don't you dare call it that!"

"Okay," he stabbed a finger at the night table, "we've got the precautions right here in the drawer. I've never liked the goddamn things, but maybe before they go bad –"

Stella was pinching at the silk of her nightie, looking at her fingers with a dizzy smile.

"Well, why don't we just throw them away and do without?"

Art glared at her.

"That's not funny, Stell."

She felt foolish, suddenly.

"Oh, forget it. Anyway, you've been drinking and –"

"That's right," he said savagely. "I couldn't even if I wanted to."

She sat up suddenly.

"What is it, Art? You think you're handicapped, or something?"

"Yeah, that's it. You hit the nail on the head. Now I'm gonna grab a nightcap, with or without you."

His voice reminded her of some quote about the Irish uttered in rage and despair, all the way down into the depths where he could be forgiven, but not heard.

Her eyes fell on his loose suspenders. She couldn't have slashed at them with his straight razor that night. Seen him shackled to his pants around his ankles if she hadn't been as drunk as he was – Stella Cevilla Ryan, the wholesome girl who never used to drink. She poked her finger down into the seam of the book where she had tucked a letter she hadn't wanted him to see.

"Who's that from?" he said

"Just a note from an old friend."

"Anybody I know?"

"Used to."

"Well, who?"

"Jo Riley. She's been divorced from Chet almost a year now, having a pretty rough time of it."

"Couldn't be half as rough as Chet had staying married to her. What does she want?"

"She wants to get as far away from Brawley as she can. Find some place to start life all over again."

Art glared at her.

"Not *here*."

Stella tucked a wayward curl behind her ear.

"Well, she thought of coming out to see us – just for a – a little visit."

"Visits from the likes of that woman could turn into weeks, a month, and then – you know her, Stell. She'll suck off us like the waif she always was. If it wasn't for her looks –"

"Art, the poor woman's in a bind. Why don't we give her a break? I don't guess a couple weeks with us is gonna hurt."

"Not on your life! That woman hates my guts. And frankly, the feeling's mutual."

"She wouldn't have written to me if she had anybody else to turn to."

Art wrenched himself aside and jabbed his finger at her, eyes aflame.

"Let's get one thing straight. The moment you bring that woman into this house, I'm leaving." He worked himself around to the end of her bed until he could hop across to his own. He yanked his pajamas out from under the pillow. "I'm tired, Stell. I'm gonna hit the sack. You gonna leave that light on all night, or what?"

He was pulling on his pajama bottoms. She knew he was through talking. Despair lay safe, unstirred by his voice, until it all blew over.

"No. I'll turn it off as soon as you're in bed."

He reached for his fallen leg and dragged it, hopping, toward the closet. He slapped the light switch off. That left her with the lamp, and as he got in under the covers she reached over and snicked it off. It took a while before you could make things out by the dim glow of the night-light in the doorway to the bathroom.

She could make out, by the faint moonlight in the window, her mother's unyielding vigil on the vanity, expecting nothing of the girl she'd had to give up at her death. No comfort ever came from this woman she had never known, never touched, was never held by. She couldn't be called upon to smile at anything she couldn't see. Only listen, as it was given to the dead to do. To think she could be made to crack a smile was like believing Art would ever cut out the booze, and they could go back to that sweltering little matchbox house on L Street, where the bedroom window wouldn't open and the Aldersons next door, being Mormons, would bend over backwards to dig you up a pipe wrench, but wouldn't get caught dead at any of Art's games. Their bed back then was leaves and straw compared with what they slept on now. Now they had a bed apiece, the best that money could buy.

It wasn't three minutes before Art began to breathe evenly. Soon he would gag on his first snore. Her mind was tethered to him still, tugging in some current. There was a fresh wind somewhere out beyond the enclosing darkness. A moon out past a fixture in a frame that so insisted on the rights of the dead.

There was a noise in the hallway. She sat up. Joe came around the corner dragging a bat and the cuffs of his PJs in his bare feet. He stood there in the semi-dark, staring at her.

"What's the matter, honey? Did you have a bad dream? Come here."

Joe shuffled to the edge of the bed, dragging the bat with him.

"Where's Dad, Mom?"

She glanced over at the hump of Art's figure under the covers.

"I think he's fast asleep already."

Joe looked at her as if she was talking to somebody else.

"Coy woke me up. She must've heard Dad coming in."

"Yes, but honey - I don't think you'll be needing that bat. It's after midnight."

Joe kept his eyes on her, as if he couldn't feel any bat in his hand.

"Then what do you want me to do?"

Stella threw the covers off her legs and swung her feet around onto the floor.

"Come on, honey, let's get you back in bed."

Joe took a step backward.

"I'll go, Mom. I'm pretty sure I had a nightmare."

"You all right, now?"

"Oh, yeah. I was gonna hit somebody with this bat. I think it was Roberta."

"Come here and give me a kiss, honey."

Joe sought her face, but missed her cheek and planted his smooch back up against her ear.

"G'night, Mom."

"Goodnight, honey. You want to leave the bat here?"

"Oh, no thanks. I got it." Joe turned abruptly and plodded out, dragging the bat.

Stella could hear him climbing back into bed. Coy in her big Doberman's body making the springs squeak, too, getting resettled.

She laid back and waited in the dark for Art's snoring to start up in earnest. Waited in the company of her mother there behind the jar of Pond's cold cream and the bottle of Tabu where she stood in the frame that might have been made as a going-away present for the baby girl she'd given birth to, never to set eyes on, forty years before. She was someplace else, now, trying to get here through the dark and airless stillness of the grave where she lay in the dress the undertaker must have thought was so becoming to her, even in death. It was the visiting hour. Stella lay as still as the girl she'd never been when, braced for a talking-to, she wouldn't dare speak out of turn.

'What have you been up to, dear, while I've been lying here rotting? Not to make you feel bad, but really, all this rushing to and fro for a man who wants to drink himself to death, and you, shelling out his allowance so you can go to your own grave knowing you killed him out of love.'

Stella flung her face aside on the pillow. She'd failed that day in her race against the dying light. In her mind a baseball sailed through the air.

Art moved on his mattress, releasing his pain into her relief that he would soon be far down into sleep. Into the first thing in the morning when he would swear to the boys, 'I'll be home a little earlier tonight, pals. Five at the latest. Don't go anywhere. We'll need all the light we can get.'

4

Tank's heart was not in the telephone number he was about to dial. He was alone in the house. It was early – maybe too early to be calling a girl. She might not even remember him. He'd had it pretty bad for her, back then - the biggest reason why he'd thought he had to have a motorcycle.

Not half the rides he'd planned to give her home had ever panned out. She liked another guy who got straight As, while Tank was lucky if he pulled off one B a semester. He pretended to be satisfied with being Poppy's friend. There was always that off-chance that friendship would break through to something better, so in his mind he never really took a back seat to that guy who'd gone into the Navy.

She seemed to like his imitations of an English gentleman, so he got busy trying out other voices to impress her. It wasn't just the voices; he could think better when he put one on, therefore talk better. Not halting, stuck for a word or trailing off a thought like you were too dumb to finish. In another voice the words just spilled out, articulate, so it felt like, actually, talking like somebody else made him feel more like himself. A paradox, they would have called it in school, then behind his back say, 'Boy, that Tank Crutchley is one weird bird.' But then at the same time they liked the voices. They thought he had 'hidden' talent and should use it in a standup comedy routine. Well, that was all before the war. Kid stuff like that just didn't sit right any more. He didn't have to talk like anybody else at all. Those three years in a world he thought he'd have to die in to get out of, those stood by him. They lingered like a nightmare in which he was waiting for something – a girl, a good job he was fit for, anything to wake him up. He'd got a Purple Heart. But in a way that medal was another voice that wasn't him, just made him feel more like he was, while the truth tossed and turned and wasn't finished with him like he'd thought the war would have to be one day, when he was out of it. He went ahead and dialed the number he had kept for Poppy in his old address book.

"Hello!" The girl's voice, unchanged, answered excitedly, as if she was expecting somebody special.

"Hi, Poppy. It's me, Tank Crutchley."

"Who?"

"Tank, remember? Senior class before –"

"Oh, Tank! How are you? Somebody told me you were home."

"Yeah, well – I thought I'd just see how you were, Poppy."

"Oh, I'm pretty good. I got a job at Woolworth's. What about you, Tank?"

"Me? I've still got both my arms and legs. Sometimes I have to pinch myself to make sure I'm really home."

"Yes, I can imagine. But are you – okay, Tank?"

Tank thought she wanted him to say he wasn't.

"Yeah, as far as I know."

"No, I mean – somebody told me you were, well, you know – something happened to you in the war."

The apology in her voice made a scar sound like it was catching. He laughed.

"Nothing a few stitches couldn't cure."

"Oh, I'm so glad! I didn't mean any disrespect."

"Oh, I know, I know."

"Listen, I hate to cut this short, but I'm due at work in twenty minutes. I've got the swing shift. They hate it when somebody's late. The other day – well, maybe we could talk some other time."

"What time do you get off tonight?" he said. "I've still got my Indian. I could give you a lift home."

"That's awfully nice of you to offer, Tank, but Warren Sutherland and I are sort of going together. He just got back from Algiers, you know. He brought me this belly-dancing outfit with a veil and everything. They promoted him to Major in Rome. God, Tank, he's only twenty-three years old. He's seriously considering staying in the Air Corps."

"What happened to Drew Pettijohn?" Tank said guardedly.

"Drew was killed on the *Lexington* in 1943. You didn't hear?"

All of Tank's old reasons for disliking Drew Pettijohn spilled into the grave that he himself had cheated.

"No," he said, and he told Poppy how sorry he was, and she told him how nice it was to hear from him again, and would he please say hi to his father for her. Tank remembered, then, that the only time he'd ever got a kiss from her was right after he did his impression of Boris Karloff.

His father had called to say he wouldn't be home for dinner. He was eating with Norbert Frost, the Police Commissioner, at the Pig n' Whistle. There was no need to worry about fixing a 'civilized' dinner, as his father liked to call them when he came home expecting some proof that his son's time had been well spent in some constructive manner.

The day was still young. Tank thought he would just go out for a cruise, see what was doing at the golf course clubhouse; drag Colorado for a while. He put on a fresh T-shirt, went out to the garage and cranked up his machine and suddenly felt good, optimistic, just to be out in the wind and the sun, even though the better part of it was smog.

What about a matinee? He didn't really feel like seeing *The Yearling*, in its second week at the Academy. *The Mighty McGurk* was still playing at the State. That didn't appeal to him, either. He glanced down at his watch, remembering his promise to those boys yesterday – how he'd meet them after school and run them home on his motorcycle.

He liked those kids a lot. Good manners, they didn't run away from things, and they seemed to look up to him - a guy back from the war. He felt good around them. He wasn't going to let them down. He'd promised, and a deal was a deal.

He passed the Pasadena Playhouse where, out front, the billboard advertised *King Lear*, featuring Morris Ankrum and Louise Turney – for a run of three weeks starting October 23. Directed by Stella Ryan, it said. Stella Ryan? Why, she was those guys' mom. All at once Tank wondered whether there would be enough room for two on the back of his saddle. He might have to take one boy home, then go back for the other. He'd let them off, wave goodbye and that would be that. He'd go home knowing he'd been as good as his word. That stuff about their playing with his guns, he wasn't so sure about that any more. Not even showing them his souvenirs. He hadn't met their folks yet. More than likely they would disapprove. It was the principle of the thing: you don't let kids play with real guns. Never mind that they weren't loaded, and were therefore, especially with supervision, as harmless as cap guns. His father was like that: you didn't dare eat off a spoon a dog had licked, even though you'd scrubbed and boiled it afterwards. Supposedly his father had met the boys' folks, but so what? Somebody might get the wrong idea.

If he was wearing anything better than Levis and a T-shirt, he'd find a nice, cool hotel bar, walk in and ask for a tall CC-Seven. Maybe he would try out his British accent on the bartender, who would then say, 'What part of England are you from, buddy?'

The thought of working in any of the cigar stores, meat lockers, van and storage companies, banks or what have you that passed him on both sides made him want to peel off and give that part of his future as much weight as the rubber he'd leave on the street. He knew he would have to get down to cases soon, nail down some kind of a job and stop freeloading on his father, who wasn't going to grease any wheels for him. On the boat coming home he had supposed that, with his dad's respect, the war might let him down a little easier than the place in the employment line where he was supposed to put it all behind him. But that didn't happen. His dad was never going to *let* him out of high school, for some reason. That was just the way he was. At least he hadn't asked him, yet, how many Japs he'd killed, or what it felt like pumping lead into another human being. That was a start.

When the light changed at the intersection, Tank turned up toward the school. It wasn't very late yet – a quarter of two. The playground, then the colonnade along the front of Burbank Elementary passed slowly on the right, glaring the color of sand in the sunlight; then there was the dirt parking lot where his dad used to pull in and let him off on days when he was late and couldn't make it on his bicycle.

The rock-studded dirt lot, where all the teachers parked their cars, looked exactly the same as when Tank had last attended Luther Burbank himself, ten years before. He roared in on his gleaming Indian, spurting dust and wrestling the handle bars to miss protruding rocks, just as the bell was ringing and kids began to pour out the side door like it was a fire drill.

A scuffle broke out at the bottom of the steps. A pretty young redhead, walking past the two boys squaring off, dropped a load of books and got between them, and they straightened up right quick. She gave them a stern talking-to, scooped up her books and while they slunk off in different directions, she started briskly for the lot, lugging her books under one arm.

He spotted Lou, now, breaking out of the swarm of kids she'd left behind around the steps. Lou was walking fast beside a tall, spindly girl who kept breaking into a trot, trying to keep up. The girl broke off, waving, then Lou came running out toward him, slowing a little to call out to the girl, "See you tomorrow, Cheryl!"

Lou stopped breathlessly before Tank, beaming.

"Jeez, Tank! We thought maybe you wouldn't make it."

"I said I'd be here, didn't I? Where's Joe?"

"Oh, his teacher got sick and there weren't any substitutes. She let the whole class go right after lunch and Joe walked home. He said for me to tell you."

"Okay. Here, put your books in my saddlebag. We'll get a move on."

Tank held up the flap while Lou dumped in his books. He mounted up, helped Lou onto the tail end of the saddle behind them and they took off. The roar of the motor made some kids stop in their tracks as they watched Tank maneuver out onto the street. As soon as they got clear of the school zone, Tank goosed the throttle up to 40. They passed the spindly girl trudging along the sidewalk and, with his hair flying, Lou waved at her. She waved back for all she was worth, her smile big and radiant.

Tank turned his head and shouted, "Is that your girlfriend!"

"No, that's Cheryl! Just a friend!"

The kind of a friend you don't want to lose, Tank thought, baring his teeth into the wind while Lou, arms wrapped around his middle, hung on tight and laid his cheek against his back. Tank liked the feel of that, the trust this boy had in him already. Something told him that these boys weren't going to be just passing people in his life. He didn't know how, or why. They had parents of their own. Lives he didn't know a thing about. He revved the throttle, air whipped his pants and rippled his T-shirt and he felt Lou's arms around him squeezing, then heard his laughter flying into the deafening wind.

The long black limo was parked along the curb. A chauffeur in a black suit and cap was leaning back against the front fender, having a smoke.

"Oh, God," Lou moaned. "Aunt Ellen's here."

The chauffeur stood up straight and gave the motorcycle a quizzical look.

"That's Stanley," Lou explained. "He drives for Aunt Ellen."

Tank steadied the Indian while Lou got off. The chauffeur's spit-shined cordovans looked tight on his small feet. Lou pulled his books out of the saddlebag.

"Thanks for the ride, Tank. I'm sorry, but it doesn't look like we can go up to your house, now."

"Oh, sure, I understand." Tank glanced at the chauffeur who, taking a drag through his holder, blew smoke through his nose and frostily regarded him. Lou was saying:

"But you could still come in and meet my Mom – if you want to."

"Maybe some other time, Lou," Tank said. He glanced at the chauffeur again, seeing behind another cloud of smoke the shifting eyes pretending nonchalance.

"Will you be home tomorrow?" Lou said.

"Should be, unless – just come on over any time you get the chance. Dad's not home until – you know, after five." Astride the Indian, Tank revved the motor. Lou shook with him and started down the walk toward the front door, saying hi to Stanley as he passed. Tank smiled as he watched Lou cut to his right off the walk, heading slowly around on the grass toward the side entrance to the house - not too eager, probably, to come to grips with his Aunt Ellen.

5

Beside Stella on the davenport the stout old lady brought Stella's hand into her lap.

"How is that possible, dear?"

"Oh, I know it's silly, but it's as if she's right there in her picture, and can hear me."

"Well, don't forget you have *me* darling."

Stella squeezed Aunt Ellen's hand.

"Of course I do."

"Actually, going to such lengths is no sillier than talking to God. Sometimes I talk to Herbert, you know, whenever I get to missing him.

"Yes, I guess that's it."

"How are you and Arthur getting along?"

Stella took in a breath, as if a doctor was listening through a stethoscope.

"I don't see him all that much. His job keeps him out on the road so long."

Aunt Ellen looked at Stella, narrowing her eyes.

"You know the last time I was here your blood pressure was up. You're much too young for that to happen. Tell me what steps you've been taking to bring it down."

"I'm supposed to be trying to get more sleep. Eat less salt, and - we had a little scare last month. I missed my period. We thought I could be pregnant."

Aunt Ellen's hand flew to her mouth.

"God forbid!"

"No, it's all right. It was a false alarm."

Aunt Ellen heaved a windy sigh, pressing her hand to her heart.

"I take it Arthur *is* being considerate of you, dear – taking every precaution."

"Yes, but he doesn't need that as a reason to leave me alone at night."

"But darling, you've got two lovely boys already. That's quite enough at your age, I should think."

"There's a little more to it than that, Aunt Ellen."

Aunt Ellen's eyes were watering. She blinked and a tear started down along her powdered nose.

"I don't regret one bit standing up for Arthur when *others* were saying he was beneath you. Of course you couldn't have known how deep his taste for liquor was back then, when he was rather on his good behavior. The Irish seem to have a weakness for the bottle." She looked wistfully across at the slits of sunlight in the Venetian blinds. A trace of cunning came into her eyes. "I had no idea that my Herbert had developed a heart condition by the time he was thirty-five. Imagine that. He never said a word. I rather doubt that I would have turned him down if I had known."

Stella thought she'd better say it, now, to clear the air.

"Dad won't be here today, Aunt Ellen. He couldn't make it."

Aunt Ellen looked up, blinking as if bringing something into focus.

"Oh, I rather thought so, dear, when I didn't see his car out there. That was prudent of him. It's really you I came down here to see. You and the boys, of course."

Suddenly the explosive roar of a motor rose and subsided out on the street.

"Mercy me, what's going on out there?" Aunt Ellen said fretfully. "Somebody's muffler has gone to pieces, I'm afraid."

Stella got up and went to the window, parted the Venetian blinds.

"There's just a man out there on a motorcycle. He's talking to Stanley."

"Will wonders never cease," Aunt Ellen pronounced. "Stanley doesn't know a soul who drives a motorcycle. I wouldn't hear of it, and he himself – you wouldn't think it but he's rather a stodgy person, even by my standards."

Stella let the slat and the streak of sunlight go.

"Well, he's leaving, anyway." Then Stella parted the slats and looked again. The unmistakable profile of a windswept Indian graced the shiny silver gas tank on the motorcycle – the very kind that Dorothy had told her Victor Crutchley kept in perfect running order during the whole time his son was gone in the South Pacific. She looked at the burly, good-looking young man astride the machine. Quite a hunk of beefcake, she thought. "What in the world . . ." she whispered to herself.

"What did you say, dear?"

Stella started back toward the davenport, saying in a cheery voice, "I think Stanley is admiring that person's motorcycle out there."

"He would," Aunt Ellen said firmly. "He once owned one of those machines, you know. Completely out of character. Thank God that was before he came to work for me."

The clash of a door shutting came from behind them up the hallway. There was a screech of coat hangers, silence, then a rush of footfalls that brought Lou around the corner into the room, looking flustered.

Aunt Ellen thrust out her arms.

"Lou, darling! *My* but you're sprouting up! Come over here and let me get a good look at you!"

With a shudder Lou started over, walking stiffly. He moved into Aunt Ellen's embrace. Her squeeze made him arch his back and lose his footing. Her kiss, tight-lipped and bristly, found his lips and he withstood its wetness holding his breath and squeezing his eyes tight shut. He gasped as soon as she let go. Aunt Ellen said:

"I haven't seen that brother of yours today. He's not hiding from me, is he?"

"No, ma'am." Lou looked at his mother. Stella said:

"Did they tell you at school that Joe got out early today, honey?"

"Yeah, that's why I – well, anyway -" Lou looked back toward the front door. "I didn't see him outside."

"I think he went out to collect some more popsicle sticks," Stella said. "Did you see who that was out on the street with Stanley, honey?"

"Out on the street?"

Stella looked at him. She kept looking at him until he said, "Oh, yeah! That's Tank from up the street. He gave me a ride home."

"Gave you a ride?"

"Well, it was supposed to be both me and Joe, but then Joe got out early and he couldn't come."

"You're talking about a ride on his motorcycle."

Lou stood there, nodding.

"How did that come about? You mean he just –"

"No, Mom. You remember yesterday when me and Joe were up at Tank's and we were gonna see his souvenirs? Well, we ran out of time so Tank said we could come back today and if we wanted to, he'd give us a ride home."

"But you didn't say a word to me about that."

"I know. We really didn't think he'd show up."

"Is that so?"

"Tank's okay. Mom. Really."

"That may be, but we're talking here about a motorcycle."

"Joe didn't come, though."

"What's that got to do with it? If you're talking about *two* on the back of a motorcycle - d'you know how dangerous that could have been?"

"Yes, Mom."

"Now I don't want to hear another word about it. No more rides with strangers on a motorcycle."

"But Mom, Tank's not a stranger. Not to us, anyway. He might still be out there. Why don't you come out and see what kind of a –"

"That's Tank?" Stella said.

"Why yeah, Mom. I thought I told you -"

"Honey, this is the first time I've ever really seen him."

Past the window and the thick wooden barrier of the front door the long trombone blat of the motorcycle blew into the street, then began to recede. Stella glanced that way, but stayed put. Aunt Ellen spoke up as if it was her turn in a quiet, reasonable roundtable discussion.

"I wouldn't be too hard on the boys about this, darling. Boys love adventure. Rather as you loved risky things at one time, when I countermanded Toots' order for you to stay off horses, after that spirited Arabian threw you. Think of all the adventures you would have missed if Toots had got her way. Oh, you'd know how to bake a muffin, all right. You never would have got to go to Mills because what are *ladies* good for in the kitchen?" Aunt Ellen sniffed righteously, blessing everybody's face with her indignant eyes.

Stella sighed. She felt calmer, suddenly, under the shelter of Aunt Ellen's dictatorial wing, come to her again from when she was a girl and even her father, always eager to please Toots, had fought for her soul.

"Ah, that woman," Aunt Ellen went on, with a furtive glance at Lou that arched her eyebrow scarily. "You know I had a real set-to with her one time. You were with me, darling, but you were very little – barely two, I b'lieve. It was about your mother's picture. Clara thought it was high time Harry took it down. Picked that time to light into him so I'd catch it, too – but what she didn't know was, I wouldn't have missed it for the world! The look on your father's face!" Aunt Ellen slapped her knee. "I saw no yes dears anywhere near it." She fixed her eyes, shin-ing with glee, on Stella, as if she meant to leave it at that. Stella saw that Lou was leaning toward her, transfixed, too.

"What did he say?" she said.

"He said simply 'I forgot.' Like he'd forgotten to shave. Well, I laughed so hard my hand failed as it never had before to gag me. One more bone for Toots to pick and she could pick it clean for all I cared. Red as a beet, she was." She stopped and looked at Stella's smile, then took her hand. "The only quarrel I ever really had with your father, darling, was his fear of crossing Toots. So natural – that fear - even for the manliest of men." She looked aside, fiddling with her purse strap. "I seem to remember some small traces of that in my Herbert."

Stella noted the twinkle in Aunt Ellen's eyes that watered down her pride, then saw that Lou was getting antsy.

"Tank's gone, now," she said. "Tell him, though, the next time you see him, your father and I want to meet him, one way or another. Until then, no more rides on motorcycles. Is that clear?"

"Yes, Mom."

Aunt Ellen reached out and took Lou's hand.

"I've brought you and your brother a surprise," she said. She dragged her large handbag closer on the cushion and began to root in it. "Now just a minute. I can't have left them - we'll have to ask Stanley before I leave. I *told* him to remind me. Or did I? No matter. I'm sure I must have left them in the car."

Lou clasped his hands behind his back and said, "What are they, Aunt Ellen?"

"Why, they're two of the very finest decks of playing cards you'll ever see, with wonderful stallions and mares of every description. Invaluable for trading."

Lou's eyes lit up.

"Joe's gonna love those, Aunt Ellen!"

"I hope you will, too - if I can *find* the darn things. Brand new, both decks. One I b'lieve has a number of dogs on the faces. We'll ask Stanley on my way out. I'll have to be getting on the road, now, darling. I'm not one bit fond of night driving. Watching Stanley peer into the murk after dark is an experience I never want to repeat."

"I'll walk out with you," Stella said. She saw then that Aunt Ellen was staring across the room at a Panther planter lamp with a ruffle-topped red shade, and it struck her as being an excuse for her to stay just a minute or two longer, as if in the short delay death could be postponed indefinitely. "Lou bought that lamp for me with his allowance."

"Is that so?" Aunt Ellen saw that Lou was beyond her reach, now, but she smiled at him. "What a thoughtful, loving thing to do. There are times when I miss having a child. Our little Cedric, you know, didn't make it past three months, for all the fight he put up. Thank your lucky stars you've got two healthy boys."

"Oh, I do," Stella said, "I sure do."

6

The ad in the morning paper read:
ASSISTANT TO THE ATHLETIC DIRECTOR. SOME EXPERIENCE PREFERRED. APPLY IN PERSON AT FLINTRIDGE PREP SCHOOL. NO CALLS PLEASE.

Tank's father had been through the classifieds already, making check marks beside some other ads – desk clerk, Yellow Cab driver, construction laborer, gas station attendant – but he had skipped this one. Tank knew right where Flintridge Prep was: Pasadena used to play them every year in football and always beat their socks off. Victor had left for the office at 7:30; now it was going on 11. Tank thought he might surprise him. Show him he could land a job that took a few brains.

He put on a nice paisley shirt, had a bowl of Shredded Ralston, and was thinking about taking his Indian up to Flintridge when he thought, no, that might not look so good. He found the key to his mother's old Packard, went out to the garage and got it started. The motor turned over a little slow, and once it got warmed up it sounded rough, but not too bad. The gas gauge read three-quarters full. Pretty old gas, he thought. By the time he got out to the school in La Canada it was a few minutes past noon.

The girl in the office just off the gym was talking with a tall, spindly boy who stood beside her desk in purple basketball togs. Tank spotted the couple of wooden chairs under the wire-embedded windows, and was on the way over to sit in one when the girl said, "Can I help you, sir?" Tank turned to see the boy backing away from her desk, saying, "Well, I'd better get going, Miss Bailey. Sure nice talking to you again."

"Same here, Ross. See you in that exhibition game Friday night."

"Yes, ma'am."

The boy jogged out. Tank watched him trot, slapping the parquetry with his oversize sneakers, onto the court where a group of other, smaller boys were shooting hoops. He walked toward the desk, and as he approached the girl she said apologetically, "Sorry, sir. That boy drops in from time to time. He's big for his age. What can I do for you?"

Tank looked at the nameplate on her desk: MARLA BAILEY. She was awfully friendly. Pretty, too, but she was the secretary. He was here to see the boss-man. He said:

"Yes, I'm here about the assistant coaching job."

"Oh yes, the ad. Well, if you don't mind waiting, Major Griffin is tied up at the moment. There's one other applicant ahead of you."

The way she said it, Tank thought, there could be something about the job that needed a boost, like he'd got here none too soon behind a never-ending line of applicants. A faint breeze blew in from the basketball court, and the sun streaming through the Venetion blinds lit up the blond hairs on her tanned arms. Her eyes were green, her nose petite, and scarlet lipstick slicked her full lips.

"I see. Well, I drove up from Altadena. I don't mind the wait."

The girl propped her chin on the eraser end of her pencil.

"Good. There are a few preliminaries I could take care of for you while you're waiting," she said. "Kind of a screening, you might say. Major Griffin's orders." She sat back and snuffed with her eyes on him.

"You say *Major* Griffin. Is he -?"

"No, he's out of the Army, sort of. Would you excuse me for a moment?"

Marla pushed back in her chair, got up and walked over toward the windows, moving gracefully in her high heels, and she wasn't wearing any nylons. She must be a beach-goer, Tank thought, to have a tan like that. She cranked open a window and turned back before Tank could lift his eyes off her legs.

"There, that's better," she said. "Oh, I'm the secretary here, if you didn't notice."

"I noticed," Tank said.

Marla lowered her eyes as she came briskly back to her desk and settled into the chair.

"Okay," she pulled a notepad under the pencil she picked up, turned back a page that had been written on, "may I tell Major Griffin that you're a veteran? And what theatre of war did you serve in?"

"Well, I just got out of the Army," Tank said. "I served with the 27th Infantry Division in the South Pacific."

"What about decorations? Commendations of any sort?"

"They gave me a Purple Heart, that's about it."

Marla looked up at him from the notes she had been writing. He thought she was about to say something when she hung an O on the air with her thumb and forefinger, wrote a little more on the pad.

"Major Griffin is partial to men who've served in the military. Now as far as experience, have you ever done any coaching? Not necessarily football. Any sport."

"Well, I'm afraid all my experience has been on the playing end. Both football and baseball in high school. I put the shot and ran the 1330 on the track team. I love sports and I know something about just about all of them except I guess tennis."

"Uh-oh. You don't happen to think tennis players are sissies, do you, Mr. –"

"Crutchley. Call me Tank if you like."

Marla sat back, grinning.

"Okay, Tank, I'll do that. Now about tennis players –"

"Well, they need coaching like anybody else, don't they?"

Marla laughed, and Tank wasn't sure why. There was some delight in her eyes, but some uneasiness, too. She glanced at the pebbled glass door marked DIRECTOR, then lowered her voice to say, "I'd like to give you a little tip, here, Tank. Kind of a heads up, if you know what I mean."

Tank looked at the pouty wet slickness of her lips, the way they moved when she spoke, going slack so you could see how white and clean her teeth were. He didn't know quite what she was getting at, but he said:

"Sure, I'm pretty new at this. I went right into the Army out of high school." And then in his mind he said to himself, what are you doing, dum-dum? Bragging about how wet behind the ears you are?

"This has nothing to do with your lack of coaching experience," Marla said. "None of our other applicants have anything on you. I'm telling you this because I think Major Griffin is going to like you. You've got the qualities he's looking for. The catch is, there's no coaching position available right now. There won't be until our football line coach, Mr. Tupper, retires at the end of the season. You'll be offered assistant to the athletics field groundskeeper, with maybe some janitorial chores thrown in to round things out. And oh, you might want to remember – Major Griffin played tennis in college."

Tank looked at her, trying to square what she was saying with how she said it.

"So what's the deal?" he said. "Did I come all the way up here to be told to turn right back around and walk out?"

"Sshhh! The coaching job will materialize eventually. I don't want you to turn around and walk out, which if you got all this from Major Griffin you probably would. The best he can offer you is your foot in the door, but I don't think you'd like his way of shaming you into accepting menial labor."

"But it's still pretty much a crap shoot."

Marla shrugged again, this time with a smile he couldn't quite decipher.

"If you like."

Just then the pebbled glass door at the back of the room opened and a man walked out. He had a long face and shuffled along in baggy gabardine trousers and a two-tone bowling shirt. Marla followed him with her eyes across the room. He walked past her without saying a word. Abreast of Tank he shook his head woefully, made a throw-away gesture with his hand. He opened the side-entrance door and walked out.

Tank looked at Marla, she looked at him. He got the feeling that, if he walked into that office and took the sad sack's place, he was volunteering to be had —as if all the other applicants Griffin hadn't hired had played it smart by turning him down. A man's tinny voice erupted from the squawk box: "Marla, I'm ready for our next applicant, if anybody's there."

Marla reached across her desk to depress the flipper, flailing one of her outstretched legs and leaving Tank with a view of her tan clear up to her lean, smooth thigh.

"Sergeant Crutchley is here, sir. I'm sending him right in."

Marla slithered off her desk. As soon and she stood up and pulled down her skirt, as if demurely, she widened her eyes a little, looking at Tank, and pointed at the pebbled glass door.

"Right in there, Tank. Good luck to you."

Her bright eyes and the boldness in them filled a hollow in him that he hadn't realized was there. All those moves around a girl that, meant to get her off her high horse, gone to scrap and rust. But now Marla's eyes, not leaving him back there at all, pushed all those alibis into the hole, and he smiled at her, and saw her wink at him before he walked to the door, put his hand on the knob and walked in.

❧

Victor was watching Spade Cooley on their new Philco TV set when Tank got home. Feeling good about his prospects up at Flintridge, Tank said in a chipper voice, "How's it goin', Dad?"

Victor barely glanced at Tank as he grunted, "Okay, I guess," and popped a crackerjack into his mouth.

He had a pile of typescript in his lap. Tank sat down on the couch and reached for the *Silver Screen* on the coffee table, which he had already gone through once. On the TV four drugstore cowboys leaned in toward the microphone and sang, "All day I rake, the barren sands, without a taste of water . . . cool water . . . *wah*ter . . ."

Victor tossed the sheaf of typescript onto the coffee table. Tank said: "What's that, Dad?"

Victor lifted a slow-burning glare until it found Tank's face.

"That's my reward for telling Dorothy how much I loved her Creole gumbo the other night. She's written a book, and wants me to look it over."

"I didn't know Dorothy wrote books," Tank said.

"She doesn't," Victor said caustically.

Tank could hear the baiting in his dad's voice. Some bone to pick that threatened reprisal if he didn't go along. He had it in him, though, to pretend that didn't faze him, wasn't too hard at all to recover from.

"What's it about?" he said.

"About? Why don't you ask me if it's any good? "

"Okay, is it?"

Victor sat back, sprawling as if he was in his editorial office, ready to approve or disapprove a story.

"As a sentimental potboiler, it's not half bad."

"Well – then are you gonna help her get it published?"

"Very perspicacious of you, son. I guess with a little editing, maybe I could put it over. The thing is, I'm not ready to take on any serious involvement with a woman at this time."

"Well, you – I mean Dorothy's pretty nice, isn't she? Pretty nice looking, too. That son of hers is a pain, but she's real nice, I think."

Victor sat up, leaned his elbows onto his knees.

"I joined a neighbor lady for a meal. Can I do a thing like that without being accused of tryna get into her pants?"

"I didn't say that, Dad. Sounds to me like you had a good time, anyway."

Victor snatched up the box of crackerjacks and made a ramming motion out of sitting back again.

"You want to watch taking certain goddamn things for granted, Tank. Let's say Dorothy decides to barbecue some burgers, or she opens up a can of pork and beans. What then? Do I tell her to feed it to the dog?"

"I don't know. I thought you –"

"What you thought was, Dorothy's got me handcuffed to her gourmet chow. If I get hungry for some Mexican, I can still drop into Gordo's. If I want Greek, I'm not too cheap to patronize Papa Dragotis's. Savvy?"

"Okay, Dad – have it your way. All I thought was, it's nice to have a lady interested in you, you know."

"Check the facts before you say a thing like that, Tank. Now, I'm not saying I don't *like* Dorothy. But that's got nothing to do with how far I'm prepared to go to get this steamy romance into print." Victor reached for the typescript, hefted it and let it flop back onto the table. "I'd hate to think I bit off more than I can chew with this goddamn thing."

Tank could hear behind his father's bluster something lurking like a pacing back and forth.

"Is something else wrong, Dad?"

Victor gobbled a crackerjack, crunched it leaving his mouth open. Then suddenly he said ominously, "You took the Packard out today. Your mother's car."

"I don't think she'd mind, do you?"

"That's a pretty flippant comment to drop about the dead, son."

"I didn't mean it that way, Dad."

"Of course you barely got to know her before she passed away, so we don't need to enshrine that car she practically never drove, or make reference to her in hushed tones. What I'm talking about is the liberty you seemed to think you're entitled to take."

Tank didn't know what to say. Victor raised a finger like a schoolmaster calling for silence.

"When you were here before the war, Tank, that car was always off limits. We had that agreement. Do you remember that?"

"Yeah, but that was –"

"When you want to go out tooling around, use your motorcycle. The Packard stays here for emergencies."

Victor's tone stung Tank, and he said:

"Dad, I wasn't just tooling around. I went up to La Canada to apply for a job. I was gonna take my bike, but the reason I took the Packard –"

"Remember, you're the one who said you had to have a motorcycle when we were discussing cars. You're gonna have to live with your mistakes, Tank."

"Mistakes?"

"You weren't the motorcycle type. Not then, not now."

Tank began to feel hot. His heart pumped harder, faster.

"How do you figure, Dad? You didn't think I should have gone out for football, either. But that turned out pretty good, don't you think?"

"If you want an automobile, get yourself a job and buy one."

"That's what I'm trying to tell you. I went out to apply for this job. I took the Packard so people wouldn't think I looked like some greaser on the bike. Plus I could wear some nice clothes and I wouldn't have to mess up my hair in the wind, or with a cap."

"So did you get the job?"

"It looks real promising. They need an assistant coach. It's supposed to work into something better after, you know, I'm there a while."

"Doing what?"

"Whatever they want, till the line coach they've got now, a Mr. Tupper, retires here in another couple months."

"I see. With no guarantee you'll move into that job when it comes up."

"Not exactly. It's written into the contract. I saw it. What's more –" Tank wondered how to phrase it, so his father wouldn't think he was thinking like a kid again, using youth to get away with playing dirty pool, or see pie in the sky. " – they seem to like me in that office. I never coached, but I know football. My war record impressed the guy who does the hiring. Plus –"

"Your war record, eh?"

"Yes. What's that supposed to mean?"

"Nothing."

"I was gonna say, well, I was talking to the secretary, who's seen all these applicants that got rejected. She said she's got Major Griffin's ear, so he won't get any second thoughts about me."

"That was quick. What's her name?"

"Marla Baily."

"Interesting. While you were out I took a call from a young lady by that name. Calling from the Athletics department at Flintridge Prep. She asked for you but I told her I was your father and if there's a message, I'll pass it on to you."

Tank sat up straighter, eyes losing the desultory blind behind which he'd been listening.

"So what was it?" he said.

"She said she'd rather talk to you, if I didn't mind. I didn't tell her that I did."

"Was that all?"

"No. I guess I got a little miffed with her. I mean for Christ's sakes, I'm your father. If she's calling in the first place, it's got to be good news. Who is this girl, anyway?"

"She just wanted to talk to me, that's all."

"Well then, pick up the telephone and call her back."

Tank glanced at his watch.

"It's a little late. By now she's gone home."

"I wonder what you're getting yourself into. Shit, I can't remember the last game Flintridge Prep won at anything. Maybe they could use a scapegoat for their lousy football showing this year."

"I guess I'll find out tomorrow, unless she was calling to tell me they picked somebody else."

Victor pushed his glasses up onto the bridge of his nose, scooped up the typescript from the coffee table.

"Oh, by the way, you had some visitors today."

"Visitors?"

"I just wonder how they can show their pusses around here after what they did."

"Did what? Who?"

"Those kids. Boy, they can thank their lucky stars I didn't call Art Ryan. He would've had a shit fit, paying for a pane of glass that big. Apparently they're under the impression that you're going to show them all the Jap stuff you brought home from Saipan. You want to be careful about making promises to kids like that, Tank."

"So what did you say to them, Dad?"

"I told them you're not home. You weren't, so what the hell else did they need to know?"

"Yeah, but did you –"

"What're you doing with these kids, anyway?"

"Doing? I like them, that's all. What's the matter with that?"

Victor gave Tank a long look, as much as to say, 'you have to ask?' He said, "You should get out more, that's all I'm saying. Find some friends your own age."

"Dad, I can't just wave a wand and – listen, don't take it out on Lou and Joe if they're just kids? Can they help it?"

"You're telling me don't take it out?"

"No, I mean, so they're excited about seeing the stuff I brought back from the war. Heck, if I was their age, I would be, too."

There was a look in his father's eyes, burning like a match that would soon go out, that seemed to say, 'But you are.' It whispered like there was no sound at all, and you couldn't tell exactly where it came from.

"Lou and Joe, is it?" Victor said. He licked his fingers and turned back a few more sheets of the typescript. "Let's hope you're not barking up a wrong tree."

The cowboys on the screen sang, "Keep a'movin' Dan, don't you listen to him Dan, he's a devil not a man, and he spreads the burning sand with water . . . *Wah*ter . Then can you see that big green tree where the water's runnin' free and it's waitin' there for you and meee . . . Cool, clear *wah*ter . . ." Tank got up.

"I think I'll head on into my room, Dad. I'm feeling kind of tired."

Victor squirmed around in his chair, not looking up. He nodded faintly and went back to flipping through the typescript.

In the half-light from his old lamp atop the dresser, Tank slumped onto the same bed he had slept on clear through junior high and high school. It felt strange to be here all over again, the stillness and the comfort all the same. The model frigate he had never finished stood on the book case, draping its threads of rigging over the lacquered decks like a boyhood dream he had never taken the extra pains to sail away in. Now in the closet, stacked with his father's doomsday cache in the event that Stalin decided to drop an atom bomb on the United States, his old kangaroo football cleats hung from a clothes hook, still caked with the mud from his final game – a tie in which he'd shone, making him think they should have won. In the other room his dad, through with him for the time being, sat like a tether from whom he could only stray so far. Something was wrong. This wasn't the way it was supposed to be. He looked over at the picture of his mother on the dresser, black and white, and she was smiling just the same as she used to every day and every night from the same place, but now it was as if *she* had been the one waiting and praying for him to come home, not his father who was actually alive to feel pain. The warmth of her touch and her gaiety with which she'd made them pals now rested across her shriveled breast in the depth of the earth and the dark that would never again disturb her.

Now he was back in his mind on the heights above Tanapag, that moment just before the screaming started. They'd been told to be alert, but nobody expected that the Japs were capable of penetrating this far behind the front areas of the battalion. They could see the beach down past the trees and some of their bulldozers and artillery. It all looked calm down there, clear out to where a couple of LSTs rode in the gentle surf. When it came, it was unreal – a tidal wave of hopped-up Japanese that, after the machine guns opened up, got even louder, not quieter. They knew that something horrible was coming, like smoke that forest animals start running from. The howitzers cut loose. The Japanese were running, falling, peeling off like skin from one monstrous centipede, and the machine gunners kept trying to get their corridors of fire that weren't blocked off by mounds of corpses. The 105s weren't stopping them, just blowing holes in the sheet of bloody flesh that grew back almost as soon as it flew apart. Some of the staff officers started yelling at the typists. Somebody shoved a rifle into his hands. "Come on, you stupid son of a bitch! Or would you rather throw your pots and pans at them!" They got behind some crates of C-rations. How many tins of corned beef would it take to stop a bullet? He took aim at what didn't look too much like a human being, because just then a grenade went off in its hand. A sudden boom like a handclap trying to silence him. A shredded stump and half a face disappeared in smoke. He fired into them the way he had been taught. Those screams, they seemed to reach out like cobra spit. It wasn't real. It needed previews, a cartoon, the news that was The Eyes and Ears of the World. It begged for time to say a prayer and put affairs in order. He saw his father sitting down to his morning coffee and the newspaper, and wanted to tell him, "Dad, please look this way. I'm going to die."

It wasn't anybody's fault but his, he knew. He must hang up the remnants of his uniform, the shadows he was dressed in, cast by the blistering sun and the Japs you hardly ever saw, maybe a dead one that could be a booby trap, and when would it be *your* turn to shoot one? Or when would you feel, for an instant, that bullet you would never live to remember?

7

The door came open a crack, eyes peered out at them. It swung wide open and Tank stood there smiling – looking, Lou thought, extra happy about something.

"Hey, I was just thinking about you guys! Come on in." Tank stepped back into the vestibule, swinging the door with him.

A waft of beer floated down on Tank's breath. Stumbling a little back into the vestibule he said, "Come on, you guys, we'll go out back. Follow me."

Lou followed Tank into the living room, with Joe dogging his heels, looking around for signs of Mr. Crutchley's fearful life. A scent of pipe tobacco seemed to swoop like some malicious bird under his nose. The portrait of a cavalier in a cock hat simpered from its place above a davenport that stood on pediments of life-sized lion's feet. They passed an archway through which Lou caught a glimpse of a beer bottle on the breakfast table beside a vase of orange Marigolds; beyond that the sparkle of late sunshine sprinkling leafy shadows through the window down across the sink. They wound on through the room that showed few signs of a woman's touch, watched by the Chinese figurines behind the breakfront's glass. Suddenly Joe pulled up short and stood stock-still, pointing at a blond young woman on the wall above the mantle, who looked wistfully down upon the guests she couldn't see.

"Who's that?" he said. In his voice there was a touch of reverence as if they were in a church, noticing the rivulets of blood that ran down Jesus' tortured, rawboned body.

Tank stopped and turned to see what Joe was looking at.

"Oh, that was my mother, right about the time she died."

So that's what haunts this house, Lou thought, and he felt something escape from around his heart like vapor, while things in his mind began to get a little straighter.

Tank moved on, rounded a corner and the boys trooped close behind him down a hallway where, passing a closet, Tank barely slowed down to tell them that was where his two Samurai swords were stowed that he would show them later, maybe. They all went out the screen door at the back of the kitchen, then down to a gravel path that wound through a cactus garden to a flight of steps at the rear of the garage. They climbed up to a padlocked door. Tank produced a key from his pants pocket, fitted it into the padlock and gave it a twist.

A breath of pine sawdust and creosote stirred out across a jumble of old furniture, rusty lamps and garden tools in the murky room that looked like somebody's attic where people got things of questionable value out of sight. Tank made his way over to a battered metal locker, made a racket yanking it open and hauled out a big bolt-action rifle slung with a bandolier. He thrust it out to Lou.

"It's heavy, Lou, but go ahead - aim at something. It's not loaded."

Lou sagged backwards raising the rifle. He squinted down the sights at a Chinese clay pot on the warped old kitchen table at the far end of the room.

"Can I pull the trigger?" he said.

"Oh, sure! There's no bullets in it."

Lou squeezed the trigger. "Bam!"

Tank was peeling back the oilcloth from a pistol that looked like a German Luger. Holding it by the muzzle, he handed it to Joe.

Joe cradled the pistol like a kitten he'd been told he could take home.

"This is called a P-38," Tank said. "Don't be afraid of it, Joe. I took the clip out. The chamber's empty."

Joe took aim with one eye shut and made the pistol jump as he said, "Pow!" With big shining eyes he looked at Lou. "Boy, Lou – wouldn't it be neat if we could play with *these*!"

Lou was quick to say, "He didn't mean that, Tank."

Tank said, "Well, I guess we'd have to clear that with your folks, first, don't you think?"

"You mean it?" Joe blurted.

"Our dad's got a gun in his drawer," Lou said. "He said the only time he ever fired it was at track meets."

"Well, I'll have to meet your folks one of these days here, pretty soon. I've been gone so long, it's like I'm kind of a new face in town."

Lou handed back the rifle, saying, "Thanks a lot, Tank," and Joe glanced at the pistol in his hand before he gave it up.

Tank started with the guns toward the metal locker, slowing a little as he passed a wooden toolbox supported by two sawhorses, about the size of a coffin for a child. He went on and stood the rifle in the locker, laid the pistol on the shelf above.

"What about the Samurai swords?" Joe said.

"Oh, those." Tank banged the metal locker closed. "They're so darned sharp, Dad told me to leave them alone, so I'm sort of pretending I don't have them, for now."

"That's okay, Tank," Lou said, but he wondered just what kind of a hold Tank's father had on him. Probably just that there was no good reason not to put the swords away and leave them alone, no matter whose idea it was.

The boys started toward the doorway. Lou was the first to notice that Tank wasn't with them. He looked around and there Tank was standing back beside the toolbox, just standing there. Then all at once he laid his hand on the dusty top and rubbed it around as if, inside, something was locked up like the war itself that kept better with a lid on.

Lou said, "What's in there, Tank?"

Tank seemed to be thinking, as if he wasn't sure. Then, "Can you guys keep a secret?"

The boys both nodded eagerly.

"All right. It's a dead Jap."

Joe took a small step backward, eyes glued to the seam of the lid and the rusty hasp, and Lou felt drawn to his awe. Not just drawn but beholden to it, for he wasn't sure that what was really in that box didn't just depend on how good a salesman Tank was. If there really was a dead Jap in that box, God almighty! What kind of a souvenir was that?

Joe was sold.

"Jeezo, Tank! How does it – I mean, how long d'you think he'll last in there?"

"Well, it's not stuffed," Tank said, "like some animal on the wall. It's more like dried out, the way those Pharaohs got preserved in Egypt. The thing about a mummy is it doesn't like fresh air."

"Did you shoot him?" Joe said.

"No, I'm pretty sure I didn't. He got killed in a Banzai charge, along with a lot of other Japanese soldiers."

"So d'you think, I mean – could we see him?" Lou said.

"Well, the thing about these mummies is, the longer they stay closed up, the better. Right now I'd have to go downstairs for the key, too. I think it's somewhere in my father's study. And Dad –" Tank looked at his watch.

Lou saw then that Tank looked slightly faint. He seemed to be reeling a little, his face was pale. Then he stood up straight and color rushed into his face.

"I guess you guys better skedaddle, then," Tank said. "It's getting on toward four."

"Well, the next time you come over, Tank," Joe said, "why don't you bring your guns? That's when you could meet our Mom."

Lou looked for the grin on Joe's face, because that was how it sounded. Too afraid of sounding serious, he'd said it like a joke. Miraculously Tank didn't laugh.

"Well, sure – that's an idea," Tank said.

Out on the street they hurried along and all at once Joe said, "You know what we forgot, Lou?"

"What?"

"If Mr. Crutchley doesn't know the mummy's in that box, what if he gets in there for a tool or something, and there's a dead Jap staring up at him?"

"That's none of our business," Lou said. "Anyway, I guess Tank's got that figured out."

"Yeah, but it kinda makes you wonder. What d'you do with a dead Jap?"

Lou thought about that. What made Tank go to all the trouble of bringing home a thing like that? What did the MP say who'd checked him off the boat with all the extra poundage? 'Got a howitzer coming on the next boat, soldier?'

No, Tank wouldn't take the chance of lying to them. Not if he didn't want them to think he was crazy. In the war he must have been the kind of a guy the other men looked up to, and were always glad of having along on patrols. Looking at him, before you heard him talk, you'd think he had to be a tough guy. But there was something else that Lou couldn't put his finger on, and the mystery brushed his heart like a bug in the dark that might be harmless and might not. He said to Joe:

"You have to hand it to Tank, Joe. Anybody who can smuggle a dead Jap into the United States has to be pretty smart."

8

The thicket of shrubs and trees that bordered the length of the yard was infested with Jap snipers, and they had to be cleaned out to make it safe for the rest of the company to move through. Tank said:

"Now remember, you guys - watch out for all those other snipers up there, not just me. Here, Lou. Think you can handle this?" He held out the Japanese bolt-action rifle.

In Lou's hands it sagged, but right away he hefted it up to port-arms, saying, "What about you, Tank?"

Tank looked down at the P-38 in his hand.

"Here, Joe. I'll trade you for that Daisy. I've gotta have a rifle, you know, up in a tree."

Joe took the pistol, beaming, and Tank relieved him of the Daisy air rifle with the rubber knife lashed to the barrel for a bayonet.

"Wow! I took this off a dead Jap, Tank. How does that sound."

"Pretty reasonable, I'd say," Tank said. "Okay, Lou – you're the lieutenant. Joe, you be the platoon sergeant. Turn your backs, now. Count to twenty. I've gotta find a tree to climb." Tank took off for the jungle while Joe started counting.

As soon as Tank hit the thicket, spiny branches snagged his T-shirt, scratched his arms and sprang back, disturbing the bees on the guava blossoms. His Wellington boots slipped on acorns and oak leaves. Rotting avocados lay all over the twig-littered ground under the tree he picked to climb. The fruit had gone to green powder in the broken black shells left of the skins. A two-way traffic line of ants disappeared around the back of the limb he grabbed. He slung the toy rifle across his shoulder and hoisted himself up. Joe was counting " . . . one-thousand nine . . ." Tank climbed up into a nice sturdy saddle, twisted the belt webbing around his forearm to steady the rifle and drew a bead on Lou. Get the lieutenant; that was the idea. Make the rest of the platoon run around like chickens with their heads cut off. And then it came to him.

It came like it had lain in a vault, all wound up to be placed on a projector one day, and today was the day. But no suspense beat in the hearts of any audience. You could lie forever under that sweltering sky that pressed down with the promise of only needing you to die to belong. Where the mosquitoes raced the Japs to get to you first; then the snakes, starving now that they had silenced all the birds, would sometimes in their zeal rear up like cobras, weaving and red-eyed, and you would keep track of the heads you'd sliced off, as if the Japs were in for the same thing, when their time came.

The sound of a car down on the street grew louder. It was coming this way. Tank looked through the foliage to his right. The gleam of chrome and a battleship grey hood flashed through the shrubs and the Pepper trees. Oh, no! Not now! And he watched the car that seemed to be slowing for a turn into the driveway. He shut his eyes tight, as if that would banish the car, or keep it going straight. Her note to the boys in the kitchen had read, *Be home around four-thirty. Be sure to stir the spaghetti sauce for me on the stove.*

Tank opened his eyes. The car hummed on past and turned left around the cactus garden and the driver goosed the engine past Daddy Banks', then Dorothy's house. Tank felt lightheaded, like he couldn't hang onto the limb anymore with one hand and keep the Daisy in the other. He wasn't really afraid of being here when she got home. That wasn't it. He knew he would have to meet her eventually. He'd got that all mapped out, the truth and a credit to his judgment.

But this - caught in the act like he was every bit as much a kid as they were - that wouldn't look good. How do you set *that* straight? 'Oh, all this is just to tide me over until . . .

"Twenty!" yelled Joe. Tank looked. The boys were crouching, starting to move out. He waited until they were right at the edge of the lawn before he opened up. The boys hadn't seen him, and they hit the deck and they were trying to see what tree he was in. As soon as they spotted him, and Joe yelled, "There he is!" Tank pulled off a round. Lou jerked and grasped the side of his leg. "I'm hit!" he cried out.

Tank cut loose again, aiming at Joe this time. His aim was off. Lou winced and clutched his shoulder. The Japanese rifle dropped onto the grass. Joe picked it up and the barrel swayed as he took aim and started blasting. Tank screamed and slithered onto the next branch down. The branch cracked and he hit hard and sprawled onto the mess of leaves and dried-up avocados. In a twisted position he lay still, leaving the toy rifle within inches of his right hand. Pain shot through his other hand. He felt a trickle of blood running between his fingers.

"Way to go, Sarge," Lou croaked. "Go check and see if he's dead. We're not taking any prisoners."

Tank could hear Joe coming. As soon as he got close enough he sprang up onto his knees and shoved the rubber bayonet into Joe's belly. The flabby blade bent double just above Joe's belt, but he just looked down at where his guts were supposed to be spilling out, rammed the bolt back, rammed it forward, took aim and shot the sniper through the heart, point blank. Tank arched his back, collapsed and died. Joe called back to Lou.

"He's dead now, Lieutenant! Real dead!"

The pain in Tank's hand now began to throb. He thought it was time, and he sat up, and with a glance at his hand, said, "Oh, shit."

Joe bent over him to get a better look.

"Jeez, Tank. You're bleeding."

Tank reached back into his pocket, pulled out a handkerchief and wrapped it around his hand, making a fist to hold it tight.

Joe said worriedly, "Let's go in and you can wash that off, Tank."

"Oh, it's not that bad," Tank said. "I'll take care of it as soon as I get home."

"Well, can't you come in for a minute? We've got some lemonade made in the fridge."

"Well –"

Joe didn't wait. He said, "Come on, Tank. You'll feel better after some nice cold lemonade." He tore off toward Lou, slowed to tell him what had happened, then made a bee-line for the house.

On the radio a single shot rang out from Tennessee Jed's long rifle, its ricochet whistling into some misty frontier valley – the way Tarzan's yodel made a jungle chatter. In the kitchen Joe slammed the fridge door and bottles in there clanked. Lou reached back from where he sat beside Tank on the bed and dragged his big illustrated Bible book onto his lap. Leaving it unopened there he said:

"Can't I get you a band-aid, Tank?"

"Naw. I can wait till I get home."

"Stay a little longer, won't you? You can say hello to Mom."

That was just what Tank, right now, didn't want to do. He looked down at the back of his hand where blood had made a big stain on the handkerchief and thought, what a fine how d'you do this is. Any minute now she'll be here, and here he was like a vagrant off the street in need of medical attention. He'd better grab his guns and leave before she pulled in. Yet wouldn't it look a lot worse, he thought, if she came home and he was right in the midst of running off? Why not stay here like he wasn't scared of anything and face the music?

Lou scooted a little closer to Tank and asked him who his favorite character in the Bible was. Before Tank could answer he said, "Mine's Samson."

Lou turned to the picture where Samson was jacking open the jaws of a lion while off to the side a couple of Philistines in a chariot watched behind a restless horse. Lou asked Tank whether he thought a person could kill a lion by pulling its jaws apart like that. Tank said he didn't think most humans could, but Samson, God gave him superhuman strength for feats like this, and Lou said yeah, who else could push the pillars of a temple down, or kill a whole canyon full of his enemies with the jawbone of an ass?

"Come on, you guys!" Joe called out from the kitchen, "Come and get it!"

In the kitchen Tank saw the big crock pot simmering on the stove, steam puffing out around the lid. Whatever was inside smelled terrific. Through the breakfast nook window, past the rose bush scratching at the glass, the palms that lined the front yard cast smog-faded shadows on the street.

Joe had the lemonade poured into three Dixie cups that stood beside the pitcher on the sink board.

"I had some already," Joe said with a guilty look. "Boy, does it ever hit the spot!"

"Which one's mine?" Lou said.

"They're all the same," Joe said with a faint whine in his voice.

Just then Tank thought he heard a car door slam through the screen door off the laundry room.

Looking up, Lou said, "Uh-oh, I think Mom's home already."

Tank tightened up inside, as if a wind had suddenly come up to blow away all the reasonable explanations for his presence. He listened while the tapping sound of high heels came briskly up the walk along the back yard, slowing on the steps. The screen door creaked.

"Boys! I'm home! Oh!" Her eyes fell on Tank, and he was looking back at the pretty woman in the doorway, lugging a sack of groceries. She came in looking fresh in black slacks and a pale yellow blouse and set the groceries down beside the dish rack. She looked prettier now that he was seeing her up closer than before, with her platinum blond hair, large blue eyes and a lot of freckles on her arms. Lou said:

"Hey, Mom! Tank's here! He came over for a – he's visiting."

"Hello there, Tank," Stella said.

Tank nodded.

"Mrs. Ryan."

"Tank hurt himself, Mom," Lou said hurriedly. "We were outside –"

Stella's eyes fell upon the bloody handkerchief that Tank was keeping tight around his hand with a clenched fist. She cocked her head a little, her face smoldering with caution, then took a step closer to him.

"How in the world did that happen?"

"Oh, I –"

"We were outside playing, Mom," Joe said, "when Tank – well, we shot him and he fell out of a tree."

"Oh, my goodness! Playing for keeps, huh?"

"Tank brought over some of his souvenirs, Mom," Lou explained. "He said we could play with them - if it's okay with you."

"Is that so?" Stella's smile slipped a little. "What kind of souvenirs?"

Before Tank could get a word out, Lou said, "Well, there's one big Japanese rifle, and a pistol. That's all. Tank left the Samurai swords at home."

"I should hope so. So these guns, Tank – you're talking about *real* guns?"

Joe hurried to say, "There's no bullets in 'em, Mom."

'Well, I'm glad to hear that. And you, Tank? You –"

"I've been with the boys the whole time, Mrs. Ryan," Tank said.

"Oh. Playing with them?"

"Well, I thought I could fall down once in a while like a wounded Jap. Be the enemy, you know. Give them a break."

Stella reached out and mussed Lou's hair.

"How come it's always the real stuff you guys like to play with?" She looked up at Tank. "I took a trip around the world once. I got a souvenir from just about every country I visited. Austrian riding boots in Vienna, mother-of-pearl opera glasses from London. We were in the Sudan, my great aunt and I. I picked up this little black voodoo doll. I mean that's what it turned into once I made a pincushion out of it. The boys've got it in their room, now. Joe tells me the riding boots make a pretty good Nazi out of him."

"I was Field Marshall Rommel with the opera glasses," Lou put in proudly.

Stella leveled a solemn look on Tank, saying, "You have to be sure none of these guns is ever loaded, Tank. I'm sure they never are, but –"

"Oh, they haven't been loaded since the war, Mrs. Ryan. Of course I'm always double-checking. Any time you'd like to look them over . . "

"Well, no . . ." Stella looked at Lou. "What's the matter with your cap guns, honey?"

"They're not real," Lou said flatly.

"Oh, you guys and the real thing."

"Tank played the Jap," Joe said. "We shot him out of a tree and he fell on something sharp. That's how he hurt his hand."

Stella stepped a little closer to Tank. "Let's have a look at that, Tank."

She took Tank's hand and, gently raising it a little, peeled back the blood-soaked handkerchief and made a face at the gash across his knuckles, where a flap of skin stuck up like a trap-door spider's hatch. "Ouch! That looks pretty nasty. You guys sure do play for keeps out there."

Tank said, "That's what a Jap sniper gets for going up against the U.S. Army." And right away he looked for the dud that must fall like a shadow across Stella's face. Yet while her mouth was set, unsmiling, her eyes came up and, right there so close to him, still holding his hand in hers, he could almost hear her asking him to notice how pretty she was for a woman her age. How her looks erased the years, the lines, the false color of her hair. And how there was a sort of tapping at the windows of her eyes, and he was supposed to look up and see a face, just meant for him, that others couldn't see. She blinked and turned away and suddenly it was all gone. She said to Joe:

"Honey, go back to the big bathroom and bring me the band aids and the bottle of mercurochrome."

"Okay, Mom."

Joe took off. Stella led Tank over to the sink, saying, "Let's get a better look at this thing." Lou followed and watched while Stella ran some cold water onto the gash. She suddenly said to him, "Don't you have a room to clean up, honey?"

"Me? What about Joe?"

"The both of you. I want you to bring your dirty clothes out to the hamper, too. They don't belong in your closet."

Just then Joe came back with a tin of band-aids and the little dipper bottle of mercurochrome.

"We've gotta clean our room, Joe," Lou said in a tone that warned Joe not to get too happy.

Joe's shoulders slumped.

"Right now?"

"Yep, right now," Stella said.

"Oh, awright. Come on, Lou. I'll stack up the comics if you vacuum."

The boys both started to trudge away. Before they were completely through the doorway Stella said:

"Let me dry that off for you, Tank."

She tore off a paper towel from the roller, folded it over Tank's knuckles and gently held it there for a moment. She dabbed on some mercurochrome with the glass dipper. The gash, with all the blood cleaned off, turned out to be worth only two band-aids. She pressed the warmth of her palm down over the back of Tank's hand to make the tape stick. Tank glanced up into her eyes and tried to take pure kindness from the gesture, but he felt short of breath. As soon as she let go, he raised his bandaged paw and said, "My ticket home." He gave his head a twist, then looked down at his watch.

"Oh, boy! I'd better get a move on. Dad said he might fire up the barbecue tonight. He mentioned steak."

"Why don't you and Victor come on over and eat with us?" Stella said. "I'm having some people over from the cast of the play I'm directing. We're putting on *King Lear* down at the Playhouse. Morrie Ankrum's got the lead. He'll be here with everybody else."

"Oh, I don't know," Tank said. "That's nice of you to offer, ma'am, but –"

"Call me Stella, why don't you," Stella said.

"Okay – Stella."

She crooked her finger at him, waggled it and started for the stove, saying, "Come over here a minute. I want you to sample this and tell me if it's not the best spaghetti sauce you've ever tasted." She lifted the lid from the pot on the back burner, steam poured out and she picked up a wooden spoon and stirred the sauce inside. She dipped some out and, cupping her other hand under it to catch the drips, moved it toward Tank's mouth. "Open wide," she said, opening her own mouth as if Tank was in a high chair. "Careful, now. It's hot!" She blew on the steaming, dripping morsel.

It wasn't supposed to be this way, but it was, and his heart began to pound like a jungle drum while the walls of a dream closed in around him, built by the years he'd been away from girls. Her pretty legs stepped into his mind, her full bust swelled under that pale yellow blouse. How far could this have played if Art was here? He heard a stupid laugh somewhere, and a stupid voice was saying, "Whew! I think I burned my tongue."

"Did you? Oh, no! I'm sorry, I didn't think it was that hot."

"Boy, it's good, though. *Really* good."

"Well, thank you. Do you like anchovies in your Caesar salad?"

"Anchovies? Sure, but - "

"Believe me, Tank - that's all you need to qualify to talk to theatre people."

"Well –"

"Just come, won't you? You and your dad. Seems like the kids have taken *quite* a shine to you."

"I like them too," Tank said. "I'll talk to Dad about it."

"Yes, and if he can't make it, bring yourself."

Bring myself, Tank thought. Leave Dad home and come alone.

"I might just do that," he said.

Tank said goodbye and turned to go. Stella saw him as far as the living room where, just at the turn for the hallway, she said, "Go this way if you'd like to say goodbye to the boys on your way out."

9

On the TV Ina Rae Hutton licked her lips and raised her trombone to lead her all-girl band in their final number, *Caravan*. The night outside was warm and balmy. Tank felt it in the air that blew in through the open window. He hadn't told his father about Stella's invitation. Then Victor announced that he was going out tonight and don't expect him back until late. That settled that.

He got up and shut off the TV. It was a long shot, this late. Maybe the boys would still be up. The shirt he picked out from his closet was that silk one he had got for Christmas, 1942. He hadn't liked it, then, but he did now.

He turned on the porch light, went out and locked the door behind him. Nobody else was out as he walked down under the streetlamps, passing Dorothy's house and then her lush rose garden. He heard the yip of a coyote far off. No dog answered.

At the top of the Ryan's front walk he looked down across the lawn for people outside holding drinks, cars choking the driveway. Nobody moved in the lighted windows. The lights that blazed through the Aspens towering over the stucco wall along the patio spread down onto the one car in the driveway and the one person, a woman, who stood back on the grass, waving at the shrill goodbyes from the back seat and the hands that poked through the open windows. A man's voice from behind the steering wheel bellowed, "Saddle my horses! Call my train together! Degenerate bastard, I'll not trouble thee! Yet have I left a daughter!"

Tank saw then, as the woman turned, that she was Stella, in black slacks and a white blouse. He watched her as she walked up toward the patio and went through the gate. That must have been the last of them, he thought, and with a sigh he turned for home. Then he didn't know what it was, what got his feet to moving back the other way. Not reason, not any wild guess. All he knew was the sooner he got going down there toward that light, the better. He felt in the mood.

Floodlights at intervals along the edge of the roof lit up a man slumped over his hand on a highball glass on the redwood table. He sat there alone, with an air about him of being shackled to his loneliness by the litter of sparerib bones and crumpled napkins on the paper plates left on the table. He wore suspenders. Strands of his wavy hair dangled across his forehead from a crooked part down the middle.

From a Victrola somewhere behind the open French doors the Army Air Corps Choir, whose beautiful harmony Tank remembered, was in the midst of *The Whiffenpoof Song*. He looked to his right where water dripping from an algae-bearded gargoyle plunked onto the dark surface of a fish pond. The mouth of a goldfish gulped a soaking crust of bread. Movement to his left became a voice that seemed to mumble out of a coma:

"Hey there, pal. You forget somethin'?"

Tank stepped toward the man.

"No, I just got here," and he led with a smile he felt unsure of – the sudden intruder like a hobo in the neighborhood, smelling leftovers.

"Why, hell – you're the – no, you couldn't be. My old pal Don Swinney is dead, I think." The music drifted out from the Victrola, 'Gentlemen songsters off on a spree, gone from here to eternity, God have mercy on such as we . . .' "But you look just like him. How the hell can that be? Back from the dead, Don?"

"No, sir," Tank said desperately. "I'm –"

"Champs of '34, my ol' zip lads. Don was my left Half, built like a brick shithouse, and he could run like a gazelle. If you weren't wearing that flattop, you'd be him to a tee. I'm not so goddamn sure you aren't."

Tank shoved his hands into his front pockets. He decided to go along with the illusion until it got corrected on its own.

"I played some football myself, but that was before the war."

"My old pal Don went into the Navy and came back with a plate in his head."

"Oh, then he's not dead?"

"Did I say he was dead? Now wait a minute –"

Just then Stella breezed out of the living room, carrying a Martini glass filled with an amber liquid.

"Tank, for God's sake! We'd given up on you. What happened?"

"My dad couldn't make it, and I –"

"Oh, never mind. Better late than never! You're here, that's the important thing. What about a drink?"

She was tight, Tank saw. He knew it shouldn't shock him at the same time that it did, and he held up his smile against that kind of fey excitement about her that made him look over at the man he knew now must be Art. There wasn't much expression on his face. If anything a kind of soulless, deadened smirk. Interest hanging on by a thread.

"Well, yes, thanks. It's a little late, but –"

"Art, here's the boy I've been telling you about. What do you think of him?"

Art tossed off a laugh. Tank heard it like an urchin asking for a place in out of the cold.

"And here I thought he was Don Swinney, back from the dead. Then I realized they didn't kill him in the war at all. I must've meant the dead of that day we beat El Centro 13-12 for the title, and ol' Don made All-Valley halfback."

Stella rested her chin on a finger.

"What was so dead about that day, Art?"

He stared at her incredulously.

"What the hell're you talking about?"

"Oh, never mind. There *is* a resemblance, kind of. But Art, for God's sake give the past a rest, okay?"

Art ignored that, reached out a limp hand toward Tank.

"H'war you, pal? My wife didn't tell me you were coming."

"I did, too, Art! Tank and Victor – don't you remember? I told you I invited them."

Art thrust an iron grip into Tank's hand that got the jump on his squeeze back.

"Pull up a chair, Tank – I mean a bench. I hate like hell drinking alone, and Stella – at heart she's still a teetotaler. I taught her everything she knows about the art of getting blotto without showing it."

Stella raised her glass up like a torch.

"Then what do you call this, wise guy? My third Shirley Temple?"

"A thousand pardons, effendi," Art said, waving a Moslem flourish up the front of his face.

Tank looked at the bottle: he could use a drink right about now. Stella started for the open doorway.

"Well, if you boys will excuse me, I've got dishes to take care of. Oh, Tank – what're you drinking?"

"We got plenty here, darling,' Art said. "Bring Tank a clean glass, would you?"

Stella hesitated before saying, "Glad to," with a curt smile.

As soon as she was gone, Art said, "Forgive me, pal - I *do* remember, now. Lou asked me where you were, and I had to say I didn't know. Say, how's that hand of yours?" Art looked for the hand that Tank had under the table, on his lap.

Tank brought it out, exhibiting the band-aid across his knuckles. He watched Art's face, afraid of the next thing he might say – 'What's this I hear about your putting real guns into the hands of my kids!'

"Oh, heck. It's hardly a scratch, really."

Art shook a finger at him.

"That doesn't excuse you from looking so much like Don Swinney, pal."

Tank smiled wanly, saying, "I'll take that as a compliment."

"How's your old dad getting along these days?" Art said. "The last time I saw him was – hell, you were still overseas."

"He couldn't make it tonight was because he had to meet a guy down at the Blue Onion. Apparently this guy had some dirt to spread on Dave Beck – you know, the union boss."

"Yeah, we'll probably read about it in his Sunday column. I'll never forget the way he raked MacArthur over the coals for going so easy on the Japs after the war."

"Dad's got pretty strong ideas that way," Tank said.

"As soon as Dorothy showed up with Ricky tonight, I thought sure your dad would be there with her. But no dice."

Tank understood, and said, "Dad sees her from time to time. Keeps telling me it's nothing serious. You should hear him talk about her cooking."

Art laughed, then fingering his glass with a thoughtful, solemn look downward, he said, "What about you, pal? What've you been up to?"

"Well, like just about everybody else in my shoes, I've been out looking for a job."

"I hear there's no shortage of those around – if you're not fussy."

Tank nodded, dropping a smile into his lap.

"The trouble is, I'm fussy."

"Hell, you should'a seen me the day I got laid off at Douglas Aircraft. Of course all the girls I'd coached in calisthenics went with me. They went home to their hubbies. I came home to my rich wife."

Tank felt like Art had accidentally nudged him into a snake pit. The only way out was to pretend they weren't there.

"It's not that I haven't got any bites, yet," he said. "I went up to Flintridge Prep the other day and applied for a coaching slot they'd opened up, thinking maybe not too many other guys had any more experience than I did. I got my hopes up too soon. Whoever takes the job will have to wait till the current football line coach quits at the end of this season. Meanwhile he'll be assigned to mowing lawns and cleaning up around the gym. I guess I would have told them to shove it if it hadn't been for the boss's secretary. She tells me she's got the boss's ear. Dad thinks he's got my number, and maybe he does. A pretty face isn't gonna sign my paychecks."

"I hate to say this, but he might have something there."

"Boy, I hope not. I love football. That's pretty much all I've got going for me on my application." Tank let a smile linger in the air of manliness they both breathed.

Just then Stella came through the doorway from the living room, carrying a glass full of ice. Art said hurriedly, "Come around tomorrow if you can, pal. I might be able to give you a few pointers on coaching."

Tank had time only to gape before Stella came up to him, saying, "Have you ever done any acting, Tank?" She swayed a little, grinning down at him. Art said:

"What's that got to do with the price of tea in China?"

"Oh, Art – would you please mind your own business?"

Art rolled his eyes at Tank and said, "But for the please, I'd be the biggest gossip in this neighborhood."

Tank tossed off a smile at Art before he said to Stella, "I was pretty terrible at acting back in high school. The only part I ever got was this detective, from Scotland Yard, because I'd fooled around some, imitating the Queen's English."

"You're kidding!" Stella said.

"No - "

"We're losing our man playing Gloucester in *King Lear*. Why don't you give it a whirl?"

"Why him?" Art said.

"Actually," Tank began, "with all the –"

"Come on, Tank," Stella prompted excitedly, "let's hear a sample of that accent. Wait a minute. Repeat this line from Glouscester, okay?"

"Okay," Tank said.

Stella waved her finger like a wand.

"*'The King is mad; how stiff is my vile sense that I stand up, and have ingenious feeling of my huge sorrows.'* Got that, Tank?"

Tank took a breath, grasping for the runaway line.

"The King is mad; how stiff is my vile sense that I – oh, shoot! I lost it."

"Never mind! That's great, Tank! You've got the job!"

"He's got other plans," Art said sullenly. "He won't have time to get up on wooden horses and swear allegiance to a windy monarch."

Stella looked at Art suspiciously, but said pleasantly enough:

"You might let Tank answer for himself, Art. Then we'd know what he's got time for."

Tank saw that Stella was looking at him intently, so he said, "I can't make any promises, Mrs. Ryan, but I'll –"

"Just think about it, won't you, Tank?"

"Oh sure, I will. I'll take that drink now, Art, if you don't mind."

Art picked up the bottle, poured into Tank's glass until ice rose tumbling to the top.

"How's that, pal?"

Tank picked up the glass and took a long, thirsty drink. Art said:

"Now don't forget tomorrow, say around noon. Just come on down to the basement. If I'm not there, go up and knock on the back door. Stell or one of the boys will let you in. Okay by you, darlin'?"

Stella gave him a cockeyed look of tentative alarm.

"I'm afraid I don't know what the heck you're talking about, Art."

Art spoke slowly, as if to a child.

"Tank's coming over tomorrow. He's got a chance for a job coaching football. I can give him a few pointers he might find useful during his interview. Other than that," Art broke open with a big smile, "come in your sweat clothes, pal. You can get a workout in– for free."

"Well, thank you," Tank said, not quite knowing what he was getting himself into.

He felt his ability to speak now losing ground to a wan smile. The kind of a smile that made you more of a listener than a talker:

protective, like a barrier between you and the next guy in a public toilet. Or worse, the shell of a car in which you were impossibly driving too fast down a shady lane, racing for home. You had to get there, or else. A dog runs under your wheels, you feel the bump and have to stop. Yet if you don't get home in the next few minutes something terrible will happen. You'll mess your pants. The kind of a nightmare you have to open your mouth to wake up from, but you can't.

He drank down his whiskey while Art poured himself another Scotch. He watched the glass fill up, knowing he'd had enough. His rubber eyelids rose and fell; his eyes spun, trying to focus. Where was Stella?

She'd gone back into the kitchen. Tank couldn't remember if he'd said goodnight to her. She must have read his mind: two men against one woman. She'd seen how he liked Art – a man you could say made her unhappy. She stood restlessly somewhere outside the vault of his imagination - almost as tight as Art was. In the morning it would all evaporate. Art wasn't such a culprit, really. Something else kept her from being who she wanted to be.

It felt so good to be down in that drugged world of hope and mercy. The anesthetic was in full swing, and he thought of those steady, reliable old streetlights by which he would soon see his way home, feeling for the key in his pocket. No weak flashlight needed to pick after the tracks that filled up with the unrelenting rain, a snake slithering past, his fear of a flare before he reached the bunker. No, he'd see the front porch light flickering through the breeze in the cherry tree; and it was so late, he could count on his father's bedroom window to be dark. At times like this, while the booze coursed through his veins and all was well with the world, there were no hangovers that couldn't be put off indefinitely.

༄

She could hear him coming along the hallway on his crutches, and plunged her hands into the dishwater, feeling for another glass. She didn't want him around her right now. She dreaded the silence he brought in with whatever else he wanted. A drink? No, she heard ice tinkling in the one he had already. The dread seemed to embrace his presence for the chance it gave her to ignore him. What she hated she wanted, just for a while. His crutches creaked behind her. He hopped on his one slipper, gripped the table and slung himself in behind it, clearing his throat loudly.

"Still doin' those damn dishes, darlin'?"

"There were a lot of them," she said, "but I'm almost through." A glass slipped from her hand and fell to the floor, but didn't break.

"Here, lemme get that for you," Art said. He braced himself to get up.

"No, no – sit still. I've got it." With dripping hands Stella picked up the glass.

"Why don't you leave the rest till morning?" Art said. "We'll hit the sack."

"Why should I? I'm not sleepy, yet."

"Not sleepy?"

She turned to look at his face. He stared back, chewing on the inside of his lip.

"You go," she said. "I'll be in later."

"Okay, are you accepting my apology, or aren't you?"

"Apology for what?"

Art sighed loud enough to blow a match out.

"That I didn't share your enthusiasm for Tank Crutchley's acting ability."

"Oh, is that all?"

"You put the kid in a bind," Art said.

Stella's hands stopped like propellers in the dishwater, as if he had cut her engine. She leaned on them.

"Art! I gave the boy a chance to be in a play. He's about the right age, nice looking and, well – that British accent did the trick. You'd think he was born and bred in England."

"Is that a fact?"

"What're you so worked up about? You like him, too, don't you?"
Art took a breath. She could tell he was holding himself in.
"We'll see."
"What, when the booze wears off?"
Art lifted his glass as far as his chin, gave up and lowered it.
"Why do I always feel like you're so much smarter than I am, Stell? I never used to feel that way."

She turned to look at him, looking for the man she used to love, like a doctor feels around for a hidden wound. But then the doctor says, I'm afraid I've got some bad news for you.

"Why don't you go to bed, Art. I'll be along in a minute."

"Yeah. This stuff tastes like gasoline, anyway." Art grunted, pushing crablike on the table as he struggled to slide out. He hobbled up behind Stella, parted her hair where it fell across her ears and kissed her there. "Goodnight, darlin'. See you in the morning."

"Okay," she said, barely turning, feeling the wetness from his lips on her neck, the way it tickled as it dried, and the emptiness of his departure washed back into her mind a night, long ago, when, trusting her that much, he had told her he was in big trouble. There was talk of his being fired for taking the boys across to Mexicali for another victory celebration, contributing to the delinquency of minors.

His slow progress down the hallway, to the loneliness of sleep without her, put off for another night the hammer's blow, and she looked down at the distortions of her face between the suds in the dishwater. The face that, looking back at her, vowed to look so much prettier in the morning.

10

Lou came out of the bathroom, rounded the corner and almost collided with his mother in the washroom, where she was loading dirty clothes into the Bendix. Lou sidled past her, saying, "Sorry, Mom. I'm goin' back down to the basement before Tank has to leave."

"Okay, honey."

Lou pushed past the screen door and started down the steps under the olive tree. He'd made up his mind in the bathroom that he would have to stick close to Tank and his dad, whatever they were doing, hoping and praying Ricky would shut up.

The sun got hot again in the glare of the stucco past the shade, and he could smell that Clorox smell coming out on his skin, then the heavy, steamy scent of gardenias. He looked out at the strips of sunlight falling through the slats of the lath house at the back of the garage. At the edge of the grass, a little smoke drifted out from under the tin hat of the incinerator. He thought maybe Tank would leave sooner if he wasn't there. Dad had poured himself a drink, and Tank had said he didn't care for one. Suddenly Coy pranced up behind him, nails clicking on the pavement. At the head of the flight of steps that led down to the basement door, Lou commanded, "You stay here, girl. Sit! That's a good girl." Coy sat. She pointed her ears and cocked her head as Lou said, "I'll be back soon."

He could hear the voices in the basement. As soon as he pushed through the door, there was Ricky wailing away at the big Everlast bag that swayed and twirled at the end of the chain it hung by from a crossbeam.

"Hey, Lou!" Ricky called out breathlessly. "Any time you're ready!"

Lou ignored him, heading for the benches and the weights in front of the big mirror where Tank, laid out on the supine bench, was just heaving a barbell off his chest while Art stood watching behind the uprights. Lou was glad to see his father didn't have a glass in his hand any more.

"Jeez, Dad – how heavy is that?"

"Two eighty," Art said in a voice that bore down on the words as if they weighed that much, too. "Tank's goin' for ten reps. He's comin' up on six."

"Wow!"

Behind Lou now the big bag shuddered on its chain. Ricky said:

"What's the matter, Lou? Chicken? Come on, let's go a couple rounds! I'll go easy on you!"

Tank grunted, arching his back as he strenuously pushed on the barbell and it inched slowly upward, tipping a little this way and that.

"Atta pepper!" Art stood back from the uprights.

Lou glanced back at the wiry boy who had come over from next door and wouldn't lay off trying to get him into a sparring match. He wondered how Dorothy felt about what hot stuff that military school had made out of her son. He glanced at himself in the mirror and said, "Can you and me and Tank play three-cornered catch with the medicine ball, Dad?"

"Just a second, pal. Let Tank finish these reps, here."

A big red blanket, tacked to some foundation pilings, hid part of the crawl space back behind the lighted area. Against the concrete bulkhead that held the dirt back, the large framed mirror leaned almost upright. You could see, by the light skimming the dirt from the ventilation windows, the black joints and elbows of the water pipes. There on the ledge stood a highball glass in a terrycloth sock.

There was a clank, the heavy barbell came to rest across the uprights and Tank slid forward and sat up. He had on sweat pants and a white ribbed undershirt damp with sweat. Lou thought Tank had just about the biggest, tightest arms he'd ever seen. How many years would it be before his arms would get that big? His dad was saying:

"Christ almighty, Tank, you wanta go for three-hundred? I think you could do it, pal. Easy."

"Maybe not easy," Tank said, and his eyes flicked onto Lou.

Lou felt Tank's smile like a letter from him, from all those tough and hot exotic places where he'd been, and had escaped now, safe and sound, as if he'd never been.

"I'll tell you one thing," Art said, "you should be *playing* football, not coaching it."

"You think so?" Tank said, and Lou picked up on the faint mocking in his voice.

"Hell, yes, I do," Art said. He turned aside, looked up toward the ledge where his drink sat in the semi-dark. He pulled up his chest, then, the way he'd always said a man should stand or walk, and Lou took a breath of him.

"Hey, Lou!" Ricky called out tauntingly, "You gonna come over here and spar with me or what? I promise I'll go easy on you."

"No thanks," Lou said.

"Why not? I need a sparring partner. You're just about as tall as I am, now. I'll bet you've got a pretty good reach."

"I don't really feel like it right now, Ricky."

"You're not chicken, are you?" Ricky danced around, throwing punches at the air.

Tank got up from the bench. He said to Ricky, "How old are you, anyway, Ricky?"

"I'm going on sixteen," Ricky said with a rebellious squint, lifting his chin like Mussolini did, Lou thought.

"And you, Lou?"

"Twelve," Lou said.

"Kind of a mismatch there, wouldn't you think?" Tank looked at Art, and Lou wished for a moment it was his dad who'd said that; but he was glad Tank said it, anyway.

"C'mere a minute, pal," Art said, and he drew Lou closer to him by his shoulder. "Remember that bully you were telling me about at school? Forest somebody or other? Okay, I'm gonna show you what you can do the next time he tries to push you around. Tank, toss me that pair of gloves over there, will you?"

Tank hesitated, glancing at Lou, and for a moment Lou thought he was saved, because his father seemed to think the world of Tank.

"Come on, pal," Art insisted. "Toss me those gloves. Both pairs."

The gloves, brand-new, lay on a bench at the edge of the canvas mat. Tank went over and picked up the two pairs by the laces they were tied together with. He brought them over and Art untied the laces and gave one pair to Ricky and laid his hand again on Lou's shoulder. "Here you are, pal. Put these on. I'll lace 'em up for you." Art held the cuffs of a glove out for Lou to push his hand into. Lou looked into the eyes of the man he loved so much and said:

"No, Dad. I don't feel like it today."

"Listen, pal. You might not feel like it the next time some bully messes with you, either."

Lou turned away from the smell of scotch on his father's breath. Tank said:

"Maybe you should lay off, Art. He doesn't want to."

Lou felt his father's hand bearing down on his shoulder, the fingers squeezing.

"You might think if you're a nice enough guy, a bully will back off and leave you alone. But see, your average bully doesn't operate that way. He loves to step on nice guys. He'll step on you until you surprise him with a right cross, you get me?"

"Yes, Dad, but when the time comes, I don't think I'll have any –"

"You have to know how to handle yourself, pal. You have to be prepared."

Lou tried again to edge away from the scotch on his father's breath as if, by getting far enough away, his father would come back into focus as the man he wanted him to be.

"Come on, Lou," Ricky prompted. "It's a cinch. We'll just fool around. Nobody's gonna get hurt."

"I'm not afraid of getting hurt," Lou snapped.

Suddenly Art was pulling down the gloves on Lou's unwilling, floppy hands, and Ricky eagerly began to get into his.

"Here, Tank," Ricky said, "lace these up for me."

"You know how to say please, son?"

"Yeah, sorry. Please."

Art got behind Lou, leaned over his shoulders and started to manipulate his arms.

"Here's what you want to do, pal. You lead with your left, see. That's the fist you jab with. Jab! Jab! Jab! And while you're throwing those jabs, you keep your right up like this to guard your face. You've gotta dance around. Stay on the balls of your feet. Bob and weave. Keep jabbing your way into an opening, then throw that right cross. That's the combination. You got it? Left jab, right cross."

Ricky was stiffening his upheld arms while Tank tied his laces. Seeing that, Lou felt like he was in a nightmare, where Tank was in the wrong corner. Ricky pulled away dancing as if a ring announcer had just declared, 'In this corner, the Bantamweight champ-peen of the world, Ricky the Wrecking-ball Mulvihill!'

All at once Lou felt different inside. He'd never been afraid of Ricky, but now it was more than that. He hated the sight of him and wanted to take him on and knock his block off. He didn't need his dad to tell him how to do it. Maybe it wouldn't be so easy, but he didn't care. Tank spoke up.

"Now wait a minute, Art, you're feeding your kid to the lions, here."

What Lou heard was, 'Wake up, Art. You wouldn't do this if you were sober.'

Art reached for Tank's shoulder. His tone was quiet, soothing.

"Shall we not over-react here, pal? Lou's okay. He can take it."

Tank searched Art's face for a moment, lowered his head. Before he could say anything Lou said:

"No, it's okay, Tank. I'm gonna be all right."

Coy suddenly barked outside the door, then started scratching at it. Art ignored the noise and said:

"Come on over here, Ricky. Here's what I want you to do. You take it easy, see? I don't mean pull every punch. Just don't get in there and try to show off. You understand me?"

"Yes, sir."

"Okay. Now, Lou, you don't want to let Ricky's punches land. Either you block 'em or you dance out of range. Keep those jabs going. Keep your right up around your face. Don't give him any openings. Watch out for the gut punches, too. Stay on your toes." As soon as Art stepped back, Ricky brought his guard up stiffly and started dancing around, staying just out of range.

At first Lou stood there, crouching with his dukes up and only his eyes moving as Ricky danced this way and that, snuffing and making a face to go with the threat of his clenched, weaving gloves. Art got behind Lou and started urging him to move in. When Lou didn't go, Art gave him a shove. Ricky caught him with a jab to the forehead that rocked him backward.

"That's okay, pal," Art said. "Get in there, now. Keep jabbing with that left."

Coy's barking at the door was frantic, now. She climbed up until her snout smeared the glass.

Ricky clinched with Lou. He threw a sledgehammer into Lou's gut, and Lou doubled over, gasping for breath. Ricky danced back, looking for the invitation to deliver an uppercut when the door flew open and Stella stood there, letting no more than a second pass before she shouted, "Art! God damn you! Stop it!"

Coy bolted past her, a growl rumbling in her throat, looking for somebody to chew on. Art stood bolt upright and gawked at Stella, then at his son doubled over in pain. Stella went over to Lou and took him by the shoulders and drew him back against her bosom. She walked straight over to Art and slapped him viciously across the face. Art took the blow with a strange, almost immobile jerk of his head, while the flesh under his chin quivered. He stared at Stella, gulping.

"Now wait a minute, darlin' –"

"Just what the hell do you think you're doing?"

"I was trying to teach him how to handle himself with his fists."

"Against a sixteen year-old boy who's on a boxing team?" Stella spotted Art's drink on the ledge. She marched over to it, picked it up and dumped it into the dirt behind the wall.

Lou looked up at the helpless guilt in his father's eyes and felt so sorry for him he wanted to say something. He wanted to take the guilt upon himself, because it was him, really, who had decided to fight Ricky. Him who'd thought he could take him.

Ricky was pulling off his gloves in disgust, the first one clamped down with his chin against his chest. It dropped onto the ground. Coy pounced and started mauling it.

"Coy, no!" Lou yelled. Coy dropped the glove and looked up, panting and wagging her stub of a tail.

Ricky shook his finger at the dog.

"Coy, sit! You sit right now! Don't do that!"

Coy looked at Ricky, still panting as if his supposed master was shouting aimless gibberish. Stella came over to Lou.

"Go on upstairs now, honey," she said.

Lou didn't want to be left out of what was going to happen. He thought as soon as he left them alone she would lash out and his dad would stand there and take it. Then they would be another step closer to something he didn't want to think about. He couldn't bear to think that, by rolling over and doing as she said, he might make things that much worse. He said, "I'd like to stay here and work out with the weights a while, Mom."

Stella shot a fiery glance at Art.

"All right. No more boxing, though. D'you hear?"

"Yes, Mom."

"Come on, Coy," Stella commanded. She started for the door. Halfway there she stopped and turned abruptly.

"Have you made up your mind, Tank, about trying out for the Gloucester part?"

Tank looked up.

"Yes, I'm sorry, Stella, but I can't. I just won't have the time. I'm starting a new job."

The tone of Tank's voice made Lou look at him. It didn't sound like Tank. He was smiling, a little, but very little. His mother wasn't. She glared at Tank, taking some time, then as if she'd got enough of that she turned and marched for the door. As soon as she went out and up the steps Ricky said:

"Sorry, Lou. I shouldn't'a caught you with that sucker punch."

"Yeah, don't worry," Lou said. "It won't happen next time."

Ricky smirked, then chuckled and jived as much as to say, 'If I were you I wouldn't wish too hard for any next time.'

11

"Let's stop for a short one at the Black Cat," Art said. "They've got terrific burgers in there, too. Homemade relish, the works. Outa this world."

Tank didn't want to, really. He'd rather keep a clear mind for tomorrow morning – his first day on the job. The groundskeeper wanted him there by seven sharp.

"But don't you figure Stella's waiting dinner for you, Art?"

"I think we deserve one lousy snort. We sold a leg, didn't we?"

Streetlights dimmed the pale balance of the day out over the distant ocean. Art pointed at the small bar coming up on the other side of the street. It featured on the roof a frazzled-looking cat that kept pawing, in shifting frames of neon, a swizzle stick in a Martini glass. Art swerved across into the small parking area, nosed up to the hibiscus bushes that lined the wall under the bar's two curtained windows. As soon as he turned off the motor, he said, "We're not gonna be here all night, pal. Just long enough to light a little glow. Comprende?"

Tank decided to believe him. Art had asked him along on a trip out to the County Hospital, where he was assigned to talk a convict out of his objections to prosthesis. When the man finally gave in, with the help of a pretty nurse, he said, 'Yeah, I can see why they don't want no hopper in the chow line holding things up.' And then to the nurse, 'For you, doll baby, they can take both legs.'

Tank followed Art into the semi-darkness of the bar that smelled of stale cigarette smoke and grilled hamburgers. The bartender, a pallid, fragile looking gentleman with washed-out eyes, came over treading carefully on the duckboard. Art's salutation left no doubt that he was a regular:

"Hey Raleigh, old pal! Fix me up with a nice tall Whitehorse and soda, will you?"

"Comin' right up, Art." The bartender turned his wan smile on Tank. "What's for you, pardner?"

"CC-Seven," Tank said.

On the jukebox the Andrews sisters were singing, 'Shoo-shoo Boogie.' Tank looked along the semi-circle of the bar at the few other men leaning over their drinks, the arc of fingers holding lighted cigarettes. Way over at the end of the curve by the wall, a young man in uniform lowered his eyes. He was about Tank's age; slight build, dark slick hair. A sultry look came onto his face as he took a drag on his cigarette. He seemed to be resigned, yet at the same time annoyed at something. The lack of women in the place, Tank guessed, and tried to place his uniform – gray wool with black hash marks and trim. Silver wings embroidered over his left pocket, a gunnery sergeant's chevrons on both sleeves.

The bartender set their drinks on the bar. Art rolled the ice around in his Scotch.

"I suppose you wonder why I drink this lousy sucker juice the way I do, Tank. Me, with a lovely, rich wife, two swell kids and . . ." Art's steel-blue eyes waited bitterly without begging Tank to care.

"No, I'm not asking, Art," Tank said.

Art took a swallow of his Scotch, grinned at Tank like a used-car salesman about to launch into his pitch.

"Stella hasn't said a word about your progress at the Playhouse, pal. How's it goin' with that?"

A lump came into Tank's throat.

"There isn't any progress. I've decided I can't do it."

Art reared back, lifting his eyebrows.

"What, not your cup of tea?"

You wouldn't have seen it in a photograph, or at a distance. But there 12 inches from his face the lie in Art's eyes had no place to run: he was only feigning surprise.

"It's not just that," Tank said. "I'd feel like a phony. Plus the more plausible excuse – my new job. That's what I told Stella."

Art threw his head back in assent, and you could tell he didn't like it – having to swallow the hand he'd shown, his last-ditch feeler for something going on between his wife and this unlikely young man. How unlikely, Tank thought, he'd never know.

A distance opened up between them. Art swung around, picked up his drink. The sip he took was slow and meditative, while over the glass as he began to lower it something attracted his attention, and he smiled at whatever it was. Tank followed the smile to the end of the bar where the young man in the strange uniform was in the midst of returning it, saluting with his glass.

"Somebody you know?" Tank said with an effort to sound casual. But the fire had too recently been lowered under his blood.

"Now how would I know a GI in a uniform that looks like he flew in the Lafayette Escadrille?"

"I can't place it, either," Tank said, hoping to get Art off his high horse.

Art took a drag on his cigarette.

"He must have seen us walking in – pegged me for some guy who lost a leg in the war."

"I doubt that. So you walk slow. That's no reason to think you're on a peg leg."

"You think I'm too old to have fought in the war – right?"

"I don't know, Art. Why don't you ask the pretty boy over there?"

"Yeah, why don't I?" Art said.

Tank felt suddenly like he'd been caught out doing something he shouldn't. Like some spy had been placed in their midst, and he was only making it worse by going so far as to think so. Then it was too late. The bartender was walking past on his way toward a man calling for another drink. Art stopped him.

"Hey, Raleigh - you see that kid over there in the corner? Whatever he's drinking, tell him the next one's on me."

"He likes Greyhounds," the bartender said.

"Okay, don't let him pay for the next one. What kind of a uniform is that, anyway?"

"Beats me. When he come in, I thought RAF. But he don't sound like no limey to me."

Oh, shit, Tank thought. Now we get a close-up dose of the guy he felt instinctively should be left to himself. He was okay at a distance – a conversation piece. Let him go on looking picturesque there on his stool. But Art seemed to want to prove something. Cast his net out on a wider swath for one more guy he could do a favor for, and gain through charity what he'd been denied in the war, as if what little friendship they had gained so far wasn't good enough, or was oddly incomplete because he hadn't taken Stella's bait. And now friendship wallowed in this play-acting after all, cheapened, coasting on its rims.

The bartender poured grapefruit juice from a can on top of the ice and two shots of vodka in a tall glass, then carried it over to the young man. As he set the drink in front of him, leaning over to tell him where it came from, the young man looked up at Art, smiled and flung a pointed finger at him in gratitude. Art made the OK sign with his fingers, the young man started to get up, now he was coming over. Tank watched him: his last chance to give the guy an even break. On the surface of it, there was nothing so unsavory that stood out. Still the feeling clung, it wouldn't go away. He looked too slick, too greasy. A flash impression that probably was unfair. Call it prejudice; Tank didn't care. If there was one thing he had learned about GIs in the last three years, it was that you couldn't cure an asshole by putting him in a uniform.

The guy slid up onto the stool on the other side of Art and told them he was Ray Strawn, forget the Sergeant part, his promotion to Mister just went through. Tank thought the kind of shifty, world-wise cheapness about him deserved a nice tight vice around his hand, and that was what he squeezed Strawn's moist, flaccid fingers with. Too tight? Too much pressure? He didn't wince, seemed to recover nicely. On the handsome, ruddy face there were only two real flaws: a slight bump on the bridge of his nose and a few small acne scars, or possibly small pox craters in his cheeks.

"That's quite a grip you got there, fella. What're you, a blacksmith?"

"Sorry, I guess I don't know my own strength," Tank said amiably.

Art gave him a look, then said to Strawn, "We've had one hell of a time placing your uniform, pal. I don't think I've ever seen one like that."

"Yeah, I get that from a lot of people. I'll be out of it in about ten more days, that's all I give a shit about it."

"What threw us was the wings," Art said.

"Well, I never flew anything but a kite," Strawn said. "I rode the machine gun seat in a torpedo bomber."

"Then you're -?"

"Yeah, Marine."

"No shit! I've read about those Avengers you guys flew in. I'll bet you had your share of close calls."

"We had a few."

Strawn's modesty was too cool, Tank thought. Too much of a wise-ass thumbed his nose at all the credit you want to give a guy who had braved the odds against living through the war in a torpedo bomber.

"Correct me if I'm wrong," Art said, "but the mortality rate among you boys in those Avengers was pretty high, wasn't it?"

Strawn let out a brittle chuckle.

"Well, let me put it this way. We just barely beat out the kamikaze pilots when it came to our chances of getting home alive."

Art shook a friendly finger at Strawn.

"I'd say you're god-damned lucky to be here, Ray."

"Luck or whatever," Strawn said. "I'm here. The sooner I can get out of this fuckin' uniform, the better."

Art sat back to clear the view between Strawn and Tank.

"So you two guys have something in common," he said, leaving them like game contestants to have it out for the right answer.

Reluctant to have anything in common with Strawn, Tank said, "What did you have in mind, Art?"

"Why hell - the both of you fought the Japs in the Pacific Theatre, right?"

"You weren't a Marine," Strawn said, more as a statement than a question.

"No. 27th Infantry Division," Tank said.

"27th . . . hmmm. Ever get to Bougainville?"

"We put in there once to resupply, and mop up after –"

"Don't tell me! Hellzapoppin Ridge."

"Could be."

"Hey, man," Strawn said, "you wouldn't forget a place like Hellzapoppin Ridge, even if you'd only heard about it."

"What about you?"

"Me? I flew off carriers, mostly – the Saratoga, Princeton – until after the 21st Marine Regiment took Hellzapippin Ridge. After that I got stuck on Bougainville for pretty nearly the rest of the war. Give me a carrier any day."

Tank swung toward his drink on the bar, putting into the movement the fee of escape from any dog-face-jarhead rivalry with Strawn, and he remembered the death he'd seen on the slightly troubled faces of the Japanese soldiers half buried in sand on the beach at Tanapag, like driftwood. He saw death bloating our own boys in the gentle surf, the maggots going in through the bullet holes. The helmets hiding faces, too hot for the heads of living people. He saw death stampeding toward him, 4,000 tanked-up, screaming Japanese, and they were firing howitzers into them point-blank and still they came, as if from some factory that turned them out like toys, and somebody had forgotten to shut off the machine.

"So what are your plans now, Ray?" Art said.

Strawn shrugged.

"I've got a train ticket home," he said in a drained voice, "One way, if you can call that a plan."

"Where's home?"

"Buffalo, New York."

"What're you doing way out here in Altadena, California?"

"We got sidetracked - me and a pal who'd rather not call Buffalo home, neither – by a couple chicks we met in a dance hall."

"I'll bet you can't wait to get home."

"Oh, yeah. Can't wait. My old man'll prob'ly come upside my head for bein' late."

"Oh, come on. He'll roll out the red carpet."

"Yeah, and bill me for it."

"You don't sound too crazy about getting on that train, pal."

"I'm not. There's nothing in Buffalo for me, except my old job down at the lumber yard. That and my old man's big mouth, and my Ma – she's had the same suitcase packed in the bedroom closet for the last ten years."

Art shook his head, then drained his glass. "Hey, Raleigh! Hit me again over here, will you?"

Tank put his hand on Art's shoulder.

"Don't you think we better skedaddle, Art? I mean, if you don't want to miss dinner."

"Relax, Professor. The night's still young."

"Okay, you're the doctor." Tank said flatly.

"Right. And the doctor says if I come home sober, my wife might not recognize me."

Tank saw how Art's eyes shifted onto Strawn when he said that, as if he was letting this stranger in on some nasty secret he was halfway proud of, or that brought him somewhat down to Strawn's level. He said:

"Would that be such a bad thing?"

Art took a long drag on his cigarette, blew the smoke out just to the side of Tank's face. He lifted his eyebrows slightly, turned to grin at Strawn.

"So where do you figure on parking yourself tonight, pal?"

"Oh, I'll find some new fleabag down around Olvera Street. The toilet backed up in the one we're in now. It's only five minutes away from Union Station. Me and my buddy, we'll have to get up early to meet the Santa Fe in the morning."

"Good luck to you, Ray," Tank said.

Art was flipping a fingernail against the side of his glass. At last he said, "I've got a pregnant idea. Spend the night at our place. Save you a trip all the way back down to L.A."

"On the level?" Strawn said, and his eyes flicked out at Tank and back, like a snake's tongue taking his temperature.

"Hell, yes. You've paid your dues in that Avenger. It's little enough to offer a guy like you a sack for the night. But it's entirely up to you, Ray."

A dreamy look came over Strawn's face, like a child wandering off in a department store, forgetting about his mother, as if all the glittering new toys were there to be tested, not paid for, and if you broke one, well, you hadn't really meant to. Tank wanted to puke, and he almost said, 'What about your wife, Art? Doesn't she have some say in this?' But he kept quiet, telling himself it was none of his affair, but beginning to wonder why he actually thought it was.

"What's the matter, pal?" Art said. "You look like you've seen a ghost."

"Maybe I have," Strawn said. "Where I come from, helping thy neighbor ain't so much a thing of this world."

"Well, I assure you I'm as real as the material in this leg, here." Art rapped on the thigh section of his artificial leg.

Strawn stared down at Art's trousers.

"Is that -?"

"The real McCoy," Art said, "Milikan's Miracle Plastic."

"Art lost his leg in a hunting accident back in '36," Tank said. "You'd hardly know it, though, the way he walks."

"Jeez, you could'a fooled me," Strawn said.

The bartender came over, saying, "Three more for you gents?"

"We're gonna call it a night, Raleigh," Art said. He laid some cash on the bar, told the bartender to keep the change, then: "Comin' along, Ray?"

"Yes, *sir*! Thank you very much!"

Outside Tank hurried ahead and got into the back seat of the Cadillac before Strawn, walking slowly beside Art, reached the car. Strawn got up in front with Art and draped his arm across the top of the seat and said, "Wow! Some wheels you got here, Art. D'you have to lower a drawbridge to get to your front door?"

"No, but the password for the snarling Doberman is 'Down boy.'"

Strawn laughed stridently while Tank, in the back seat, kept silent. The cat stirring its drink on the roof splashed alternating red and blue light down across the dashboard and the seats, carving gaps in Art's movements as he maneuvered the car out to the edge of the lot. He waited there for a couple of passing cars, then pulled out onto the boulevard and headed west.

It was cool out, the car was closed up, and they were passing the block-long stretch of Madman Muntz's used car lot when Tank smelled it. He thought Art must smell it, too, although he gave no indication. The only thing different was that Ray Strawn was in the car, so it had to come from him. You'd think he had an open pack of limburger in his pocket, the stench was that strong. But who in his right mind would carry around a stinking block of ripe cheese on his person? The only other thing it could be was his socks. Strawn's arm bent from the elbow where it had been resting and he gingerly patted one side of his pomaded hair, and Tank thought, who cares if you look like John Garfield if you've got toe-jam a dog wouldn't nibble on? Then he thought maybe he should give the Marine an even break. The stench of limburger about a man wasn't necessarily a sign of bad character. On the other hand, you couldn't really write off personal hygiene when it came to adding up a person's good and bad points. Something else about him got Tank's goat. Or was it Art? He thought hotly, what does he need, a whole platoon?

Art cruised home along the street that passed the Country Club. He was slowing for the driveway when Tank said, "Just drop me at home if you don't mind, Art."

"You sure you don't want to come in for a bite to eat?"

"No, thanks," Tank said, and he thought he saw in Strawn's smile a hint of satisfaction.

The man hadn't really done a thing to him; it was just instinctive. Some people just rubbed you the wrong way. He wanted to warn Art, say something to his father. But he could hear Victor's saying, 'So what? Even if it's true, what good does it do to know?' And Tank knew then, those words were his. The kind you'd always have to keep to yourself: 'You're headed in the wrong direction, Art. You missed a turn back there. The way you want to go is over here.' But Art didn't want to be okay. His hands were lashed to the wheel. He didn't even need to see where he was going. That's how he wanted to go, blindfolded, and the booze could sit there beside him, keeping him company.

From the sidewalk Tank waved and stood there for a moment watching the car recede, leaving a thin cloud of red exhaust to dissipate into the dark street. He suddenly felt hungry. There was some roast beef left in the fridge. As soon as he hit the kitchen, he would make himself a big, fat sandwich. Then try to forget the stench that lingered in his nostrils while he ate it.

12

It wasn't as if it was anything new, sitting there under the floor lamp with the book in her hands, waiting for him. The only difference this time was that it seemed to her like Art was doing this on purpose: he *wanted* to see how much she could take. And what was there to do about that, other than to keep it in reserve for their next quarrel? When a thing that once got under your skin and worried you sick becomes old hat, then what?

She sighed and looked down at the printed page that might as well be Chinese. She heard the sound of a motor outside, lights flashed through the windows and then dimly hovered in the patio before they went out. She looked up, holding her breath and tensing in her neck, listening. There were voices, Art's and somebody else. She got up and went to the French doors where she knew he would come in. She had to head him off. She didn't care: she wasn't having any stray dogs in the house tonight.

She opened the doors and stood there in her dressing gown, leaving the patio light off. They were out there, just beyond the gate, talking in low tones. Art came through the gate first, then the stranger – a man dragging a heavy duffle bag. She caught only a glimpse of his face before he turned to shut the gate. Art was reeling a little as he came on laboriously. The stranger, in a uniform, dropped the duffle bag and hurried to Art's side, offering his arm, but Art brushed it aside, saying, "I'm okay, pal." She saw now that the man was handsome, his eyebrows dark and nicely shaped. He might as well be trash for the way she felt – resenting Art for dragging home somebody out of nowhere, on some drunken whim. She drew her dressing gown together just under her throat.

"I've got a friend here with me, darlin'," Art said. "Meet Sergeant Ray Strawn, U.S. Marines. How're we fixed for leftover spaghetti?"

"Art –"

All she had to say was, I'm sorry, no. We don't have any room. She couldn't have Jo Riley in the house, but he could drag in any old stranger off the street. Sorry, no dice. She saw that the handsome face was looking at her. It might as well be plastered to a wall, yet barely aware of it she relaxed her fingers on her dressing gown, it fell slightly away and the dark eyes jumped off the wall and she found herself, just briefly, looking at his lips that told her he was young – could be as young as half her age. She said guardedly:

"Art – d'you know what time it is?" She glanced at the young man. "Please keep your voices down. Our two boys are asleep."

"Oh jeez, I'm sorry, ma'am." Strawn said in a grating near-whisper, crouching humbly. "Listen, this ain't right. I'm not gonna put you folks out in any way. I'll just turn around and catch a cab back to the city."

She was to remember these first words out of Ray Strawn's mouth. The kind of shading of dissimulation, like some flattering trick phrase out of the Fuller Brush man's slick mouth to gain entrance, and to sit on your furniture like he was an old friend, and open up his satchel full of things a woman couldn't do without in this wondrous, modern world. Art was saying:

"Let's at least break out a bite to eat, darlin'. You've gotta be hungry, Ray? Aren't you?"

Strawn shrugged, leaving the matter open. You could see his wary eyes feasting on a plate of spaghetti right enough.

"I'm good with a taco down by the hotel. If I could use your phone a minute, ma'am – I'll call that cab."

It struck her like a little jolt of electric current, his switching to address her. Stella stared at his trace of a smile, that strange familiarity that youth brought to the face of a man she didn't know from Adam. The woman was supposed to have the softer heart. He'd got his way before, she could tell, with that face. That soft touch leaving it to her: what to do with a boy down on his luck. No, he'd got her wrong. She'd better throw this fish back in.

"Yes, just come right through here." She stood aside and pointed. "You'll find the phone in that little alcove on your right."

"Now wait a minute, darlin'," Art said. "What's the problem with heating up a little food, I mean – for a guy who fought for our country? Ray, tell me. How long has it been since you've had a home-cooked meal?"

"Me? Oh, heck – I can't remember. Must've been before the war. Not that the stuff my Ma turned out was anything to write home about."

"See there, Stell? Let's give old Ray something to write home about. Can't you see the guy needs some meat on his bones?"

Stella looked at the young man standing there beside his duffle bag, just smiling. The smile could be forlorn, except it wasn't. She couldn't see any lack of meat on his bones. He stood with that cocky weight-shift telling you he'd take what he could get. And why do men in uniform look so handsome - especially the young ones? What all can a man wear on his sleeve, and what that looks so plain to see may not be there at all?

"Well, okay – but we'll have to shut the kitchen door so we don't wake up the boys."

"Oh, yeah." Strawn's head ducked meekly into his shoulders again, the raspy whisper prepared for a stealthy trip to the kitchen. "Mind if I leave my duffle bag out here, ma'am? That way I can grab it on my way out."

His eyes belonged to her, she saw now. Well, what was a little diversion at twelve midnight when it might have stretched out into that same old gag on rage and fury put to bed for crazy dreams to handle?

"Forget the cab," Art said. "I'll run you back into town."

"Art, you're in no condition to drive that far." And then Stella realized what she was saying. "You could drop him at the bus stop, if they run this late."

"Don't worry, ma'am," Strawn said, "I've got the money for a cab. I kinda like a taxi ride. Especially here – out west. Back where I come from I'd sooner walk. Easier to forget you got noplace to go." Strawn threw his head back slightly, laughing.

Stella took a step back onto the rug.

"Well, before you go, you'd better have a bite to eat. I'll show you where the bathroom is, if you'd like to wash up."

"Why, sure. Thank you."

Stella put together a fresh Caesar salad, warmed up some leftover garlic bread under the broiler to go with the spaghetti. She fixed a plate for Strawn and Art, then sat with them at the table in the breakfast nook, nursing a cup of hot chocolate. Strawn mopped up his plate like he hadn't eaten a decent meal in a month.

"This is sure kind of you, ma'am," he said with his mouth full. "Puts my Ma's cooking to shame."

"Oh, I doubt that," Stella said. "There's more where that came from if you're -"

"Oh, jeez no! I'm gonna burst here in a minute, ma'am."

"No room for Angel Food cake?" Art said. "You're gonna be sorry, Ray."

"Well . . ."

Stella had the cake already out of the refrigerator. She got up and cut a piece for Strawn.

"What about you, Art?"

Art shook his head mournfully.

"I'm goin' with my discovery long ago that cake and Scotch don't mix."

Strawn flung his head back in appreciation of Art's wit, and Stella blinked at them, rather enjoying this strange midnight interlude.

Strawn dug into his cake, smiling as he ate it as if suddenly he'd found a lot more room in his stomach than he'd bargained on.

"Coffee?" Stella said.

Shaking his head, Strawn patted his stomach.

"No, no. I'd better call that cab before the dead zone hits, here."

"Just how far do you have to go?" Stella said.

Strawn gave her a hesitant look.

"Down to Olvera Street. The place we found last night wasn't that bad for where it's at, they tell me. Trouble is, the toilet backed up."

"Clear down by Union Station? God, won't a cab cost you a fortune?"

"What else am I gonna spend my fortune on?" Strawn joked.

"Forget the cab, Ray," Art said grimly. "I'm driving you."

"And pile up on the freeway," Stella flared, "*if* you get there alive?"

"So maybe we should call an ambulance?" Art said lazily.

Strawn's eyes were darting between the two of them. He didn't know what to do. He didn't want to impose, but he was so weary – you could see that. It wasn't just rhetorical, either – Art's being too drunk to drive. You could turn the man out, and he would disappear, never to return. Gone in a cab that would become a train on a track to his problem, not yours. There were thousands of them. Why this one?

"You know we *could* let the sergeant stay the night, Art. I don't like it - that long drive out so late just isn't safe. I think the best thing is for you to get a fresh start in the morning, Ray." And she realized that, for the first time, she had said his name.

Art's head came up, wobbling a little. Whatever word was rolling down from his mind was too slow and Stella wasn't looking at him anyway.

"Oh, heck, Mrs. Ryan," Strawn protested, "it's no skin off my teeth, takin' the cab."

"We've got a spare room, just sitting there," Stella said, and she looked at Art, who said:

"If you guys don't need me any more, I'm gonna hit the sack. Meet you in dreamland, darlin'." The scotch seemed to be pulling the shades on Art's red, unsightly face as he got up and made his way back past the Bendix, then down the hallway toward the bedroom.

Strawn cleared his throat.

"Could I help you with these dishes, Mrs. Ryan?"

Left alone with him, Stella felt that he was just too young to be afraid of. Young and handsome somehow added up to that familiarity again. There was that little titillating danger, though, still running to and fro between them. Pretty silly to make anything out of, she thought.

"Oh, no. I'm leaving them till morning," she said with a smile.

"Well, thank you for the great meal. The last spaghetti I had came out of a can." He seemed to be watching her, then, for laughter, and she gave it to him feeling girlish like it was the thing to do, and this air of pleasantry she was so unused to might not die out.

"I'm glad you liked it."

"I guess I'd better grab my duffle bag outside. Be back in a jiffey."

"Sure, just meet me in the hallway. I'll be getting out some clean sheets for your bed."

At the end of the hallway Stella was pulling the sheets and pillow cases out of the linen closet when Coy ambled out of the dark of the boys' room, yawning. She spotted Strawn, gave a flabby, muffled bark, and went over to investigate his crotch. She gazed up as much as to say, 'It doesn't seem to be here, so where's the dead rat?"

"No, Coy!" Stella clapped her hands lightly. "Come here, girl. It's all right, Sergeant Strawn. Coy won't hurt you. Go on and pet her if you want."

"Well, I guess I'll take a rain check on that. Say Mrs. Ryan, y'know –" Strawn labored with a smile. "- as time goes on I'm feelin' less and less like a sergeant. Why don't you call me Ray? Even if it's only for one night."

From behind the closed door of their bedroom Stella could hear Art snoring already.

"All right – Ray. Do you like dogs?"

"It's not a matter of likin' 'em. I got bit by one when I was a kid, but then my old man bought one for me on my tenth birthday. It came from the pound – a little runt of a thing without much hair, full grown, too. The only thing about Flash was, he didn't know when to shut up. Yip yip yip yip yip until you'd think there couldn't be another yip left in him. That's the little breeds for you – yappers. I told my old man I wanted a St. Bernard, so he brings home a mouse. Go figure."

Stella was observing Strawn's eyes while he spoke, the way his mouth moved, how he held his body, almost everything except what he was saying. She vaguely understood what he was saying, and just as vaguely disapproved, but she couldn't hold it against him. Some people and dogs just didn't naturally mix. She herself, no matter how sorry she might feel for the high strung small breeds, could get annoyed with their yapping, too, and wouldn't own one if you paid her. She said:

"Coy's not really our dog. She belongs to our next-door neighbor, Mrs. Mulvihill. She's really taken to my two boys. She might as well be ours."

"Is that a fact? Vicious, ain't they – when they wanta be? I seen a couple Dobermans at the car impound back home – the way they come at that fence like they could bite right through it. Boy, I wouldn't want to tick one off, that's for darn sure."

Coy walked up to Stella, stubby tail wagging. Stella reached down and patted her broad back that shivered to her touch.

"Coy's not that way – are you, girl? Once you get to know her, she's as gentle as a lamb. Well! I'd better get those sheets on your bed."

Stella went to both the windows in the spare room and lifted them to let in some fresh air. She smelled something funny, wasn't sure where it was coming from. Coy might have tracked something in. The window that opened onto the roof of the garage was where the boys liked to sneak out and lie in wait for the next stagecoach, Jap patrol, or some unsuspecting regiment of cavalry. A scent of gardenias wafted in on a breath of the cool night air. There, that was better. Much better. She wouldn't want a guest to think she was a sloppy housekeeper. Too lazy to clean out something dead from a dark corner.

She went over to the bed, turned back the spread and got busy putting on the clean sheets. Just as she unfurled the bottom one across the mattress, Strawn hurried to the other side.

"Here, I'll catch this side for you."

"Oh, thanks."

The two sheets were on, the bedspread pulled up. Stella stepped over to the chair, picked up the two fresh pillow cases. She came back and was stretching across the bed for the nearest pillow when Strawn said, "I'll get the other one." But he didn't do it right away, and that made her look up as she dragged the pillow toward her, and there were his eyes locked on what she suddenly knew was spilling out of her nightie. She'd always known, since she was seventeen, that if a man was on the fence about her looks; her skin not dark or smooth enough, eyes not cat-like, manner too reserved and nothing really of the vamp about her, her breasts made up the difference. It happened time and time again, and now in a kind of dreamy, harmless vindication, she lingered there a moment, giving him an eyeful, while Strawn's eyes darted right and left as if he wanted to drop it in the nearest mailbox, addressed to himself.

Stella finished with the pillow, plumped it and said, "Well, all set! Oh! Here's the alarm clock on the nightstand if you need one. Looks like you'll have to set the time and wind it."

"Sure, I'll take care of that," Strawn said.

"All right. The bathroom's just a few steps down the hall to your right, Sergeant."

"Ray," Strawn corrected.

"Yes, Ray. Oh, your duffle bag –"

Strawn snapped his fingers, stepped out into the hallway and grabbed the duffle bag and swung it, bumping against his leg, over beside the nightstand. Stella was moving toward the doorway. She placed her hand over the light switch on the wall.

"Shall I turn this off for you?"

"Why, sure. Thank you."

The light above the bed went out. Shadows painted the room with softer colors from the lamp on the nightstand.

"Goodnight," Stella said. "I hope you sleep well."

"I can't see why I wouldn't," Strawn said.

13

Lou blundered into the kitchen, sleepy-eyed, ready to make the coffee. The smell of coffee was in the air already and he wondered if the clock was wrong. The sound of something like a heel knocked back against the hollow seat in the breakfast nook. He saw the man, then, sitting there alone, leaning over a steaming cup. He needed a shave. Under the table his white ankles showed above a pair of loafers. The face turned to him, Lou didn't know what else to say but, "Hi."

"Oh! How's it goin' there, pardner? Lookin' for your mom or dad?"

"No, I came out to make the coffee."

"Ah! Your mom saved you the trouble this morning – on account of me. I'm a coffee hound if there ever was one."

Lou looked over and saw the percolator on the stove, not the pot into which he poured boiling water on top of the coffee mashed in with the egg whites and the shells. He was wrestling in his mind with what to say next when Strawn said:

"I guess you've gotta be wondering who I am."

Lou stood where he was, just inside the doorway.

"Well, sir –"

"Ray Strawn. Your old – ah, your father was kind enough to let me bunk here with you folks last night. I was gonna leave early to catch a train, but damned if the alarm clock didn't go off, and then I – I guess I got lazy. Who might you be, pardner?"

"I'm Lou," Lou said.

"Lou the coffee maker, huh?"

"Yeah."

"Hey, that's pretty good! Helping out your mother like that."

"I like to do it," Lou said, smiling in case that sounded too abrupt.

"Well, whatever. It's still a load off, ain't it?"

Lou nodded. Strawn kept looking at him so he said, more out of nerves than curiosity, "Are you supposed to do some work for my dad?" Remembering the tall, austere man they'd taken in for a few days to do some painting on the gate out by the fish pond next to Dorothy's, about whom Dad had said, making sense of why he wore a long black coat and never smiled, that he had fought with the Danish underground against the Nazis.

"Oh, no. I won't be here that long. If I was I might, though. I could use the bread. What happened was, I just got out of the Marines. I'm not quite out, but I will be in a few days. We was kind of a different branch from the guys most people think of when you say Marines. You ever hear of the Flying Leathernecks?"

"I think so - in the newsreels."

"Yeah, that was us. I sat behind the pilot in a torpedo bomber, manning a machine gun."

"Gee whiz! How many Jap Zeroes did you shoot down?"

"As many as I could," Strawn said. "But I want to forget all that. They're makin' us wait a mile too long, kid. You wouldn't believe the formalities, the paperwork. We got another name for it."

"So you still have to wear your uniform a little longer?"

"Well, I had it on last night, and I have to get back into it this morning. These civvies I'm in here – they don't hardly fit any more. I'd look pretty funny in 'em on the street." Ray stiffened one leg out from under the table. "Would you believe these pants fit the day I joined up? And my Ma told me I was all through growing. I need some new threads somthin' fierce. Something I can look good in, you know, when I go looking for a job."

"I'll bet you'd look as good as anything in your uniform," Lou said.

Strawn looked at him skeptically.

"Believe me, kid – I'm not gonna miss that chunk of wool except – okay, I have to admit, whenever we got liberty the chicks went for it. Now you've gotta think of other things to get their attention – like a job." Strawn hung his head and shook it ruefully. "It takes the brass a century to stamp a signature on one simple piece of paper. You're out, goodbye and thanks for the memories. That's all I ask. Don't get me wrong, I was as gung-ho as the next guy when I first joined up. You're lucky, kid. Lucky you never had to get into it."

"I don't think so," Lou said.

Strawn chuckled.

"Hey, you got something against bein' alive?"

"No, but *you* made it. *You're* alive."

There was a movement in the doorway, Lou turned to see his father, draped in his robe and flopping his one slipper on the linoleum, coming through on crutches. As he looked up, his eyes popped open.

"You still here, Ray?"

"Yeah, sorry, Art. I screwed up and overslept."

"Missed your train, huh?"

"Yeah. Now I'm wondering whether Dom left without me. We was supposed to meet up at the station."

Art started over to the table, saying, "Try calling the hotel."

Strawn reached back, pulled out his wallet.

"I think I got the number here, somewheres."

Art leaned his crutches against the wall, hopped to the bench across from Strawn and slid in.

"Lou, old pal, pour me a cup of that java, will you? Black this time."

"Sure, Dad." Lou went to the cupboard and took down his father's favorite cup.

There was a flurry in the doorway, a waft of *Tabu* laced the air and Stella strode in briskly in a pale yellow dress and white high heels, the radiance of her face set off with eye-liner and mascara, rouge and ruby-red lipstick. Art looked her over.

"What's the occasion, darlin'? You running late for the Ax Grinder's Ball?"

"Can't a girl freshen up in the morning?" Stella said breathlessly, and she pranced nervously toward the coffee pot, and when she got there, brushed her hand across something that Lou saw wasn't there while she toyed with a wayward, absent smile. "Here, let me pour that for your dad, honey. Or is this for you?"

Lou stood away from her a little. Her hand trembled slightly, pouring. The way she'd fixed her face and that dress he'd never seen her wear gave off a kind of nervous brilliance, like a sparkler that can't last too long. He wondered where she was going, this early in the morning when she usually kept her robe on, didn't comb her hair or scrub off last night's cold cream.

"No, it's for dad. He said no cream and sugar."

Stella's fingers fluttered, wincing from the cup.

"Oh! Well then, here - you take it over to him, honey."

Lou felt as if she wasn't exactly talking to him, just flashing him the brittle smile needed to disown the coffee.

"Ray missed his train," Art said.

Stella half-turned, flung him a troubled look.

"Yes, I know. That was my fault, really. I shouldn't have trusted that darned old alarm clock we haven't used in ages."

Strawn was shaking his head.

"Don't blame yourself, Mrs. Ryan. I fell dead asleep before I had a chance to even wind that clock. When I finally woke up and realized what I done, I didn't want to be calling cabs and causing a ruckus at five in the morning. Luckily, my ticket's good till the end of the month."

Lou set the full hot cup on the table beside his father's hand.

"Thanks, pal," Art said.

"I know what I'll do," Strawn said. "I'll call up that fleabag and see if Dom checked out." He fingered out a small calling-card from a slot in his wallet. "The Rosarita Hotel. I'm gonna play hell with that spic behind the desk, if he's the one that answers."

"How come?" Stella said.

"He can't speak English worth the beans them people eat. Well, what can you expect for three bucks a night?"

It struck Lou, then, how mildly his mother was taking the way Ray talked, smiling at just about everything he said. She'd smile, not looking at anybody, as if the way he spoke was colorful, a step up on kids, like her own, who mustn't ever say spic about a Mexican: they were human beings the same as us. She stood there nervously fingering the coffee pot. She turned the fire down under it, like an actress onstage, pretending the audience wasn't there.

Art took a swallow of his coffee, made a face.

"What happened to the java, Lou? Tastes kinda funny."

"That was me," Stella said. "Lou wasn't up, yet. Ray was, so I used the percolator."

"Y'know," Strawn said, fingering his chin, "What good's a call gonna do? I gotta get down there myself."

"Could be a wild goose chase, Ray," Art said, "if your pal flew the coop."

"But can you trust anything a spic says on the phone? They could say si, si till the cows come home, even if you ask 'em if they want a punch in the face."

Lou giggled, Strawn's eyes darted at him appreciatively.

"So what do you want to do?" Art said.

Before Strawn could answer Stella said:

"What you could do is rest up a while, Ray – as long as your ticket's good till the end of the month."

"Boy I don't know, Mrs. Ryan," Strawn said, shaking his head woefully, "I've put you folks out enough as it is already."

"That wasn't the idea last night, Art, was it?" Stella said. "Or did I misunderstand, because Ray told us how much he hated going back to Buffalo?"

The struggle in his father's face, Lou saw, twisted oddly, his smile knotted up. His pleasant tone ran with a streak of acid.

"Ray knows how much we'd like to help him out, Stell. And we respected his wishes. Otherwise you wouldn't have made sure he had the alarm clock, would you?"

Strawn leaned across the table toward Art, his face a boiled red oath of sincerity.

"The best thing I could do right now," he said, "is to get down to that fleabag and pick up where me and Dom left off. You don't leave a bud high and dry the way I did."

"You don't think you should try calling first?" Stella said.

"Like I said," Strawn said, "you can't get a straight answer from a spic."

"I'm sorry, Ray," Art said, "but you'll have to find some other way into the city. I've gotta get on the road here in a few minutes. I'm due in Riverside by nine o'clock."

"Oh, I completely understand," Strawn said in a weakened, faintly tearful voice.

Stella leaned back against the sink, bracing her hands against the edge, her face brightening with a smile that seemed to Lou the last forgotten touch she needed to complete her makeup.

"It seems like such a shame that Ray has to put all his eggs into going back to a place he doesn't like. What's a ticket like that worth, anyway?" Stella looked down at her shoes on the linoleum, brought them a little closer together, pointing her toes.

Strawn shrugged.

"That ticket's about all I got, Mrs. Ryan."

"Yes. Well, there should be some alternative, I think. Don't you?"

"That's my problem," Strawn said, "How did I know I was gonna get to like sunny Southern California this quick?"

Art was drumming his fingers on the table, squinting at the window and the stillness of the roses lit with morning sunshine. He rolled his shoulders, rubbed downward from the tip of his nose to his chin, drawing his eyes shut. He opened them with a flutter.

"I'll tell you what. We could make you an offer, Ray. Stay with us another week or so. Get the lie of the land. It shouldn't take you long to find a job and get into a place of your own. If it doesn't work out, well – the rest is up to you, pal."

"Well, shoot, Art – this is just – just really swell of you! I promise I won't overstay my welcome. I'll go out first thing and get myself a car, any old beater to get me around in. I'm not out to mooch on you folks, so please, if I ever get in the way, just say the word and I'll take off. I'll pay you rent, too! Just name it! Just as soon as I can nail down a job!"

"Well, it may not come to rent, pal," Art said. "I'm sure you'll be able to afford a nice little place of your own before too long."

"Oh, sure! What am I thinking? My buddy, Dom, he might want to throw in with me, if I can find him. If I can't, well, c'est la vie."

"Fair enough," Art said, and his tired eyes came to rest on Lou, as if without words he was trying to tell him that what may have sounded like defeat wasn't, really. But it was, Lou saw, and he smiled at his father, hoping he would understand.

14

Tank pulled the telephone closer, dialed the number Marla had written on the back of the invoice. They had been talking about a movie, but it had grown to be too late. She answered before the second ring, like she'd been waiting right beside the phone. She didn't sound put out about the time, but Tank apologized anyway, saying, "Sorry this is such short notice. I guess we'll have to skip that movie. If you'd rather wait till –"

"Stop it," she said. "There's always Eaton Canyon, if the gate's still open. Did you forget?"

Tank wanted to say how could I as her voice reached through and fired a rocket from his groin into a night alone with her.

It was their third date. The others had been preliminary courtesy calls, so to speak, hardly any different from the way it used to be with a girl in high school. He'd walked her around the campus once during lunch hour, they admired the Azaleas and the stately old Eucalyptus trees and talked about maybe going horseback riding one of these days, using the nearby stable, and Tank warned her that if they didn't have a docile nag for him to ride, he'd be in trouble, and she called him chicken playfully, implying she knew darn well he was the opposite. The next day he took her out to Irv Engle's opulent drugstore for a soda, where they sat at the counter and had liverwurst sandwiches, too, with the crusts trimmed off; then he followed her as she wandered around admiring the luxury scented soaps and the Richard Hudnut beauty products that she declined to buy, saying she had plenty of a different brand at home; so while she walked ahead Tank picked up the set she had looked at the longest and just as they were leaving stopped at the cash register and she was almost outside before she saw what he was doing and came back chiding him, but arm in arm with him outside in the sun she went up on tiptoe to kiss him, and told him what a wonderful guy he was, and he had to admit, in the warmth spreading under his heart, that for the sake of how far he seemed to be getting with her, he was.

"See you in about ten minutes," he said into the phone.

"I'll be waiting outside."

They were lucky. The gate to Eaton Canyon stood wide open. The smell of eucalyptus, oaks and greasewood floated through the open windows as they took the dirt road into the picnic area. The quarter moon out held the trees and the rocks in the river bed in a misty glow, and glossed the tops of the picnic tables as Tank drove past them.

He parked under a big oak tree. Marla sat right up against him, like they were going steady. There was a scent of lemon in her hair. Tank turned off the motor, leaned forward and looked up through the windshield at the stars above the ridgeline.

"Well, here we are," he said.

Marla slid forward a little and let her head fall onto the back of the seat.

"It smells so good up here," she said.

Tank looked over at the slope of her nose, the moon in her eyes under her long eyelashes. He looked at the tenderness of her mouth, the luster of her lipstick. She let him look a while, then turned toward him, her cheek against her hair and nothing in her gaze but him.

"You must be so-oo glad to be home, Tank. After all you've been through."

Tank didn't think he ought to just agree.

"Well, I'm lucky. Too many other guys went through a hell of a lot more. Too many of them got killed."

"Thank God you didn't." He could feel Marla's eyes like the fingers of a blind girl on his face. She snuggled closer to him, laying her hand and then her chin on his shoulder. "Your luck is my luck, buddy."

Tank's eyes strayed onto the curve of her tanned leg in the dark. He looked away, she peeled off into his mind for him to stare at, in wonder, until he could turn back with his arms around her, his lips on hers and the feel of her all along the dream of who she was.

"What were those places like, Tank? Those islands in the South Pacific."

He didn't say anything right away: the old frustration washed over him, as if they were competing for the truest moment of silence. All he cared about was the warmth of her body, the miracle that she was real – her eyes, the sweetness of her breath. Finally he said:

"Well, I guess it was about the way you would imagine. Hot and sticky. Crabs that popped up out of holes. The smell of coral always in the air, like sulphur. In the jungle, the mosquitoes ate us alive. I guess them and the heat were about the worst things, now that I remember."

"Not the Japanese?"

"Well, sure – them. I mean, you know – day in and day out."

She laid a finger on his lips. His voice hovered in space. She wriggled over onto her knees on the seat, her hand caressed his cheek and then her mouth closed down upon him and he reached around her and kissed her and his throat was filling with all the aching desire he'd built up since he'd first seen her in that office, looking so fresh and perky. He thought it was a miracle. She was too pretty, too real to be in his arms. He had forgotten how to kiss, but it was coming back.

They made out for what seemed like an eternity. He felt her fumbling with his belt. He buried his face in her breasts and pulled her dress up over her hips. Her legs were soft and cool against the heat of his face. There was a taste of her bath on her nipples. She sat there in the middle of the seat, pushing herself out to the edge while he came over onto his knees on the floorboards. It came on like a rocket taking off for those stars they were supposed to be here gazing at, and she was down there moaning and making those sounds, over and over, with his name on them.

They were parked a little behind the oak tree, but there was a moment when light swept in through the windshield, and Tank thought it was the cops. But the shadow on the ceiling shot just as quickly back outside. He peeked out and saw somebody's car turning around, and they sat there listening until quiet came back into the dark.

They were both sweating like horses. He sat back up behind the wheel, fixing his pants, and she threw her head back and rolled it from side to side, shaking her hair out, and finally she looked at him, not bothering to pull her panties up, or her skirt back down, saying in a husky voice, "God, Tank. I like you."

"I like you, too," he said, meaning much more than that. It wasn't even ten-thirty, and here they were, like they'd been going steady for the last five years. She was staring at him now with her head thrown back against the seat, her lips parted. He said, "What is it?"

"I want to tell you something, Tank. Promise you won't laugh."

"Okay."

"I've never had a feeling like this in my life before. Never anything this wonderful, until now." She scooted closer to him and put her hand gently on the place where his desire sat on its rims.

"You know, Tank," she went on, "promise me you won't tell anybody."

"I promise."

She moved her hand around a little. It's not true that you can't get blood from a turnip, he thought.

"It's you. A man who's been in battle." She wanted to say something else, but she just blinked and shook her head as if words would fail her again and he would have to pick up on what she was trying to say. He looked at her and said:

"In combat?"

"Try not to think less of me for this, but it's –" She hooked one of her smooth, long legs over his knee, pulling him closer. She started doodling with the hair on his chest. In the dark, she couldn't clearly see the big scar up by his shoulder.

"I shouldn't admit this to you," she said, "because you might misunderstand." She dragged her finger down to his belly-button. "But I'm going to. You went to war and survived all those horrors that we here at home could only read about, or sit through, watching the newsreels. I just admire you so much for what you've been through. Well – I guess admire's not exactly what I mean. It's *you*, but – " Her hand strayed a few more inches downward.

"What?" he said.

She rested her head under his chin.

"It really turns me on, Tank - that you've been in the war."

He understood what she was saying, but said, "If I hadn't, would it make a difference?"

She sat up abruptly.

"Oh, I knew you'd take it all wrong! I shouldn't have said anything. You'd still be you, of course. Without that, all the war in the world wouldn't make you into superman."

Tank felt afraid, now, that he'd gone too far, letting her believe what he *could* be, but wasn't. He didn't want to spoil things and take the chance of losing her. Or was it that she made him think of what he'd let the boys believe, and how they, too, thought he was some kind of a super-hero.

"I'm just saying," he said, "everybody's got secrets. What if I'm not all you might think I'm cracked up to be?"

Marla said almost angrily, "Will you just shut up! It's like you're – you're mocking me, Tank."

"I'm not mocking you. I'm serious. If a rumor starts to circulate about me -"

She pulled back a ways, blinking.

"What kind of a rumor?"

"I don't know. That the war did something to me. I'm retarded. Something like that."

"You've gotta be kidding! Who'd start a rumor going around like that? And why?"

"Well, I've been home almost two months, now. I'm not exactly going places fast. The only real friends I've made are a couple of kids."

Marla shoved on his shoulder playfully.

"Get out of here! What's so bad about that? Half my friends are kids, too, up at the school."

Tank saw that he had gone too far and better stop, now, while he was ahead. He looked at his watch.

"You want to go out to Irv Engle's for a soda?"

"Okay. But do you think they're open now?"

"Might be."

She held a kind of wicked half-smile on him.

"Okay. Otherwise we might get into real hot water with our parents."

Tank kept himself from watching her as she got dressed, and she sat right up against him again as he drove out to the drugstore, but they found that it had closed just half an hour before. She snuggled up to him.

"Might as well just take me home," she said.

He walked her up to her porch and kissed her there, a long kiss that took her deep down into him and he wondered if he was beginning to love her. Then he was alone in the car, alone with what he knew he had to do. He owed those boys, and suddenly it seemed like an assignment he'd thought up from another life, an obligation which, if shirked, would bring that terrible old feeling down upon him and he couldn't use a woman to get out of it. Not Marla. Not anybody.

15

"Stella," the voice said.

She jumped and turned to see him standing just outside the shadow, squinting in the full sunshine, in a ribbed undershirt, while the sun played on his lush dark hair that shone with pomade.

"Oh, Ray –"

"Sorry, I was looking for you," Strawn said, and he raised his arms and stretched. "Boy, did I catch my share of Zs. Me and Dom kind of tied one on last night."

"That's okay," she said. "It's Sunday. You don't have to go to work." She looked at him, waiting, and he looked back at her, as if he was stuck for telling her why he'd come out looking for her.

She hadn't heard him stealing up behind her, as if the heavy, sultry fragrance of gardenias was a padded wall. She moved on past the Birds of Paradise, stirring like a paddle wheel the strips of sunlight across her bare shoulders. Close to her foot a water bug threaded a step from a lily pad onto the dark water under the stoic stone Buddha.

His hair, she noticed, was not neatly combed but left a little mussed, that added something to his youth. She saw that he was wearing flip-flops. You could call him unkempt but somehow that made him easier to look at. He said:

"I've got this load of dirty laundry and thought - if you wouldn't mind showing me how to operate that washer –"

"Oh, for God's sake, Ray," she chided, "I'll wash your clothes when I do ours."

"Every washer's different, that's all. I wouldn't want to break yours."

"Like you really could," Stella said. "These new machines are as simple as can be."

"My ma had one of those contraptions with the wringer. Simple as long as you kept your fingers out of them rollers."

Stella laughed. She caught a whiff of his skin, then, a little variation of that good smell that the sun brought out on hers. She'd been so consumed with being alone, suddenly she felt exposed by the skimpiness of her sundress. It was hot out. She'd put it on just to stay cool, that was all.

Strawn took a big breath of the tropical air from in where she stood that met the blazing heat on his shoulders out on the walk where he was.

"Boy, it sure smells good in there."

She pointed at the bush on which several gardenias were in glorious white bloom.

"It's these. They seem to overwhelm the scent of all the other flowers in here."

Strawn shuffled in out of the sun, threw his head back and breathed in deeply, swooning.

"Man oh man! You could get drunk on that." He crossed to another stone, gingerly planting his foot so as not to smash the enclosing moss. Strips of the sun knifed through the slats above. She watched how the dizzying quiet of a kaleidoscope moved on his shoulders. "Seductive, aren't they," he said.

Stella held her eyes on him. He just smiled, as if they were talking about a change in the weather. She felt like reaching for a gardenia. She couldn't touch the petals, or else they would turn brown, like death brought to a moth, once you disturbed the powder on its wings. She decided not to and he was so close, then, she locked her arms across her breasts, saying, "I could stay in here for hours, sometimes."

"Yeah, they've got a gardenia perfume, you know. It don't smell near this good."

She thought about cutting the biggest flower and taking it inside, but water wouldn't save a gardenia. They made the best corsage you could ever want. She remembered how nervously Art had pinned one on her gown in the Avalon Casino Ballroom. From then on it became her favorite flower.

It was like they were in a crowded elevator. His face was inches from hers, and you couldn't do anything about it until the doors jerked and trundled open. She knew there was no escaping him as his face tilted, then, and her whole body ached for that collision with his longing while the gardenias surrounded them and made them feel alone. He shut his eyes, she saw the slack, soft hunger on his lips before they touched hers, and in a corner of her mind Art moved uneasily. She pressed her body up against the power of this stranger she had known forever. He wanted her. That's all she cared about. His hand groped downward from her back, unerringly. Struggling, she whispered breathlessly, "No," but yes ran through her body as she arched her back a little, waiting for his next kiss. He pulled her toward him almost brutally. Still holding her he flung his head back.

"I know," he breathed, "I know. What'll we do? There must be someplace – someplace away from here –"

She hadn't any breath left to answer. She could only shake her head. He said:

"Upstairs. Can't we -?"

With a gasp she said, "No, the boys. And Art –"

He pulled her up against him in a final grip against defeat.

"I want you, Stella. I can't take it any more. I love you. You believe that, don't you?"

"Yes, yes!"

He wrapped his stranglehold around her again, unwilling to give up, as if something would come to him.

"Why don't we just – we'd be alone for a little while, anyway. Somewhere gone from here. There's gotta be someplace around here where we could just – you know, a park with trees and – just the two of us. Of course the kids, too. Don't say Art any more. I don't want to hear his name."

He was breathing so heavily, the veins on his forehead bulged, and she saw his readiness pumping down there under his belt. The gardenias looked on, unmoving, giving off their intoxicating scent, and the idea clutched onto sanity like a helping hand after a bad fall. There was nothing wrong with it. It cleared the air. It brought everything out into the open where things should be.

"I do know of a place," she said. "Not far away. A park with picnic tables, nice trees."

He stood away from her, eyes brightening.

"Y'know all that stuff in the fridge I brought from the plant? That big ham and the cold cuts? Well, I could pick up some beer and a couple bottles of pop for the kids."

"We'll have to leave a note for Art," she said.

"I said –" He pinned her to the fury of a scowl.

"We can't just ignore him, pretend he's not there."

He let up in his eyes that seemed to jitter with uncertainty.

"What kind of a note?"

"Tell him where we've gone, that's all. We've got the kids. He can meet us out there if he wants to."

"You think he will?"

"I don't know. Maybe not."

Ray started to nod, smiling at the perfect sense, how plausibly on the up and up it sounded, as if Art's feelings meant something to him. They could both conspire in the same deceptive world to treat with decency the man with whom she'd lived for fifteen years. How could she blame Ray for impudence when she knew she wasn't going to shut him down? She'd been waiting for so long to say yes. There just hadn't been anyone to say yes *to*.

"Okay, lemme run out and get that six-pack and some pretzels," Strawn said, glancing at his watch.

"The boys are over at the Cahill's house. I'll call them, then they should be here by the time you get back." She felt aware of a rising anxiety to hurry up and leave before Art got home. You never knew what time he might show up.

"The kids can bring along their mitts and stuff," Strawn said. "Heck, I'll hit 'em a few myself." He lifted a finger decisively. "Now we got a good reason to use up all those cold cuts in the fridge! I'm gonna keep 'em coming from the plant, too, plus the ham and bacon when they can spare some, and they don't really have to tell me when that happens. I'm in like Flynn over there. You'll never have to pay for another ham again, Stella."

"Never again?"

He stared at her.

"I mean as long as I'm here. Of course I don't expect to be packin' meat for the rest of my life, neither."

"Of course not. You're a lot better than that, Ray."

"I might as well pick up some Fritos for the kids, too."

"Oh, Fritos are their favorite," Stella said.

Strawn hesitated a moment, as if he'd forgotten to say something, and Stella thought, swallowing her vanity, that in this rush he might try to kiss her again. A kiss in the rip-tide under the calm of a little recreation that would carry them out to a sea where some miracle would come along to rescue them, and sail them away to Shangri-la.

"Well, I'd better get busy," Stella said, moving past him toward the safety of the kitchen that made her heart beat faster, anyway.

On the dry grass out toward the shady road some boys were kicking a soccer ball around. Farther out another boy with a bat was hitting fly balls to a couple of others staggered to catch the long balls and the pop-ups. The expanse of the huge oak tree above barely stirred in the faint breeze.

"I don't see the boys anywhere," Stella said. "Where in the world could they have disappeared to, anyway?"

Across the picnic table from her Strawn guzzled from his beer bottle.

"They're around," he said. "Shoot, you know how long it's gonna take 'em to count up a hundred squirrels?"

"I know, but – shouldn't we be eating soon?"

"Aw, let 'em have their fun. You ready for a beer?"

She didn't really want to be drinking when Art got here, if he showed up.

"In a while, maybe."

"What's the matter? Sorry we came?"

"Oh, no! I could be doing laundry."

Strawn laughed.

"Yeah, with all that extra I threw in."

"I wonder if he got the note," Stella said, stopping his laughter cold.

It was as if Strawn's next word should be 'Who?' so he wouldn't have to think *his* company wasn't good enough.

"Well, if he doesn't show, he doesn't show," Strawn said.

Just then Lou and Joe ran up, both out of breath. Lou was pointing.

"Look, there's Dad!" he said,

Stella looked out toward the road that wound through the park and saw the Cadillac slowly pulling off to the side. The door on the driver's side swung open, Art lifted out his artificial leg and let the heel drop onto the grass. He turned around on the seat and got out backwards. He stood up straight, waved and went back to the trunk, opened it and pulled out a glove and a bat – part of his treasure of props that he kept in there. He slammed the trunk down and started toward them, weaving a little and then righting himself. There was the crack of a bat from somewhere and a fly ball sailed toward him. Joe shouted:

"Look out, Dad!"

Art ducked, dropping the bat, at the same time looking upward for the ball. He was trying to stuff his hand into the glove. The ball was coming down. He made a stab for it, lunging forward onto all fours as the ball plopped onto the grass about a yard away. Lou and Joe took off running toward him. Joe got there first, then Lou was there in time to help, each grabbing an arm until they pulled Art to his feet. Joe picked up the ball and viciously pegged it back at the boy who'd socked it - so hard it landed several yards behind the boy's upraised glove.

He's been drinking, Stella thought. The boys were walking with him, now, Joe carrying the bat, the glove still on Art's hand. Strawn got to his feet and stood beside her – the welcoming committee. She said, "Are you okay, Art?"

"Yeah, yeah. I should'a had that ball, goddamn it. I lost it in the sun."

"That kid sure wasn't looking where he was hitting," Strawn said.

Art glanced at him, turned his attention to Stella: "I didn't find your note till I was about ready to call the Playhouse to see if you were still there. A drink seemed appropriate. Then damned if I didn't stumble on the note and I thought, for Christ's sakes. Now I've got to drive across town under the influence. What a revolting development."

Looking at Lou's eyes glued to her, Stella faltered. Strawn slapped the table and said:

"Well, heck – siddown, Art. We got some good chow, here. Cold cuts practically fresh off the hogs. Lemme crack you a beer."

Art made his way to the far end of the table on Stella's side and slid in, helping his leg over the brace.

"It's Pabst, Art," Strawn said. "For my dough Pabst beats Schlitz all to hell." He slammed his knee up against the table getting out, hurried over to the cooler and fished a dripping bottle out of the melting ice. "Try one. It'll tide you over."

Art looked at the bottle that Strawn was just about to open. He raised one hand.

"Hold on, Ray. I'm not really much of a beer drinker."

"Oh, no? I guess you gotta be from the working class to acquire the taste."

"Like the steel mills on Lake Michigan where my brother and I worked to pay our way through college?"

Strawn's eyes flared with discomfort, riding on the crimped line of a grin.

"Steel mills, eh? Did you get to join the Union on a summer job?"

"No, but we thought it was a gold mine," Art said, "in spite of our advantaged life. Our mother made all our college clothes for us, by hand."

Strawn snuffed.

"Lucky you. My Ma still can't hardly darn a sock."

Stella felt something like smoke in the air from some electrical accident: Art hadn't tacked 'pal' onto anything he'd said to Ray for the past several days. Almost as if he was backtracking toward the night he'd dragged Ray home from the Black Cat, where he could return him and get his money back.

"You wanta play some catch with us, Dad?" Lou said.

"Lemme take a rain check for now, pal. Maybe a little later." He reached into his pants pocket, pulled out a small flask.

"Got something there a little stronger there, Art?" Strawn said.

"For emergencies," Art said.

Strawn jived a little, nodding, then said, looking at the boys:

"I'll toss a few with you guys."

"Where's your glove?" Lou said warily.

"No problem. I used to catch bare-handed all the time."

Everybody looked at the glove that lay beside Art's hand. Giving it a flip, Art said, "Here, use this if you want to."

"Naw. That's yours, Art. I like catching bare-handed, anyways."

"Suit yourself," Art said. "I know how it is, sticking your hand into somebody else's sweat."

Stella gave him a startled look.

"I'm sure Ray didn't mean –"

"Ray told us what he meant. We don't need a dissertation to clear that up. Am I right, Ray?"

Strawn eyed Art with a smirk to which it seemed to take effort to confine himself.

"Right."

Art reached for the pack of cigarettes in his shirt pocket, tapped one out and felt for his matches in the same pocket.

"So how did it go today, Art?" Stella said. "That was quite some drive for you – all the way down to Gardena and back."

Art lit his cigarette, sparked ash onto the tip taking a drag.

"I'll tell you later," he said ominously.

Stella wanted to say, 'What's the matter with now?' But she would only aggravate that pressure she felt building in him, bring on some other sarcastic retort.

All at once Strawn bolted to his feet, scooping up the baseball from where it had rolled from Joe's hand against the picnic basket.

"Come on, you guys! I used to be a pretty darn good sandlot catcher!" He nimbly hopped over the bench and started to fling the ball from one hand to the other, smacking it against his palms.

Lou lowered a look at Joe, who frowned back, eyes rolling aimlessly this way and that.

"Dad, don't you want to –?" Joe began.

"Hey, Joe! Think fast!" Strawn lobbed the ball at him, then took off sprinting into the clearing. Joe bobbled the ball and dropped it. Out on the grass Strawn began to unbutton his shirt. He tore it off, sailed it onto the grass, then took a stance like a shortstop, hands on his bent knees.

"Come on, Joe! Burn one in! Gimme all you got!"

Stella took in her breath at the sight of him out there naked to the waist – so lean and smooth and muscular, his skin burnished by the sun, that made her think of where he must have got the tan – those islands broiling in the South Pacific. She thought of the way he must have looked in the air behind his machine gun; or on the ground again, getting out of his gear and another day in which death hadn't got around to him. She'd got him into her system and she couldn't get him out. Not while just looking at him made him run so hot through her body, draining into the center of her being where she could almost feel him pouring his own longing into hers, as if already he was hers, and she his.

Art was watching as if casually, puffing on his cigarette. Stella felt his crapulent nearness to her, reeking of the cigarettes and the bourbon on his breath.

"Come on, Joe!" Strawn badgered, "toss that baby! Fast ball comin' down the pike!"

"You haven't got a glove," Joe demurred.

"Am I complaining? If I don't catch it, that's when I'll need a glove."

Joe wound up and threw with all his might. The ball hit the ground in front of Strawn and hopped into his mid-section where he bobbled it but held on. Stella clapped and Joe, glancing at her, let out a nervous laugh.

"Way to go in there, pal," Art said, but Stella couldn't tell which one he meant. He blew out a lungful of smoke, reached for the flask and started to unscrew the top.

"I got fired today, Stell."

She wasn't sure she'd heard him right. He could be joking, just to get her attention. Strawn picked up the bat.

"Get out there, you guys! No, way on out there! I'll sock you some long ones!"

The boys grinned at each other before they took off. Strawn got ready, waiting until they were out as far as they would be in left and center fields in a ball park.

"Okay, heads up!" Strawn called out.

Stella watched the muscles rippling in his back as he swung. The ball in the air began to drift toward Joe. He called for it, causing Lou to pull up. She could see the smile at the corner of Strawn's face. The way he leaned on the bat with one arm, watching. That copper glint rounding his shoulder down across the wedge of muscle into the craggy shadow on his arm. She knew Joe wouldn't miss the ball, and he didn't. He was becoming quite an outfielder, that boy.

The silence beside her called her back to the effort of caring about what Art had said.

"I'm sorry, Art. What did you say?"

"Skip it. It's no big deal, as deals go."

"No, no - I was watching the boys and I –"

She saw that he was pouring from the flask into the top that, upturned, held a shot of whiskey.

"I said they fired me," he said. "They told me there's no appeal. Don't come back."

"What happened?"

Art shrugged.

"Somebody said I was drinking on the job. Had it in for me, I guess – I don't know who. Never mind all the goddamn legs I sold for the bastards."

"But Art –"

"Of course you have to agree with them. I mean let's face it, you can't do your job with liquor on your breath. On the other hand, you can't do it without."

It was so hard for her to care now, as she had cared back over the thousand times he'd got into some jam, dragging his raging selfishness around like tin cans. The crowds that had once roared for him left her heart as empty as the Brawley stadium. Now she couldn't bring herself to do it any more - to bear the sight of him, in youth and glory, coming in out of the heat; feel the refuge of the swamp cooler stirring her hair as she got up to pour him another drink and tell him, meaning it, 'I love you so much, Art.'

She looked out at the powerful young man, about to swing the bat again. The wraith beside her raised a flask to his lips, drank the crippling poison that meant more to him than her, and waited for her pity that might not be there now, but it would come.

How true it was, Stella thought, that he drank to keep the leg shot off. Every leg he ever owned.

16

On the other end of the line Stella heard a bang that sounded like a door slamming.

"Oh, for God's sake, your father *is* here." Toots' voice faded from the phone. "Harry, Stella's on the line! Where in the world did you go?"

Stella made out her father's saying in the background, "Just out to pull the truck into the garage."

"Well, here's Stella. She wants to talk to you."

Her father's voice was brusque, businesslike.

"Hello, honey. What's on your mind?"

"How're you, Dad?"

"I'm all right. Haven't heard from you in a while." His voice maintained its clipped, standoffish tone.

"Yes, but – how're you doing?"

"As well as can be expected."

"What do you mean?"

"My sciatica's acting up. Flared up that day I was supposed to visit you, and Toots told me I wasn't welcome."

Those must have been exactly Toots' words, Stella thought.

"Now you know that's not the way it was, Dad. I'm so sorry – I know how painful sciatica can be." She withheld the reason why she knew; now wasn't the time to bring up any of Art's sufferings. "I wanted to talk to you personally, Dad, but Toots said the phone was out up at the ranch?"

There was a pause, then: "Yes, that line's been giving us some trouble."

"Listen Dad – I've decided to hang on to the Buelton parcel. I just feel that's what I want to do."

"I see. Art, I suppose," he said flintily.

"No, actually, it's me."

"Well, all right. I was about to kiss that feedlot goodbye, anyway. Art must be happy as a jaybird."

"Dad, I told you – Art has nothing to do with this. Can't you believe I've got a mind of my own?"

"Oh, you always have."

"I love you just the same, you know. You wouldn't know it any better if I signed that land over to you."

"How are the two of you getting along these days, anyway?"

The back door slammed.

"Stell!" Art's voice was strident.

"You still there, honey?" her father said.

"I have to go now, Dad. We'll be in touch. I love you."

"I love you, too, darling. Don't be such a stranger. And keep me posted on – things."

"I will. Bye, Dad."

"Goodbye."

She hung up the phone in time to see Art storming into the kitchen.

"God damn it, Stell! I tell him he can go down there to take a workout, and what happens? He leaves the medicine ball clear over on the dirt. The weights are scattered all over the goddamn mat. He drapes a stinking T-shirt over the supine bench. Christ, is that consideration? Is this our home, or a flophouse?" Art glared at her, letting his head wobble up and down indignantly, giving her time to get the picture.

Stella made like she didn't know what he was driving at.

"You're talking about -?"

"Who else? I think our Sergeant Strawn has overstayed his welcome, that's what I think. It's high time he found another place to live. He's been working now at Armour's for damn near a month."

"Art, you were the one who made him feel like he could stay until –"

"That's right! He's driving his own car. He's making decent money. Apparently he thinks our charity will go on and on, as long as he's as snug as a bug in a rug."

"Tell him to get out, then. You brought him here, so you should be the one to kick him out."

"Am I getting any argument from you?"

She looked at him, knowing he must know, but holding out that outside chance that he didn't. She had to turn it all around. The time had come. She felt the heat under her nerves, the wastes in her heart being overruled.

"The fact of the matter is, I've been thinking, Art. We're getting nowhere. We fight almost every day. It's no good for the kids. We need a break from each other. I think we should separate for a while. Otherwise I just don't think we'll ever clear the air."

"You mean clear the decks, don't you? Everybody off the boat but the cabin boy."

She glared at him, but didn't take the bait.

"Don't you see? It's the same old thing, day in and day out. I think you need to go away for a while. We need to give ourselves some breathing room, some time to think. They call it a trial separation."

"I know what they call it," Art said, looking down at his hands that were coming apart, now, and the hurt in his eyes dove for cover in the quieting of his voice. "Okay, you're probably right. I'll go if that's what you want. Shall I break it to the boys, or would you rather do it?"

She hadn't expected this - the fateful acceptance in his face. A kind of black and grieving embrace of the end of their lives together, and for a second she almost caught her breath, not wanting to let him go.

"I *can't* any more, Art. Maybe you could stop drinking, once you're free of me."

"Oh, is that it? The boot with a little charity behind it?"

She looked at him, saw his false strength leaving him, his face a sunken shell.

"You'll be lonely for a while, I guess," she said.

"It won't hurt you a bit if I'm lonely," he said quietly.

So quietly it frightened her, and whether she feared for him or herself, she didn't know. She wanted to escape, but there was no outlet. No relief. Only the dumb plodding ahead with what she had told herself she must do.

"It's not leaping for a divorce, Art. Sometimes people just need some time apart before they can see how they can make it work when they get back together. I think you've got to get some help about your drinking. Don't ridicule me for thinking you might do it better without me."

Art stepped back, still remote, like a fighter deliberately letting his guard down.

"So once I'm gone, what happens to the boarder?"

"What do you mean?"

"Don't play dumb with me, Stell. You better watch yourself, though. He might not have the compunctions I do about getting you pregnant."

"Are you crazy? There's never been so much as –"

"Did you tell him a little kiss in the shadows will have to wait till I leave, too?"

"I'm not listening to this anymore!" Stella grabbed the edge of the table, as if to keep herself from collapsing. Art brought his hand down on her wrist.

"What is it, Stell – besides the booze? You've stood that, matched me drink for drink. It's the leg, isn't it? One legged lovers can't be expected to satisfy a whole woman."

"No!" She said it to stanch the flow of what was coming. She could say no to the one leg and the booze. She couldn't tell him what it really was. She had no words for that. How she could take the sloppy drunkenness, the grotesque handicap that she had once so easily ignored, if she loved him. But she didn't. She couldn't tell him that, and it seemed impossible – the emptiness like a room where they had loved each other for so long, cleared out. The movers had come and taken everything away.

His eyes narrowed, flicked out at her.

"Okay. That leaves only him. Just how good a swordsman is the son of a bitch, anyway?"

"I'm not listening to this any more, Art!"

"Don't tell me I fed him to you on a platter, either. You'd have found him in a soup kitchen. The funny thing is, in all these fifteen years since we were married, I never once – not *once* did I ever sleep with another woman."

She said it equably, with the icy calm of retribution:

"You've forgotten something, haven't you?"

He stared at her, incredulous, as if a terrible wind he thought he could stand up to was forcing him backward, backward toward some crime he hadn't buried deep enough.

"That day I came home from shopping in El Centro, and you were on your third or fourth scotch. I was late because I'd stopped to give a man a lift. I just told you, oh, it was a farmhand. But it wasn't a farmhand. If I'd told you who it really was, you'd be furious and hate me. Because he was your arch enemy, Percy Palmer, and he told me a story. All these years I've kept it to myself, because you -"

"Palmer? But why -?"

"He'd got a blowout on the road. He said his spare was flat, and he didn't have a pump. He looked familiar from that picture of him when he'd got elected Superintendent of Schools. When I told him who I was, he clammed up, but little by little I got him talking. I asked him why, with all the complaints he had against you, he hadn't called you on the carpet yet. He said he was waiting to see when you'd stop taking your boys across to Mexicali after the games, contributing to the delinquency of minors."

"Why, that goddamn little piss-ant –"

"He knew he wouldn't be thanked, even by the parents of the boys whose morals you were playing fast and loose with. He knew public opinion would protect you. He might as well be nothing but an earthworm squirming in the sunlight of your football glory. You'd never taken him seriously. He couldn't forgive you for that. I knew he'd never let you repent. He was going to fire you as soon as he got something on you that was so air-tight, your fans could all go hang. He'd got it already. I'll never forget it when he said, so quietly, like a snake, I'm sorry, Mrs. Ryan, but there's more."

Art stared at her, eyes locked tight in their sockets. Stella pressed on:

"Do you remember her, Art? Thelma Bryant? She was in her senior year at Brawley High - one of your cheerleaders. Some busybody saw the two of you together in your car. Somebody who thought it might be cute to tell on you. Palmer didn't say who did the squealing, but it wasn't her parents. In fact, they wanted to hush it up. When Palmer went to them, they promised to make her stop. It seems that Mr. Bryant blamed his daughter, not you. She was *that* kind of a girl. He'd whip her to within an inch of her life. But Palmer wasn't interested in saving Thelma's butt. He wanted you. He called Thelma into his office and scared her so badly, she broke down and begged him not to harm you. She'd leave you alone, never see you again. But he'd got what he wanted – her confession. Your doom was sealed."

Art sat back, shutting his eyes in defeat.

"Why the hell didn't you -?"

"Because the next morning you were at death's door in the hospital, with one of your legs gone, and I –"

Art looked up and watched her, waiting. The words he wanted trembled soundlessly between them on the past that brought him back – that man she'd loved like crazy, would go on loving until death did them part. She almost reached her hand across to him. It took all her strength to hold it back. She got up abruptly, unable to look any more at the hope that lingered in his eyes, now shimmering with tears. And then in the dining room, the nearest exit, she knew she hadn't got away at all, and she ran down the hallway toward the shrine that had long since replaced the Holy Mother, the beautiful young woman clinging to her wedding bouquet, her short life entombed in a frame like a casket in which she was still too pretty to be dead.

17

Lou heard them in the breakfast nook, talking in low tones. He stood just beyond the doorway, ready to duck into the bathroom if he had to, hearing his mother say, "Let's say six months. Maybe a year, we'll have to see." He couldn't help it. He was going in there. They both looked up at him.

"What is it, honey?" Stella said.

"I was just wondering where you were," Lou said.

Stella glanced absently at the clock over the stove.

"Your dad and I are just having a talk, honey."

"Is anything wrong?"

"No," Stella said, "not –"

"Lou, old pal," his father said. "Come over here."

"Art, not now," Stella said.

"When?" Art said viciously. His face just as suddenly softened. He scooted sideways, patted the bench beside him.

"Right over here, pal."

Lou obeyed, getting in beside his dad.

"Lou, old pal, your mom and I have been talking. I'm gonna take a little trip up north to see a friend of mine I used to know. I'll be gone a while – could be a couple months. But I'm gonna make some money."

"You mean a lot of money?" Lou said, thinking of it as a kind of ransom that could hold time to its promise.

"Well, enough to make the trip worthwhile. More than I'm making now."

Lou knew that what his dad was making now was next to nothing.

"What'll you be doing?"

"Helping out my old friend, Tommy Wyatt. He's a doctor. I'll be helping him with – whatever he wants me to do."

"Like what, d'you think?"

"He's a surgeon, so I might have to get some training from him. He'll have to fill me in on the details after I get up there."

"How far is it?"

"He lives in a town called Redding, not too far from Mount Shasta. My guess is about four-hundred miles from here."

"That's such a long way, Dad. Why do you have to go that far away to make some money?"

"Well, it's not just that. Four-hundred miles is hardly anything in this big state. You know there's a train called the Starlight that'll get you there in one night. We'll be writing back and forth, too. You guys and me."

"Mom," Lou said, "do you want Dad to leave?"

"Honey, we've had a talk about it, and this is what we think is best for us right now. Sometimes people have to be apart a while before they can start to see things clearly. You understand?" She reached for his hand on the table. He snatched it away.

"When somebody goes away, they're just gone," he said. "Like Tank when he was in the war." He left his logic to writhe helplessly like an earthworm on a hot sidewalk.

The warmth of his father's hand came down upon his arm. Lou didn't move.

"It's not your mother's wish alone, pal. We've talked this out together. We've agreed that what I'm doing is the right thing, for now. You may not understand the whole thing until – some day this will make more sense to you."

It wasn't exactly what his father said, but the quiet of his voice, the tenderness that wouldn't let him go while he spoke, like God, almost, pinning down his arm with nothing but the dream that He was there. Lou sat back.

"Can I go up to Tank's as soon as I'm finished with my homework?"

"Honey," Stella said, "your father's leaving now. Go get Joe and we can say goodbye."

"Right now? Right this minute, Dad?"

"Yes, pal. I've planned it so I can get up as far as San Francisco before nightfall."

"Joe went up to Toby and Roberta's," Lou said desperately.

"Well, then –" Art looked at Stella.

"I can explain it to him when he gets home," Stella said.

"That's right," Art said to Lou. "You say goodbye to Joe for me, pal. No, not goodbye. That's not what it is. Just tell him I had to get on the road, and as soon as I get up to San Francisco, I'll call you guys. It's like a business trip, not forever. Two months, tops. You got that, Lou?"

"Yes, Dad." But Lou could see Joe's stricken face, hear him saying furiously, 'Why didn't you come and get me? It's only up the street.' And when the explanation didn't work, the part about the business trip, Joe would get mad, the way he'd seen him do before when something hurt his feelings. You couldn't sell a lie to Joe. No matter what Dad said, how gently he was trying to put it; it seemed to Lou like he was running out on them.

In the bedroom his father said, "You want to carry this suitcase down for me, Lou? I'll be along in a minute."

Lou carried his name on his father's voice, too, spilling things he couldn't stop to pick up, down to the car. Sitting on his father's suitcase, he wondered what was taking them so long. They'd loved each other. He'd always thought they did.

Down on the grass in front of the car his father took him in his arms. The smell of cigarettes and Tweed cologne was strong on his kiss, as always. His mother took his hand and they stood back. Art got the car started. She didn't wait but walked Lou up into her bedroom and they hurried over to the open window. The car was just pulling around into the street. They watched it, coughing exhaust, until it disappeared behind the pepper trees.

 Lou wasn't looking when his mother's hand, lost in the air, came onto her mouth and he could hear the sobs and lurching in her chest. He looked up and saw the tears on her face. He thought he should be crying, too, and didn't know why he couldn't. Maybe it was just that he still had her. What made him believe that, no matter how his father's being gone felt like forever, one day soon he would come back?

❧

She stood alone, now, near the window, hoping Ray would not be home from work any time soon, that he would stay out late for any reason at all. She didn't want to deal with him this way, like now they could whoop it up.

 She'd made herself stop crying long enough to send Lou out to bring his brother home. Her tears were not all gone. She felt them filling up her heart, fighting to come back. And when they did she let her sorrow pour like a rain that washes down a street and then lets up, still roaring in the gutters. Goodbye might keep her just a little longer with that man when she had loved him like crazy. Back into one of those nights, like it was just around the corner, in that little clapboard house they used to live in, the oven it turned into in August. They'd be going out to Wu Fong's for some Chinese tonight, and talk of how his boys were shaping up out on the practice field.

 Art had never gone hunting for anything in his life. He'd never owned a gun, unless you counted that little .32 he fired at track events. Deacon Pine was going to let him borrow one of his shotguns. They hardly knew Deacon Pine from the dogcatcher, yet Art had said to her, like rolling off a log, 'I've gotta get up early in the morning, darlin'. Deacon Pine wants me to go dove hunting with him and his boy.' Just like that, as if there was something to be gained by cozying up to that phony preacher, who sometimes played around with snakes to prove that God was on his side.

She couldn't imagine what. Neither one of them had ever talked about taking up church-going. It was so unlike Art, going out to blow some harmless little doves to kingdom come, a thing he'd never done before, with a man he barely knew and that boy of his who had a few screws loose. Something about it screamed at her, don't let him go!

She should have insisted, threatened even. Done anything; thrown a tizzy.

He died that night while they were trying to save his life. They couldn't understand that he had wanted to go on. They weren't there with him in that room that shimmered everywhere with gold, pulling him onward, leaving no regret to hold him back. It was as if, when he opened his eyes to the doctor's face triumphantly assuring him that he was going to be all right, he resented her happiness. She drove home past the blistering miles and miles of cotton, melons and alfalfa, wondering how long that would last. No, she'd give him back his life without a leg. He'd never give that golden room another thought. She knew how to do it. Little things would be important like they used to be. Things like how she'd go out for a spin at high noon in her new Cabriolet, and if she had a blowout or the radiator boiled over she'd feel pretty silly about embarking on a pilgrimage to Mecca for the brand of Seltzer water Art liked with his Scotch. He'd roar laughing at that. And it would show how harmless, too, a little drink was in the evening, the same as always. Life goes on.

The empty driveway looked the way it always did when he'd gone out to sell another leg. She'd count the hours and the minutes until forgiveness hauled him in with what was left of the hate that wouldn't let him go. And then his guilt that she had so believed in failed her - but didn't she have Ray? The feel of her wedding ring clung to the bare, pale band of skin – like Art had told her once how he could feel his missing leg there under the covers. She'd never ask Ray if the gem was real, as long as it was big and bright. One size fits all. Could she get away with slipping it on a different finger? Or wouldn't that be love? To wear it like that one that Lou sent away for, with the three Wheaties box tops, and when it came its wee atomic bomb looked cheap. It wasn't silver-plated, no tiny hatch opened to a picture of the mushroom cloud at all.

There was a knocking softly on the door. Lou's voice in the hallway said, "Mom, Joe's home. Are you okay?"

"Yes, honey. Just a minute, I'm coming."

18

Strawn was in bed already, thumbing through the new October issue of *Life* magazine, when Stella came into the spare room where, as far as the boys knew, he slept alone every night.

"What're you reading?" she said. Her hair was wet, combed out to dry without curlers, and she was wearing a red silk negligee, bought just yesterday at Bullocks.

"Just lookin' at the pictures," Strawn said.

She waited a few seconds, but he didn't seem to notice the negligee. The funny thing was, Stella thought, he ate *bierkase* all the time; you could hardly tell the smell of that from his dirty Argyll socks, yet he never seemed to notice. She was getting used to it.

She just couldn't get enough of him. And Ray had told her that was exactly the way he felt about her, too. Their age difference didn't bother him if it didn't bother her. She had never felt so desirable in her life. Ray said he wanted to marry her as soon as the divorce was final. Right now she saw no reason why she shouldn't become Mrs. Ray Strawn. She'd thought about that – how it would affect the boys, but it was certainly better to be married than not. Yes, his desire came out of how young he was, how long he'd been away from women, but most of all there was her new awareness of how pretty she was, that made him want her like that, and if he wanted her that bad, well, what more could a girl ask?

He laid down the magazine.

"C'mere," he said.

She went over to him, sat on the edge of the bed. Her negligee fell away from her thigh, and he ran his hand in, dragging up the silk and drawing her down.

"You smell good," he said.

She couldn't say the same for him. She'd have a lot more to say, if she could say it. But she could never tell him. He'd take it all wrong, hearing, 'Honey, that smell about your feet – it goes better on you than a cracker.' He'd get right up and go and wash, feeling like that's what she wanted him to do. Then what? Mention the ounce of aberration that the French took *their* sex with. Don't compare me with the frogs, he'd say. I wouldn't fart in your face to save my soul. 'Honey, you already have.'

Her blood began to pound like waves in her head, the heat of his hand knifed into her groin. She turned her face to him, sought his eyes. She felt her breath brush past her open lips. Sometimes it didn't work, the follow-up; he was so awkward, usually, being romantic. How could a man who looked like he did . . . ?

She didn't know if he would care; he'd hadn't seemed too interested, so far. But these were things that mattered to her, and they should matter to him, too.

"Honey," she began, "I've got sort of a problem."

"Oh, yeah? What?" He turned another page in the magazine.

"Well, you know how hard I've been working on the play we're getting ready for."

He looked over at her, chin tucked down onto his chest, as if he might have missed something.

"Yeah?"

"I tried and tried to stay on schedule, but our understudy for Cordelia needs more work, and then we lost a player and it's taken all this time to find a good replacement. We won't be ready unless I postpone opening night another month, maybe longer. God, I feel like I've really dropped the ball."

"How come?"

She looked at him. He was just waiting, eyes like holes for pinballs to blunder into.

"Well, I'm the director. I'm supposed to be on top of these things."

"Yeah, but what's the big deal about putting it off? It's not like anybody's gonna blow a gasket, seein' it a little later."

She searched his eyes again, looking for what wasn't there, and probably she shouldn't expect. In the practical sense, he was right.

"We'll be apart more often, with me down at the Playhouse working late. I know how much you like us to have our drinks early, so we don't have to rush dinner."

"Aw, shoot, honey. Me and Dom'll go out for a beer. You do what you have to do."

She didn't like that answer, but how could she argue with the practicality? He flipped another page.

"Look at this! Damn, did they ever flatten Nagasaki. Who could live through that? Well, they asked for it, and they got it."

Stella looked at the vast charred wasteland in which, unseen, people had been turned to ash in the same fireball that consumed their flimsy houses and their once meticulously pretty gardens.

"Anyway, I just wanted you to know. Sometimes you might have to get dinner for the kids."

"Hey, don't I know how to open a can of pork and beans?"

She saw the humor he was bottling up behind his tightened grin, and she gave him a shove.

He turned aside, withdrew his hand as if it wasn't his, but something he had left there, like a hot pad in the oven.

"Shit, I almost forgot. The phone rang while you were in the shower."

The jolt caused a sudden rearrangement in her mind: it had to be somebody important, she thought, for him to put the brakes on in the middle of the road. She sat up and stretched the hem of her nightie down across her knees.

"Oh? Who was it?"

"She wouldn't say right off. Who're *you?* she says, kinda smart-like. Boy, with that southern drawl she could wring hot water out of a candy cane."

Stella tried to think of who among her friends hailed from the south. None of the girls in the cast came to mind.

"Did she leave a name?"

"Yeah. She says just tell Stella Jo Riley called. You'll know what it's about."

"Oh, God, I never wrote her back. Things got so hectic –"

"Wrote her about what?"

Stella wanted to believe now that she had liked Jo Riley, and now that Art was gone, there'd be no reason why she couldn't come on out.

"Well, this was a couple months ago. She'd finally got a divorce from a guy Art used to coach and she said she had to get out of that little town, you know, where people take sides, and she was hoping maybe we could put her up until she got back on her feet. Art never liked her. He put his foot down, said no, period."

Strawn picked up the magazine, mussed a page back.

"What'd he have against her?"

"Oh, she kept blaming Chet for ruining the life she might've had if they'd never got married. She dropped out of school to have their baby. Art always thought she ought to take a little responsibility for seducing him."

Strawn was nodding, his eyes not where they were pointed.

"You and Art musta had some time back then, huh?"

She just looked at him, maintaining a tepid smile. Strawn went on:

"I don't hold anything against Art, you know – like you do."

"Who says I've got anything against him?"

"You sure could'a fooled me, hon." Strawn kept rubbing his hand around on the magazine, smoothing the page. "Where's she from, anyway?"

"Jo Riley? Texas, I think."

"Well, I won't kick if you want to bring her out here, hon. This room's gonna be free, here, as soon as those money-grubbin' lawyers get their heads outa their asses and we can get our license and do this thing up right."

Stella searched his face.

"I don't know about letting her stay here. She might get too comfortable."

"Up to you, hon."

"So you think you could put up with that southern drawl while she told you all about Chet's bad points? I guess you could learn what not to do as a husband."

He was nodding. His face suddenly took on a remote, troubled look.

"You know that guy, Tank whatsisname? I got a funny feeling about that guy."

"What do you mean?"

"The way he likes to hang around the kids. It's unnatural."

"Oh, come on, Ray. Tank's harmless. Kind of a kid himself."

Strawn scooted back and sat up irritably.

"That's just it. A guy that age – he's not supposed to be no kid."

She stared at him quizzically, taking the time to admire his thick, dark hair. She reached out and ran her hand through it. He blinked impatiently until she stopped.

"So what're you getting at?" she said.

"No combat veteran I know of, unless maybe he's shell-shocked, gets out with a couple kids to play war. It don't happen. But then what the hell do I know?"

"Tank won the Purple Heart for getting shot in –"

"Says him. Maybe he got in the way of a bullet when he was changing a tire. I don't like him hangin' around the house – makin' the kids think he's some – I don't know – some kind of a hotshot."

"I don't think he's out to make them think anything. Anyway, the kids wouldn't understand if I told them not to play with him any more. I couldn't do that."

"Awright, awright. But don't let him snow you. He could be queer, you know."

"Oh, get out of here! With a girlfriend like Marla?"

"Could be a decoy. They do that to throw you off the scent."

"Are you kidding? Honey, you can take that thought and throw it out the window." Then it seemed to her that he could have some other ax to grind with Tank. What could that be? "Really, honey. I know it when I see a real man, or he's a little off."

"Oh, yeah?" Strawn pulled her down onto the bed. "I got something real for you right here."

"Turn the light out, will you?" Stella giggled.

"What for? Leave it on." In the light he looked at her, as if he'd forgotten something. "Maybe I better jump in the shower before we –"

"No, no!" She laughed but reached for the light switch anyway. "I want you just the way you are."

The light went out. Darkness was the space through which she felt for him, and words retreated from the lips she brought down on his face. Under the sheets the smell of his feet, revolting in polite company, thrilled her, that raw thing they had between them that made him so much more hers. It was the smell of his lust, devouring her. Her secret and the man he was. Nobody else would ever have to know.

※

"What do you think of Stella's new boyfriend?" Victor said.

They were having tea and ginger snaps at the breakfast table, compliments of a sortie Dorothy had made into Chinatown.

"I don't like him," Tank said, with no apparent animosity.

"So he flew a torpedo bomber, is that it?"

"No. Manned the machine-gun seat," Tank said matter-of-factly.

"I guess that'd take some guts."

"I guess so," Tank said. "If you call it guts to sit there and do your job."

Victor dropped another spoonful of sugar into his tea and shook his head.

"You have to wonder, what does Stella think she's doing with a guy that young?"

"*Do* you?"

"Okay, but knowing her own mind won't help much if she gets knocked up."

"How could she at her age?"

"She's only forty, Tank. Her age isn't gonna protect her."

"From what?"

"Art told me they got it from three separate doctors – no more babies. Otherwise she runs the risk of not only losing the child, but her own life. Her mother died giving birth to her. Did you know that?"

Tank looked up sharply.

"Well then, if Strawn knows –"

"Who's gonna tell him? Her? And spoil the party?"

Tank stared across at his father. All he could say was, "Christ."

Victor cleared his throat and sat back. He picked up his spoon and stirred his tea.

"At any rate, it's none of our business."

"I'd hate to see an asshole like that taking advantage, Dad."

"Sure, but what are we supposed to do? Already I think you might stop spending so much time up there with Stella's boys. It doesn't look good - your fooling around with a couple kids with the guns and stuff."

"I guess you're getting tired of making excuses for me."

Victor sucked in a breath, like he was starved for air.

"Just back off a little, can't you? You've got a honey of a girl in your life, now. You should be concentrating on her."

"What, like you think I ever had a crush on Stella?"

"You said it, son, not me."

"Dad –"

"Who could blame you? She's a damn fine-looking a woman."

"Thanks a lot, Dad." But he thought of that moment in the kitchen, the time she took to hold her hand around his wound. He could have left all the blame to her, but then Strawn came along and there was no blame any more, just a guy who'd let his ticket back to Buffalo expire in the arms of a lonely woman.

"Okay, okay," Victor said. "Don't get your balls in an uproar."

"I'm gonna keep my eye on that cock sucker," Tank said, clenching one fist.

"No, you're not. You've got a reputation to protect."

"With who?"

"You have to ask? If I had a girlfriend like Marla –"

Tank moved roughly in his chair, scooting back a little. It was late in the afternoon, going on five. Not too early for a drink.

"Dad, I'm not in high school any more."

"Did I say Marla was a bobby-soxer? Come on, man."

"You know, this tea's too weak, Dad. I could use a shot of bourbon in mine."

"Wait till the dinner hour, can't you?"

"Yeah, maybe you're right." Tank stood up, hitched up his pants. "I'm goin' out for a spin on my bike. Maybe drop by Marla's."

"Aw, shut up and have another ginger snap there, you big lug you. I want to be able to tell Dorothy how much you liked them."

"You know, Dad - she's gonna have you voting for MacArthur in the next election."

"That'll be the day," Victor said. "I wouldn't vote for him if she baked me a carrot cake with orange icing and ten cherries on top. Period."

19

Sweat dripped off Lou's face onto the grass. He'd been going at it hard since five o'clock. The next ball he decided would go diagonally to his right. He set himself, hands on his knees, waiting for the crack of the bat in his mind.

"Hey, Lou! I thought I told you not to do that any more!"

Strawn peered over the top of the patio wall, scowling. Lou was out of breath. The important thing was how lightning-quick he could turn, now; the ground he could cover in his new kangaroo cleats, sent air-mail from Dad. Now he was supposed to answer Ray while he was panting.

"It's not hurting anything," he said.

Strawn came marching around through the gate and down the slope toward him. He pointed at the grass, waving his hand to indicate the whole expanse of it.

"What do you call that? These grooves you dug up like you're carving a diagram of the confederate flag out here! I told you yesterday. How many more times do I have to tell you?"

"It'll grow back," Lou said in a weak, unconvincing voice.

"Sure, in a month a' Sundays! You can't be tearin' it up for it to grow back, and I don't see you lettin' up."

"I'm doing what Dad told us to," Lou said sullenly, "so we'll get good at –"

"What team are you tryna get so good for? The New York Yankees? You've gotta do this someplace else. Look at this yard. You might as well be diggin' up rows for corn."

Lou wanted badly to say, 'It's not your yard. You're not the boss around here.'

"When I write Dad the next time, I want to be able to tell him –"

"Not here, don't you get it? There's vacant lot you can plough up all you want to down the street."

"It's too lumpy. I'd twist my ankle in these cleats."

Strawn stared at him, red bloating in around his eyes.

"I'm telling you you've got to quit this. D'you hear?"

"But, Ray – this is our yard. I have to wear the cleats. I can't get good enough without them."

Strawn looked at him, a smirk growing on his face.

"Okay. Let's go and see what your mother has to say about this."

Lou stood there, not moving, except for the fist he drove into his glove. Still smirking, Strawn turned on his heel and climbed up toward the house. Lou followed, dawdling. In the patio he got out of his cleats and left them there; later he would bang the dirt off. In the hallway he saw Strawn waiting just outside the bathroom. Strawn jabbed a stiff finger at him.

"*Wait* for me." Then he went on in and shut the door behind him.

Lou hurried down into the kitchen where his mother was fixing a salad. The air smelled of the pot roast in the oven.

"Mom -?"

She turned to look at him, came fully around.

"What is it, honey?"

"Ray says I can't do my baseball drills out in the yard any more."

"Well, didn't he speak to you about that yesterday?"

"Yeah, but -?"

"Actually, honey - Ray's got a point. The way that grass is getting to look –"

"Dad wouldn't mind if he was here."

In the doorway Ray stood so quietly, Lou wasn't sure how long he'd been there. The smirk on his face now looked oddly sour, worn out, but there was still a seething about it.

"I thought I told you to wait for me, Lou."

"I know. I was just telling Mom –"

"I heard. Sounds like you're forgetting your dad doesn't live here any more."

"Ray, he doesn't have to be reminded of that," Stella said.

"Right. Reminders don't work."

Stella shot Strawn a frown, turned to Lou.

"Honey, I'd like you to listen to Ray, now. I know your dad sent you those baseball drills, and the cleats. And I know how much you want to follow through. But you see, those cleats really do tear up the grass. Remember the lawn is yours and Joe's responsibility, too. To keep it looking nice. You *could* put on your tennis shoes, like your brother does."

"That's right!" Strawn put in. "Joe's got no problem with tennis shoes. It's simple. It stands to reason."

"It's not the same in tennis shoes," Lou pleaded, laying forlorn eyes on his mother.

"Honey, if you have to wear the cleats, there's the vacant lot down the street, next to the Crutchleys'. Don't you think that makes more sense?"

Lou was shaking his head, and as he shook it he knew that he would go on shaking it, no matter what they said.

"Okay, Mom," he said. "I'll try that," knowing that when the time came, he wouldn't.

Ray bobbed his head cynically.

"I'll believe *that* when I see it."

Lou sought his mother's face for another look of displeasure. He saw her downcast eyes instead.

"Go get your brother, now, honey. Dinner's ready."

Lou's face filled with blood like a tide. The words came to him like a weapon he had never fired before.

"I'll get Joe, but I'm not hungry, Mom."

Strawn suddenly reared up ramrod straight, his eyes like flint being struck.

"You'll eat now or you'll go to bed without." He went to the fridge, yanked open the door and snatched out one of the toppling, clanking beers bottles.

"Go on, honey," Stella said. "Then we'll eat. I don't want things to get cold."

Lou went on down the hallway, turned into the room where Joe was sitting on the bed, petting Coy. Lou went over and flounced onto his own bed and sat there, glowering at the floor. When that didn't get a rise out of Joe he said:

"Dinner's ready. I'm not eating."

"Whatta you mean? Are you sick?"

"No."

"What, then?"

"You like Ray, don't you? You get along with him okay."

"I can take him or leave him. What's the matter with you, Lou?"

Something in Lou's heart boiled up.

"Am I the only one around that wishes Ray would drop dead?" Then he felt that he had gone too far, that he had implicated their mother. He stepped back in his mind to being alone with Strawn.

"Okay, what'd he do?" Joe said.

"I can't sprint on the lawn in my cleats any more. I'm digging up the grass."

"Why don't you wear your tennis shoes?"

"Yeah they said that - like you do. That's why you get along with him so good, I guess."

"What's he supposed to do? Let us do everything we want?"

"What'd he ever tell *you* not to do?"

"He told me – once I left my Daisy on the davenport. He wanted to lie down there and watch TV. It's not so hard to get along with him."

"Okay, go on and do what you want. I don't *care* if he doesn't like me."

"Yeah, but don't you think it's stupid to get on his bad side, Lou? You're gonna be sorry. He'll get mad right back, and then – you're in the doghouse."

From the kitchen Stella's voice rang out, "Come on, boys! Soup's on!"

Joe pushed himself off the bed.

"Come on and eat, Lou," he said, laying his hand on Lou's shoulder.

Lou shrugged it off.

"No. I'd rather starve than eat with him."

"Maybe you will," Joe said, and Lou heard in his voice again the accusation, and he thought okay, I'll starve and be stupid, too. Go on and eat and joke around and get along and wear your tennis shoes and stay on his good side. Let me know how it feels when he pats you on the back.

20

"You know what I really adore about Robert Taylor?" Marla said.

"No, what?" Tank said.

"His voice. He's got that pretty face, but he's so manly."

"What about Robert Mitchum? You're not so crazy about his voice, but he's sure got one."

Marla sucked on the straw in her chocolate malt. Tank picked up his hamburger. They were sitting in a booth beside a big bay window at Buster's drive-in, trying to decide on a movie to go to later on. It was a toss-up between *Undercurrent,* playing at the Academy, with Taylor Mitchum and Katherine Hepburn, and a pair of Lon Chaney horror features at the *Uptown.* In any case they'd have to catch a late showing, since Victor had corralled Tank into going with him for toddies at Daddy Banks'. It was a special Halloween occasion, costumes optional.

Tank looked out at the carhops in their brown slacks, the glittering grilles and bumpers nosed up under the blue neon. A big De Soto pulled in off the street. Behind the wheel a pretty woman sat alone, but she had a lot of herself to keep her company. Her lights shone in on them as she parked. She smiled as she wrestled the gearshift into neutral. A carhop stepped off the curb and headed for her.

"What're you looking at out there?" Marla sucked on her straw some more.

"Me? I don't know. People's faces."

"You're the kind who watches hula girls' hands, too, aren't you?"

"You got that right," Tank said.

Marla laughed, then swirled her straw around in her malt.

"He's kind of a strange-looking person, isn't he?"

"Who?"

"Robert Mitchum. I guess it's those lazy eyes of his. They look at you like you could never help yourself as well as he could help you."

"Tough guy, you mean?"

"Yeah, I guess so. You know with that face of yours, Tank, *you* could be in the movies."

"Where I could finally be tough."

"You'd make a perfect Tarzan, now that Johnny Weismuller's too fat to be anything but Jungle Jim. All you have to do is practice that vine-swinging yell. I mean it. You've got everything it takes."

"As soon as I come up with the talent and the luck."

"Will you stop beating yourself up! Okay, let's just say you *could* be Tarzan, the way I've seen how the girls look at you."

"Keep on thinking that. Pretty soon it'll make you forget I'm nothing but a janitor."

Marla looked at Tank, squinting a little, her face quizzical, but stern.

"I wish you'd get off that, Tank. My plan's been working, if you haven't noticed. Ever since I started calling you 'Coach' around the office, Major Griffin's picked up on it. Don't tell me you haven't heard."

"He might have, once. The rest of the time it's still Sergeant Crutchley."

"Hey! Do you think I care a hoot if you're a janitor? Anyway, you're not. You're Tank. The man I love with all my heart. The man I'm going to marry if you'll let me." She reached her hand across to him, he took it feeling a strange peace rolling across his excitement. "Darling, d'you know how lucky we are that we met? That you walked into that office and I'd get you a job shining shoes if I had to. As far as I'm concerned, there'll never be another man in my life. Not even Johnny Weismuller. You can take that to the bank."

It was as if she knew Tank needed that.

"Yes, I know," he said, wishing he could think of more to say. He'd say it, all right, one of these days, when they were more alone than this.

She lowered her eyes, then looked back up. Her head rose slightly as her mouth fell open and she leaned over close to Tank and whispered:

"Oh, my God, Tank. That guy there, paying at the cashier's – isn't that Van Johnson?"

The cash register was right across the aisle from them. The tall man with the strawberry-blond hair had on a pair of khakis, loafers and a short-sleeved tartan shirt, and he was Johnson, all right. The cashier, all fingers, was just about to hemorrhage from her shy smile. She handed Johnson his change.

"No no no! You keep that, dearie."

"Oh! But this is a five dollar bill. I'll make sure your waitress gets it."

"I took care of her already. That's for you."

The girl went ahead and hemorrhaged.

"Thanks a lot, Mr. Johnson! Gee, I –"

"You tell the cook, now, you tell him not to change a hair on those hamburgers. I don't mean that literally."

The cashier tittered.

"Come back and see us real soon, now, Mr. Johnson."

"You've got yourself a deal there!" Johnson stuffed his wallet into his back pocket, turned and looked straight down at Tank, who smiled, then felt foolish as Johnson started for the exit.

"Boy!" Marla shook her head. "The people you get to see at Buster's."

She looked so cute over there, Tank thought, grinning like an imp. He said, "What kind of a Tarzan do you think he'd make?"

She wrinkled up her nose.

"Yeah, I know. I just can't see him in a loincloth the way I can see you. Or should I say, the way I've *seen* you?"

The last showing at the *Academy* tonight would play at 8:05, while the *Uptown* had shows clear up until midnight. Marla wasn't miffed at all about the change of plans. She said, "Don't press yourself tonight. Just give me a call when you get home. I'll be up late passing out candy, anyway."

"I've got a better idea," Tank said. "Come with me to Daddy Banks'. We'll leave a little early for the movie."

"Are you kidding? It'll look like you picked me up off the street."

"Anything goes on Halloween."

"Okay, on one condition. I'm there so you can show me off."

"That was the idea."

Marla leaned forward excitedly.

"You know, we could skip the movie afterwards. Actually, I think I'd rather see the moon from Eaton Canyon and listen to the coyotes howl. You know how to talk to the coyotes, don't you, Tarzan?"

21

Tank knew as soon as he walked in that Daddy Banks, the way he was staring, had forgotten who he was. Or did Marla's being with him throw him off? But then from his chair near the fireplace Daddy Banks called out, "Vincent! Come over here and let me get a look at you!"

Buford "Daddy" Banks had come west to Altadena from Independence, Missouri in 1934, the year he retired from the presidency of the Union Pacific railroad. Nobody knew how much money he had socked away, or how he'd come through the Great Depression just as rich as if it never happened. He liked to say the house he bought across from the Ryans' was built like he was: a two-storied, ivy-covered block of granite in the neo-Gothic style. Marble columns flanked the front porch. Gargoyles emptied rain from all the gutters and the drainpipes. The shades were kept drawn on all his windows. He didn't get too many people calling. You'd almost never see his porch light on, except on Tuesday nights like this, when a few people from the neighborhood would be invited to join him for hot lemonade and bourbon toddies. Only tonight was special. Tonight was Halloween.

He was fondling his favorite conversation piece, a dangling little wooden minstrel that only he could make tap-dance on its wooden scaffold. Lou and Joe, fresh off the street from trick or treating, sat on the rug at his feet. Marla took Tank's arm and they started over. On the way he stopped a moment to introduce her to Dorothy Mulvihill, Victor's date this evening.

Tank had never known Daddy Banks when he wasn't old. Now portly with pale blue watery eyes, thin white mustache and a few wild strands of hair that clung to life on his otherwise bald head, he sat between the radio and the fireplace in a cape with a blanket thrown over his spindly legs. Stella looked up from the couch where she and Strawn sat close together, bathed in the ochre light from a Victorian lamp whose shadows seemed to fan the flames that shot from the Turner barque original that hung over the mantel. Stella twiddled fingers at Tank. He smiled, hoping none of it would rub off on Strawn, who sat close beside her.

She looked so pretty, he thought, with her hair done up and the wavy pile tilted to one side, tied in back with a big yellow bow. Strawn raised a finger-plated gun, tilted it at Tank and said, "How're you doin' there, sport?"

"I'm doin' fine," Tank said.

Marla said, "I'm Marla," and bent over to shake hands in turn with Stella and Strawn, who didn't miss the opportunity to look into her cleavage before, as she stood back, his eyes took in her legs.

Joe tugged on Tank's trouser leg.

"Guess what, Tank? It's Halloween." The smirk that Joe let linger on Tank suggested that tonight couldn't be better for letting the dead Jap in the toolbox get some air.

"It sure is, isn't it?" Tank said, then as he introduced Marla to Daddy Banks he guessed her name would last about as long on his memory as the dwindling fire spitting sparks in the hearth. On the radio Jo Stafford was singing, *I'll be so alone without you. Maybe you'll be lonesome, too, and blue . . .'*

"With a name like that," Daddy Banks said, "your parents must have known you were going to be very pretty."

"You're awfully sweet, sir," Marla said.

Daddy Banks' eyes began to wander, as if he'd run up on a dead end. He looked down at Lou, became reanimated.

"All right, Louis," he said. "Since you're the oldest, I'm giving you another chance to tell me what the spirit is that moves my little darky. But before we get into that, I've got a surprise for you." He reached around and pulled open a glass cabinet just to the left of the fireplace. He took out a box slightly larger than a cigar box, opened it on his lap and lifted out a large, heavy revolver, bringing with it a whiff of oil on gunmetal. "For many years, now, I've kept in this box a .44 calibre revolver that was used in the Civil War. No doubt it was responsible for the death of a number of unfortunate souls. I bought it off a lawman back in – I can't precisely recall the year, but no matter. The barrel's jammed and it weighs close to four pounds. Louis, I'm going to give this gun to you. You, Joe –" Daddy Banks reached down and mussed Joe's hair. "You're a little young, yet, to own a real firearm. But I'm *saving* one for you, when you turn 12 years of age, like your brother."

Joe made soulful dog's eyes as he nodded. Lou took hold of the scarred wooden butt of the revolver that Daddy Banks handed to him by its barrel.

"Boy, it *is* heavy," Lou said. "Thank you, Mr. Banks. Mom! Look what Mr. Banks just gave me!"

"Yes, I see it, honey. Buford, are you sure –?"

Daddy Banks went on, ignoring her, "Now you can't very well play World War Two with that, Louis. It'll have to be cowboys and Indians, you see, or Civil War. That gun was carried originally by a Union soldier, I was told. Not a yella belly."

"I'll take real good care of it, sir," Lou said. "Mom, you want to feel how heavy this is?"

"No, no, honey - that's all right."

"I'll take a look at it if you don't mind," Strawn said.

Daddy Banks wagged his finger, tapping down the revolver's barrel so that it sagged in Lou's hands.

"Never point a revolver at a person like that, Louis, loaded or unloaded. Even though it is a fossil, you've got to hold it by the barrel."

"I'm sorry, sir." Lou frowned at Strawn, then turned the gun around and thrust it, handle first, at him. Strawn took the gun in both hands, hefted it as if to ascertain its weight.

"Boy, it's a heavy one, all right. Too heavy for a kid to handle if you ask me."

"I won't be shooting anybody," Lou said.

Strawn looked at him, holding a smirk in check.

"Yeah, that's right. Just hit 'em upside the head with it."

Stella said, "Are you sure you want to part with this, Buford? It looks so valuable."

"Yeah!" Strawn put in. "This baby's gotta be worth some real money. I wouldn't be surprised if it'd bring a couple hundred bucks in a pawn shop."

"Its monetary worth is immaterial here, young man. I know how it is when you're pretending. You want what's closest to the real thing as you can get. Authenticity, that's the ticket. I've got plenty more where that came from. And one of them is earmarked for Joe, here." He reached for the top of Joe's head, and Joe squinched his eyes shut while Daddy Banks scrambled his hair again.

"Could I have my gun back, Ray?" Lou said.

"Why, sure! It's all yours, kid." But Strawn didn't hand it back the way it had been given to him and, watching, Daddy Banks winced.

"All right, boys," he said loudly, "let's get back to the spirit that moves my little darky!" He lifted a trembling liver-spotted hand toward the wooden minstrel on its platform on the radio.

Nobody, including Tank in his boyhood, had yet been able to figure out what kept this clackety-clacking little minstrel's feet tap-dancing, once it got started. There was nothing to wind up, no mechanical force that anybody could see to keep it going.

"I think I know what the secret to that thing is," Strawn said.

Daddy Banks stared uncomprehendingly at Strawn, as if there'd been a knock on the door, and nobody was there.

"I'm sorry, son. I don't believe we've met."

Strawn tried to chuckle away the red rushing into his face.

"We met when I first came in about an hour ago, sir – with Stella."

Daddy Banks' head turned like a periscope toward the more comforting sight of Stella.

"Stella, we seem to be missing Art. I hope that darned lock on my bathroom isn't giving him trouble."

"No, Buford, Art isn't here with me tonight. He's gone up north, on a trip."

"Up north?"

"Yes. Mr. Strawn, here, has been boarding with us for some time. He was in the war, too, like Tank."

"Is that a fact? Boarding with you, is he?"

In his mind Tank sided with Daddy Banks' failure to move on to the next slide, in which a stranger sat right there beside Stella where Art should be. Maybe Strawn could fill the hole that Art had left in her heart, but in the circles she moved in, never.

Just then Gertrude, the housekeeper, bumped backwards on the swinging kitchen door and came through, clumping in her heavy matronly heels with several steaming toddies on a tray. She marched over to Tank and Marla.

"Here you are, folks. These are piping hot, so watch out."

"Where's mine?" Daddy Banks said.

"You don't mean that, sir," Gertrude said.

"Why don't I?"

"You know two is your limit, Mr. Banks."

"Do you want me to ring Bates at this hour, Gertrude? Or get out of this chair and fix my own? I could fall down and break my hip. Then where would you be? Is that what you want, Gertrude? To visit me in a hospital bed?"

Rattled, Gertrude said in a tremulous voice, "Well of course not, Mr. Banks. But –"

Daddy Banks reached back and turned up the volume on the radio. Dick Haymes was singing *Long Ago and Far Away*. The minstrel on its little magic platform hung limp. Daddy Banks shut his eyes and swooned.

"Listen to that voice, will you? Is that velvet, Gertrude, or is it velvet? It makes me want to dance. I danced with Lily Langtree once when she whistle-stopped St. Louis. I invited her into my caboose, but she declined. The place I was going was somewhat out of her way. Put that tray down, Gertrude. I'll show you a box step you'll never forget."

"Oh, for goodness sakes, Mr. Banks."

"It's the little gibbet you've got there," Strawn said.

Silence turned a spotlight on him, then Daddy Banks.

"Were you talking to me, young man?"

"The string you've got running through your little doll's ears, there. Everybody thinks it's just to hold him up, but actually, it's strung down through one side of the gibbet, and as you tug on it from the bottom the string at the top tightens, so the whole thing jitters."

Daddy Banks smiled lazily at Strawn.

"I should remind you that this little fellow was made by the Chinese. Have you ever played a game of dominoes with a Chinaman? The moment you think you're winning, out comes the inscrutable match to spoil your fun."

"Did I get it wrong, then, sir?"

"I'm telling you not to count your chickens before they hatch. And furthermore, this particular conundrum is for the boys to solve, nobody else."

"O-kay." Strawn flopped back against the cushion and wriggled there uncomfortably. He winced at the touch of Stella's hand on his knee. Dorothy strolled over none too soon.

"Stella, listen. I took the plunge. My Velvet Troubadours are doing so beautifully in the garden, at the show the other day I sprang for the Crimson Sultan. Thirty dollars for a rose bush when the plumbing in my back bathroom is beginning to fall apart. Can you believe it?"

"If that's what makes you happy, Dorothy – shoot. If only I could grow a rose like you do. What've you been feeding them besides love?"

"Well –" Dorothy stood back plumping the back of her new blued permanent. "I'm tempted to say the same thing I've been feeding Victor."

Victor came up behind her hurriedly.

"If I seem to be blushing," Victor said, "it's because I'm still not over that Creole gumbo Dorothy spiked up for us the other night."

Tank's eyes moved onto Strawn, whose face twitched with a lifeless smile as he squirmed and rolled his shoulders, as if he needed air, or more room, sitting there so close to Stella.

Dorothy ran her hand down Victor's sleeve.

"Shouldn't we be going, Victor?"

Victor looked at his watch.

"Ouch, you're right! It's going on ten already."

"Oh, no you don't!" Daddy Banks crowed. "I've been saving up a story, and to my recollection, it's one I've never told before."

People looked at each other. Feet shuffled uneasily. Gertrude was taking in the crowd with a kind of hawk-like calculation.

A story was the *piece de resistance* of Daddy Banks' toddy parties. He was fond of saying that he had a hundred in him, half of them unprintable. Stories about buffalo herds, marauding Indians, sadistic gunslingers and Chinese laborers. This one, he said, could be somewhat risqué, if you didn't have an open mind. All at once in a loud, firm voice Gertrude said, "I'm afraid it's *much* too late for a story tonight, Mr. Banks. I've turned your bed down. You know what the doctor said about getting your rest. I won't have him scolding me again for failing to remind you."

Daddy Banks started to raise his hand, then let it fall.

"Yes, of course, Gertrude. That infernal doctor. Keeping me alive at such a great cost."

Tank and Marla were the last to go. In the doorway Tank paused, feeling Gertrude's hand on his arm.

"Hang onto that one, Mr. Vincent. She's a honey."

Tank walked Marla up the street as far as where he'd left the Packard in the driveway. She leaned back against the car. Just then a bunch of kids came along on the street. He knew the taller girl among them, swinging a flashlight, and said, "Hi there, Roberta! You guys cleaning up on the candy tonight?"

"You said it, Tank! But we're not through, yet! Bye!"

She still had dimples, like Tank remembered when he knew she would be beautiful when she grew up. She giggled, tossing her head, and her top hat almost fell off. Her prettiness glowed softly in the mannish vaudeville outfit she had on. A phosphorescent skeleton glowed on a little body, blackened pipe-cleaners lopped over the forehead of a little girl dressed up as a bee. The two smaller kids' heavy bags of candy bumped along the pavement. One turned the flashlight on Tank, Roberta slapped the top of his rubber mask and the light swept onto the street again. It wasn't long before they weren't bodies any more, just light, like the stern of a galleon on the long ups and downs of the open sea.

"Oh, Tank," Marla said. "I'd hate to fall asleep in your arms tonight. Or come to think of it I'd love to. But those hot drinks really did me in."

He told her okay, he'd see her at work in the morning. They'd catch that movie some other time. He drove her home and kissed her in the car and she said, "Those friendly mountain lions are keeping Eaton Canyon warm for us."

"I'm gonna sleep on that," he said.

22

The notice appeared in the evening edition of the *Star-News*:

> Long Awaited King Lear Opens at Playhouse
> *Morris Ankrum, as King Lear, leads a talented cast of Pasadena Playhouse students in this great Shakespearean tragedy, opening tonight. Mr. Ankrum, well-known as a character actor for MGM pictures, can currently be seen in the Raymond Chandler thriller,* Lady in the Lake, *starring Robert Montgomery and Audrey Totter; and a Topper series comedy,* The Cockeyed Miracle *with Cecil Kelloway and Frank Morgan. Mr. Ankrum is one of the many professionals who have lent their talents to Playhouse productions, thereby enriching the theatre experience for cast members and audiences alike.*
>
> *The curtain goes up on Act I of* King Lear *tonight at 8 PM. Tickets are $5.00 at the box office. The production, directed by Stella Ryan, a graduate of the Playhouse (1932), will run for two weeks including Sunday matinees.*

Marla couldn't make it to the play tonight, so Tank bought two tickets for next Sunday's matinee. His father and Dorothy had already left for the theatre, dressed to the nines. Tank thought about the boys, wondered what they were doing. Would they be there in the audience, all dressed up in their Sunday suits? Or were they home right now, alone?

It was dark out, but not late. Tank got on his Indian and rode it down to Stella's house, parking out in front so as to keep the noise at a distance. He walked up to where the lights were brightest – coming from the boys' bedroom. He was surprised to see Ricky Mulvihill in there, patting the spikes of his flattop. Coy was sitting at his feet, looking restively up at him as if he had just given her a harsh command. Lou crossed in front of them, wearing an empty holster. A leg, with a cowboy boot at the end of it, shot out on the floor. Tank rapped on the glass. Three pairs of startled eyes stared at what might be out where he was. Coy leaped at the glass and her body bounced on stiffened legs with every snarling bark at the unknown shape beyond the glare. Lou ran over and let Tank in.

"Come on in, Tank! Boy, am I glad you're here."

"Hi, guys," Tank said, glancing at Ricky. "What's goin' on?"

Ricky folded his arms across his chest.

"I'm sitting them," he said solemnly. "Their mother and Mr. Strawn went to a play. So did my mom. I'm home for the week-end, so Mrs. Ryan asked me if I'd keep an eye on Lou and Joe."

"We can do without your eye," Joe said.

"Yeah, sure," Ricky said. "The point is, your mother wanted somebody older to stay with you. I get three bucks for it, too."

"Well, Tank's here now," Lou said. "You can go home any time you want to."

"No, I can't," Ricky said, "Tank's not the one who's getting paid to stay with you."

Coy went up to Tank, pointing her ears and wagging her stubby tail. He scratched her back and she opened her mouth and started to pant, looking up at him. She nuzzled him, asking for more.

"That's okay, Tank," Ricky said. "She won't bite."

"Tank knows," Joe said.

Ricky said fretfully, "Coy's a Doberman Pinscher. The breed is known for its protectiveness. They're one-man dogs, you know."

"Who's the one man?" Joe said.

"I am."

"But you're hardly ever home, and when you are –"

"So what? Coy recognizes me as her master."

"Master Ricky," Joe sampled the title like castor oil on his tongue.

Ricky snuffed and bit down on a frown.

"I've gotta go to the bathroom."

He marched out into the hallway. The lock on the bathroom door clunked. Joe kicked out at a football lying on the floor but only tipped it, making it wobble. Lou was slipping his hand in and out of the empty holster on his hip, like something was on his mind. Without looking at Tank he said, "Guess what, Tank."

"What?" Tank said.

Lou kept silent for a moment, then said, "The other day I found something in Mom's room. Her bed wasn't made, and it was just lying right there in the open. Mom's got it in her dresser drawer, now. I want to see if you could tell us what it is."

Joe said excitedly, "No, Lou! We shouldn't be showing that to anybody!"

Lou ignored him.

"Would you, Tank?"

Tank demurred, "It sounds to me like something pretty private."

"Tank's right," Joe said.

"But he can tell us what it is." Lou said irritably.

"We *know* what it is."

"Did you know, Tank," Lou said, "that Mom's not supposed to have any more babies?"

"Well, I – " Tank began to nod.

"One time Mom asked me and Joe if we ever wished we had a little sister. Dad said we could always adopt a little girl. Remember, Joe?"

"Yeah, I remember. Hey, Ricky'll be out of the bathroom any minute. Are we going, or aren't we?" Joe glowered, like it was a chore, but Tank felt better now that they were both in agreement.

Lou led the way up the hallway, turned into the master bedroom. One large bed now took up the space where the two had been. He went over to the dresser, got into one of the small drawers at the top and after poking around came out with a little red and white piece of knitting. He held it squeamishly, handed it to Tank and said in a reverent voice, "Here it is, Tank."

In the half light Tank looked down at what seemed to be the start of a mitten. But at the base of the thumb where you would expect a dangling string of yarn, attached to a ball of it, there was a perfect little pouch. Tank wondered whether Stella had knitted it herself, or Strawn had picked it up in some porno shop, and this was all he wore at night when he climbed into bed with her. Silence stared like a toad into their midst. Finally Lou said:

"They left it right there in the bed."

"Lou, hurry up and put that back!" Joe said.

Lou was staring up at Tank, waiting. There wasn't any time. He said in the almost smug manner of a police detective adding moral outrage to a piece of damning evidence, "And they're not even married."

They hurried back down the hallway to the room where Coy lay on the folds and lumps of the nest she'd pawed up out of the throw-rug. The muffled sound of the toilet flushing grew louder as the bathroom door opened, the floor creaked in the hallway and Ricky was there, standing in the doorway. His face was grim.

"All right. I guess I can go home, now. You don't need me any more. Come on, Coy."

"Wait a minute, Ricky," Tank said. "They'll be expecting you to be here when they get back."

Ricky sighed.

"I know, but . . ."

Lou was doing it again, sliding his hand in and out of his holster. This time he looked alert, anxious. He went into the closet, pulled the light string and started rummaging around. Turning to come back out, he said, "Okay, Ricky. Where is it?"

"Where's what?"

"My big gun. You had it this afternoon. It's not here, now. So what'd you do with it?"

"I put it back there in the closet."

"It's not there. Maybe you left it outside. Go take a look."

"Out there in the dark? Heck, no! Anyway, I know I didn't leave it outside. I wouldn't be that careless."

"Just tell me where it is. Okay?"

"I'm telling you -I don't *know* where it is."

"I'm gonna count to three, then –"

"What? Go put on your Dad's boxing gloves and beat the truth out of me? I'm quakin' in my boots."

"Okay, knock it off, you guys," Tank said.

"Lou started it," Ricky whined.

"Listen, why don't we all sit down and play a game of monopoly. How does that sound?"

Ricky snorted his disgust.

"I wouldn't play monopoly with them if you paid me. I'm going home and I'm taking my dog with me. I'll tell my mother I don't want Coy to spend one more night in this house. She'll back me up, too." There was a swelling in Ricky's otherwise tough-guy voice.

"Before you go," Lou said, "just tell me what you did with my big gun."

"I'll bet you lost it yourself, and now you've gotta blame it on somebody else."

Before Tank could say anything, or stand between them, Lou leaped at Ricky with his hands stretched out toward Ricky's face. Tank could just see Lou's head slipping into the noose of Ricky's hammer lock, or caught with a sucker punch. But nothing like that happened. Lou's fingers flew like eagle's feet at Ricky's face and when they clamped on, felt for his mouth. Ricky let out a god-awful yelp and bolted for the hallway. He made too sharp a turn and his feet got tangled in the throw-rug, it slipped out from under him and he went down like a bag of elbows. Lou went after him. Again he worked his fingers into Ricky's mouth. Coy started barking at them. Tank saw the picture, then, as Lou finally got it right, and Ricky was the lion about to have its jaws snapped for him while the Philistines looked on from the chariot.

"Talk!" Lou shouted. "You rotten liar! Where's my gun!"

The one thing Ricky couldn't do right then was talk. Through his jacked-open mouth he made honking sounds, like a deaf-mute trying out a vowel. Tank pulled Lou off Ricky, and Ricky flopped onto all fours, drooling on the rug. Coy kept on barking at him.

"Shut up, you goddamn mutt!" Ricky yelled. "Who the hell do you think you're barking at!"

"Jeezo, Lou." Joe stood there, awe-struck.

"You stupid maniacs!" Ricky slurped drool back into his mouth and wiped at it with the back of his hand. "Who'd want your stinkin' gun!" He got up, slapping at his knees. "You'll be lucky if you don't end up in reform school for this!"

Ricky's hair was all messed up. He said, "Come on, Coy. Let's get out of this loony bin." But Coy just sat and stayed right where she was. "Okay, you stupid mutt! See if I care!" Ricky stomped to the French doors, went through, and they could see his head bobbing up and down over the wall as he began to run home. Joe said to Lou:

"I guess he didn't know where your big gun was, Lou."

Coy let out a few more piercing barks. Lou shook a finger at her, saying, "Be quiet, Coy."

"I'll bet he's gonna go squealing to his mom, now," Joe said.

"He might not say anything," Tank said, "if he's guilty."

"He would've talked if he was guilty," Joe said.

"Not necessarily," Tank said. "The worst thing for him now is the beating he took. He won't want to admit that."

Lou said, "Daddy Banks is gonna be so mad when he finds out I lost that gun."

"It'll turn up, Lou," Tank said. He looked at his watch. "Listen, you guys, I'd better get on home."

"But Tank," Lou said, "we'll see you again soon, won't we?"

"I hope so," Tank said, and he felt suddenly dizzy. A voice near him was saying:

"When are we gonna get to see your dead Jap, Tank? You never told us whether he's – what kind of clothes he's got on."

Tank followed Lou's voice to that sweet face looking up at him, and he almost said no clothes at all, because there wasn't any dead Jap. He'd told them a tall tale. It was on the tip of his tongue, but he couldn't come out with it. Not yet. He'd lose them forever if he did. There had to be a better time, after he'd thought about it.

"Listen, you guys. I've really gotta run."

Lou plumped like a rock on his bed.

"I know who took my gun," he said determinedly.

"Who?" Joe said.

"Ray."

"Oh jeez, Lou," Joe said. "What would Ray want with a gun that doesn't even shoot?"

"He'd take it to the hock shop. He said so, remember? He knows it's worth a lot of money."

"He doesn't need the money, though," Joe said. "He's got a job."

Tank shook his head and said as gently as he could, "Don't go accusing Ray of taking your gun, Lou. Not while you can't be sure he did."

Red poured into Lou's face. He pushed down on his mattress, bracing his arms rigidly.

"Okay, I know. He might haul off and slap my face, but he wouldn't try anything like that with you. Not if you asked him, Tank."

"Oh, now wait a minute. That's a pretty wild accusation, Lou."

"Okay, but how else are we gonna find out if he did it?"

Lou's innocent logic fell like the sound of a trapdoor slamming shut, and there wasn't any room to move, as if it was *him* who should have known, all along, that the likely suspect was Ray, and it was up to him to squeeze the truth out of him.

Just then there was the clunk of a bolt back in the pantry. The screen door banged and a voice called out, "Hey, kids! We're home!" It was Strawn's voice.

The boys both looked at Tank. Keys jangled dully on tile. Stella called out:

"Did you guys eat?"

"We're in here, Mom," Lou called out. His voice was faint, regretful.

Footsteps, a mix of shuffling and the sharp thud of high heels, moved off the kitchen linoleum, came up the hall. Strawn, in army pinks and a brown suede jacket, came into the doorway first. He took one look at Tank and reared back.

"What're you doin' here, chief?"

Stella, right behind Strawn, was looking over his shoulder. He stepped aside and they both came into the room. She had fully platinum blond hair, now, and wore a long mink coat. She was wearing a lot of makeup around her eyes - too much, Tank thought.

"Well hi, Tank!" she said cheerfully. How're you?"

"I'm fine, Stella. You?"

"Walking on air! You just missed our play. We had a sellout crowd." Her face darkened a little. "What happened to Ricky?"

"He went home early," Lou said.

"Why?" Stella waited, pursing her lips.

"Tank came over, Mom. He's better than Ricky any day."

"Honey, you know what we talked about. Ricky was supposed to stay until Ray and I got home." She looked at Tank. Strawn turned his head aside and had a little private laugh.

"What's so funny?" Stella said.

"Relax, baby. We're home, now. All the baby-sitters can go." Strawn stepped over closer to Stella and, leering, reached out and tweaked the nipple of her left breast through her blouse. "And we can have a little quiet time."

Stella slapped at Strawn's hand, biting down on a grin.

"For Pete's sake, Ray! That's not nice, in front of the boys."

"It was in front of God." Strawn winked at Tank "They pretend they don't like it, but we both know better. Don't we, chief?"

Tank tried to say by saying nothing that he had seen a lot more than he should, when he wanted to ask Strawn why it was that some of the nicest women got mixed up with the biggest jerks.

"Well, I just dropped over to say hi to the boys," he said. "Ricky was here. He and the boys weren't getting along too well. Ricky got mad and . . . he wanted to go home."

Strawn leaned over and gently squeezed Stella's arm and whispered, "I'm gonna leave you guys to the small stuff. I'll be right outside havin' a smoke, hon." He walked across to the French doors, opened them and stepped out into the patio.

"All right, honey," Stella said. And then to Lou in a demanding tone, "What made Ricky want to go home?"

"My big gun disappeared," Lou said. "I thought Ricky stole it."

"Why on earth would you think a thing like that?"

"Mom, he'd do it! But after I . . . I questioned him . . ."

"Lou decided it wasn't Ricky after all," Tank said. "But Ricky was put out, so he ran on home anyway."

"I don't blame him. Well, I guess it was a good thing you came over, Tank. Thank you for not leaving the boys alone after Ricky left."

Tank got up.

"That's okay, Stella. Listen, it's late. I'm going, you guys. Goodnight, Stella."

"Goodnight," Stella said, making the word sound like a question.

Tank caught her late smile as he turned to go, hearing behind him, "Come on, you guys. Get ready for bed. It's going on ten."

Tank made his way over to the French doors, opened one. He smelled Strawn's smoke from where he saw him leaning against the wall under the aspens, taking his time with a cigarette.

In the doorway Lou tugged at Tank's sleeve.

"*Ask* him, Tank. Please?"

Tank smiled and said, "Maybe." And he stepped outside into the familiar realm of indecision.

Into the world of the nice guy, who went along with this or that, with anything, as long as he didn't spoil his image as the nice guy, who could never step on anybody's toes, because everybody liked a nice guy, and wouldn't hurt him because he was so harmless to begin with. But he wasn't really kind, this nice guy. He was just afraid of saying something he might have to back up and, being nice, he was too dumb to back up much of anything. Nice guys are good at making themselves dumb. It was the best excuse for always being a few steps behind, for why you'd let people walk all over you before you'd break the mold and take a stand. They walked because they saw the truth, the coward pretending to be kind. They saw the nice guy caring what you thought. He made the best doormat in the world.

Tank was almost to the gate when Strawn took a drag on his cigarette and forcibly blew the lungful of smoke at him; blew it like a swipe with a broom in a dusty room. Tank made himself believe that was just the way Strawn smoked. Soon he would be way down the street in the harmless world where he belonged. He stopped. Something in him wouldn't let him go on. Something burning. A fuse that reached its end but nothing happened. He felt the nearness of a spark lurking in Strawn's smoke. It needed just the fanning of a few words.

"By the way, Ray. You remember that big Civil War revolver that Daddy Banks gave Lou the other night?"

Strawn let a quizzical, faintly resentful look linger on Tank before he said, "Sure I remember it. What about it?"

"Well, Lou's misplaced it. You wouldn't know anything about that, would you?"

"Why would I? I don't keep tabs on kids' playthings."

"No, and this is pure speculation, of course, but you didn't by any chance take that gun to a pawn shop to find out what it might be worth? I'm just asking. A Civil War relic like that, a person might get fifty, maybe seventy-five bucks for it."

Strawn came off the wall like it had shoved him. The smoking butt came out of his hand and fell to the bricks; he left it burning there.

"Oh, I get it. Perfect idea to put into a kid's head. Anything to make him hate me more than he already does."

Tank decided not to say it wasn't his idea.

"I'm just asking, Ray. So what you're saying is no."

"Goddamn right! Like I owe you any answer. No and goodbye. This better be the last time I see you on these premises, Mister Buttinski."

Tank felt now that he had crossed the line, a door had slammed and there was only one way to go. It wasn't enough to dislike Ray Strawn, turn away and leave it alone. A moment like this, he knew, would never happen again. He could take it or leave it.

"Just one more thing, Ray. Are you aware that Stella's been warned by doctors that she's too old to have any more kids? Her mother died in childbirth. Stella could die the same way."

Tank fully expected Strawn to come back at him with something like 'What business is it of yours?' But he turned in a different direction.

"Stella never said nothing about that. Anyway this is 1946. Women don't have babies in covered wagons."

"Why didn't you go back to Buffalo, Ray, where you could have found yourself some nice young healthy chick? You'd be a lot better off."

"You're forgetting something. I love Stella."

Tank stared at Strawn, thinking of the little woolen calling card his love had left on the rumpled sheets.

"Yeah, you love her so much, you're willing to take the chance she won't survive the birth of your kid."

"Who said anything about a kid? Jesus Christ. You been listening to too much of *Portia Faces Life*."

"If Art comes home," Tank said, "you won't be seeing him in any soap opera."

"Is that a threat? Now why would he come back? When he walked out of here, he left all the doors wide open. Shit, even you could walk right in." Strawn let out a gasping chuckle. "In fact when I first seen you, I knew you had the hots for Stella yourself. It was all over your face. Too bad you lost out. You're just too much of a weirdo for a lady like Stella. Any real woman for that matter."

Words jammed in Tank's throat, then, as he looked at Strawn, and he could see the raw edges of the truth feeling around his cocky smile. He was the kind of a person whose horse he would have shot, just to get him.

"What's the matter, chief," Strawn taunted, "cat got your tongue? I know what your problem is. Sour grapes."

Tank had a flash, then, of Strawn in the gunner's seat of his Avenger. The gray wall of a Japanese hull loomed beyond the bursts of flak the pilot threaded his way through, praying more than steering as the shreds of black smoke sailed past. In all the shuddering rush of being in the air with death one step ahead, Fate lost its aim, and the gunner became this wise-ass he needed no excuse to kill, as if death was looking to catch up to him, anyway.

Tank was aware that the boys were peering out the window. They couldn't hear, but they could watch. He said, "I'd have to be you if I'd made a play for Stella. Not even Stella could make me want to be you."

"Well, I can't imagine why you like yourself so much. You're such a loser and a fake. Where did you shoot yourself to get that Purple Heart? In the nuts? You must have. A real man wouldn't come around here looking to play war with a couple boys."

Tank felt a panic rising in him. Where was the goodness his father had tried to make sure he would always live by? How could he let this sleazeball opportunist turn everything upside down? But he didn't want the nice guy to answer that. He wanted a club.

Tank spotted Strawn again in the gunner's seat of his Avenger, machine-gun bullets whizzing past him by a hair, but why? Was he really a better man, just for coming home alive from that much danger? Was he good just because of all those near-misses he'd been through in the air?

Strawn pulled out his pack of Old Golds, tapped one out, and in his mind Tank gripped a baseball bat. The cigarette dropped from Strawn's lips as he swung, and pieces of his skull flew like watermelon seeds along with the red pulp that splashed all over the white stucco wall. The rest of his body slumped into a heap of lifeless waste on the bricks. The God of Wrath stood by him. The God of Samson's slaughter of the Philistines in the canyon while lightning lit up terror on the faces of the rest of them about to die. Tank felt the heat of his blood in his head, his hands, slithering up and down every inch of his skin, and it had to be this way from here on out. He didn't want the nice guy any more. He couldn't let him in again. He felt the power and the freedom at the end of a long meek road to nowhere.

Real life won't sit still for the things that happen in the movies. Was there any use in thinking he could tamper with Strawn's brakes, or toss a couple rattlers into his back seat? Let's say he picked the rattlers. So what if, when Strawn lost control of his car, he killed some other people on the freeway? What would Lou and Joe think of him for going so far as to commit a murder to protect them from a man they might hold off indefinitely with hate alone?

Tank wished God would take care of Strawn for him, like letting the slaughterhouses bear the burden of turning cattle into steaks. He thought that even God would have to agree that, as a human being, Ray Strawn was worse than any Jap he'd ever shot. But you can't put anything over on God. He wasn't a hit-man. If anything was going to happen to Ray Strawn, he was going to have to make it happen himself. And that would be murder, wouldn't it?

He turned to see the boys' eyes, stark with helpless wonder and expectation, behind the glass. He gave them the high sign before he turned and walked away. Strawn's taunting behind him was so much gibberish.

"Don't set foot on this property no more, neither! Twenty-three years old, for Christ's sakes! You oughta be locked up!"

Tank thought the year he'd gained in Strawn's mistake was funny more than anything. He turned a look on Strawn that almost escaped as words. He could tell Strawn wanted the words, was waiting for them. That alone was enough make him hold them in check. Strawn's voice nipped at him like a dog that had a person on the run.

"Any time you want to go a couple rounds of grab-ass, Sport, you name the day! Just name the day!"

Tank was already thinking of that day, a scene in which nobody would believe the guy who'd thought it up was him. Temporary insanity, maybe? He didn't really care if he got away with it. It didn't bother him that his father would have to say, through the bars in the visiting room of a prison, 'Tank, this isn't you.' It hadn't been him for a long time, and maybe never was.

APRIL, 1947

23

"Hi, honey. Where've you been?"

Stella was sitting on the davenport in the blue and white maternity dress she liked to wear more often than the others. She was holding her cigarette in that kind of lazy, sexy way Lou didn't like to look at. That and the way she was crossing her bare legs, slicked with lotion. Strawn sat across from her in an easy chair, just raising a highball to his lips. In the ashtray under the lamp beside him smoke twisted into the draft that carried it away into the general haze. Strawn's eyes came up over his glass, ice tinkled as he lowered it. Lou went straight up to his mother, saying, "Oh, downtown."

"Both you and Joe?"

"No. Joe's still out collecting popsicle sticks."

"That's right. He's got that deadline. What've you got behind your back, there?"

Lou swung his hand that held the gift out into view. He could feel Strawn looking on behind him.

"Here, Mom. This is for you."

Stella sat up, planting both feet on the rug.

"Oh, honey – thank you! What could this be?"

"Open it."

"Gee, this paper is so pretty, and the red ribbon." Stella carefully undid the ribbon, pulled the paper off without tearing it. She lifted the top from the little box and looked down at a sparkling butterfly on a bed of cotton. "Honey, it's beautiful! What did you do, go and spend all your allowance on this?"

"Not all of it," Lou said, meaning the twenty-two cents left over from the cost of the brooch.

Stella held it up so Strawn could get a better look.

"Look, Ray – isn't this the prettiest butterfly you ever saw?"

Smoke shot from Strawn's nostrils as he brought his eyes back off the cigarette he was stabbing out in the ashtray.

"Yeah, yeah. Real nice."

Stella grunted a little, sitting forward.

"Be careful, Mom."

"Oh, it's okay. Come here, honey." She brought him into a hug and kissed him. "This was so thoughtful of you. Wasn't it, Ray? This guy of mine." She took one of Lou's hands and squeezed it. He saw tears suddenly in her eyes while she was smiling. Strawn seemed to telegraph his isolation by withholding any comment. Lou said:

"Well, I've got some math to do. I guess I'd better get to it."

"Okay, honey. Dinner should be ready in about an hour. We're having lamb chops."

"Oh, boy!"

"Honey, I just love this butterfly. Thank you so much."

Lou smiled and turned away. Several steps into the hallway, where he was out of sight, he stopped. Silence filled in behind him, rode the waves of his breathing. He stood there, listening, until he heard his mother say:

"This was so nice, Ray. So thoughtful, don't you think?"

"I guess so, but are you gonna *wear* that thing?"

"SShhh! Of course I am! What did you think?"

Ice sloshed up against Strawn's lips, fell tinkling to the bottom of his glass.

"I'm gonna grab myself another drink. You want one?"

"No. It's no good for the baby."

"How bad is two if one's okay?"

"I've had enough, Ray."

"Oooo-kay."

There was the creak of Strawn pushing himself out of the chair. He slipped into his loafers and started for the kitchen.

Lou went on quickly up the hallway and turned into his room. He hoped and prayed his mother didn't think the brooch was ugly, too. All the jewels were imitation – the diamonds in the wings, sapphire body and ruby antennas. The saleslady had said, 'What a nice choice. You've got good taste, young man.'

The door rattled. Joe came tromping in from the patio.

"Darn! I only got forty-seven sticks. I need a hundred to win. Lou, if the Swell Time man comes around, get a bar, will you? Save me the stick."

"I thought they only wanted popsicle sticks."

"They won't know the difference if you lick all the ice cream off."

Lou didn't bother reminding Joe about the brand engraved on the sticks.

"Come on," he said. "I've got enough money on me for two."

24

Stella came back down the walk from the mailbox, sorting through bills. She looked up and saw Dorothy in her rose garden, surrounded by the glorious color of her Velvet Troubadours, Crimson Sultans and the pinks and yellows she refused to call 'common.' As she looked up Stella waved. She stepped off the walk and cut across the grass toward Dorothy.

"Boy oh boy, I can't get over it, Dorothy – the bumper crop you've got this year."

Dorothy raised the pair of snippers in her gloved hand.

"I have to admit I've got more than I know what to do with. Let me cut you a bouquet."

"Oh, I wouldn't want to –"

"No, no – good God! I've got loads."

Stella was afraid to ask, but thought she'd better.

"How's Ricky getting along? Is he coming home for Easter?"

"I'm not sure. He said something about a sophomore getaway to Palm Springs. One of the older boys has a car. I still haven't made up my mind if I should let him go."

Stella couldn't detect anything in Dorothy's tone that sounded like a grudge. She was snipping off the fullest, prettiest roses, fit for a county fair. Stella wasn't sure but that it was a gesture of reconciliation.

"I'm giving you long stems," Dorothy said, "so you can just cut them as you like." She stood up straight, smiling at Stella. "How's that baby coming along in there, honey? Doing any kicking, yet?"

"Not yet," Stella said. "But any day now, the doctor tells me."

"Did he give you a clean bill of health? Your blood pressure's under control?"

"Oh, yes! No problems at all."

Dorothy studied her a moment, then her face lit up.

"You know I loved the way you had your hair done up the other day in Bullocks. I saw *you* but you didn't see me. You and Ray looked so happy shopping together, I didn't want to interfere. I guess you were shopping for the future, since you were in the ladies' slacks section."

Stella felt suddenly lightheaded. Dorothy seemed to reel in her vision. The blasé tone was all wrong.

"But Dorothy, I haven't been to Bullocks since – I don't know when. That couldn't have been me."

"Oh. Well, then I guess it couldn't have been Ray, either. Come to think of it, you didn't look too pregnant. But I don't really trust my eyesight at that distance."

Stella's heart beat fast, emptily. For a moment she couldn't breathe. She brought her hand up onto her collarbones and pressed.

"Just how much did the man you saw look like Ray?"

"Well, so much I started to walk over. The strange thing was, you looked years younger, but I just thought that must be the radiance of your being pregnant. Now I can tell you – you *do* look radiant, honey."

"But would you say, regardless of me, the man with this woman was definitely Ray?"

Dorothy stepped gingerly past the thorns and blossoms until she was out on the grass where Stella stood, snippers in one hand and the other wrapped around rose stems.

"Oh, honey, I can see I've upset you. I wouldn't have said a word if – you know people's eyes play tricks on them. This wouldn't be the first time *mine* did. I didn't really go up close enough to make sure. It was just that, at the time and that distance, I thought it was the two of you right off. As I say, it had to be that radiance about you that made you look so much younger."

"You keep saying me," Stella said. "Younger, but not pregnant."

"So many clothes racks stood in the way, I couldn't see that clearly. The only thing that made me wonder was you weren't in the maternity section. There was a sale on for women's slacks and blouses, so I just wrote that off."

"I see. Oh, well. People do have their look-alikes. That must have been what it was."

"That's right," Dorothy said. "I was with my late husband once at the horse track when I saw this woman who looked so much like me, it was scary, like I was sitting over *there*, not where I was. It was so uncanny, I couldn't point her out to Ralph. Imagine that. Like if I did, we'd change places."

Stella saw the doubt, the reaching out of sympathy, in Dorothy's eyes. She felt her lips distorting with a smile that fell apart.

"Just kind of wondering, Dorothy, when you saw us – I mean thought you did – how come you didn't come all the way over?"

Dorothy looked up, staring starkly.

"Gee, I can't exactly remember. I think I thought I'd be intruding. Yes, that's it. And you – that is, the couple – started to walk away. It'd be gauche to go chasing you down."

"Yes, I see. Well, I guess I'll get back in the house and take a look at all these bills."

"Just a minute, honey. Let me cut you one more special rose."

Dorothy added another Velvet Troubadour to the bouquet and handed it to Stella.

"Careful of the thorns now, honey."

"Thanks, Dorothy. Be seeing you later."

"Bye, honey. Come on over any time you feel like talking. We'll have some tea."

In the breakfast nook Stella spread all the bills across the table, separating out a letter to the boys from Art. It was strange to see this evidence of him, and she thought of him holding his pen, licking the envelope, and his handwriting that had so thrilled her long ago when they were in love, and she lifted the letter to see if she could catch a whiff of his cologne – *Tweed* – that always fought with the smell of cigarettes about him. There was nothing but the smell of paper passed from hand to hand.

It all began to add up now – the fears she'd tucked away in the back of her mind – back in that vacuum where, eventually, she had been so sure they must be made to die of neglect. It had begun about a month ago. Slowly at first, sporadically, so you couldn't lay it to the account of any one, concrete reason. One would do as well as another. Ray's beginning to work longer hours, sometimes getting home by as late as eight o'clock. Overtime, he said, so of course his being tired by the time they went to bed stood to reason. You could reason, too, that that was why, in bed with her, he was mechanical, like it was a chore. But now of course there was a baby in the way. All men slowed down in bed with a pregnant woman, plus there was just the natural descent from their explosive beginning, the newness wearing off. One troubling thing, though, was Ray's old friend from the service, Dom de Serpa – how he would come around, now, almost every day. He and Ray would stay up until all hours talking in the closed-up kitchen, nibbling *bierkase*, drinking beer and smoking. So much for the extra rest Ray needed to deal with those longer hours he was putting in at the plant.

She saw him stuck in this dead-end job, packing meat for the Armour-Star Company. He didn't have the education to get out of it. He didn't really seem to care if he ever did find anything better. He had little interest in her work at the Playhouse. In the old circles she and Art had moved in, he didn't fit. Worst of all, he seemed indifferent to being anything like a father to the boys. Until now she had swept all these things away in the flood-tide of their physical passion for each other. But that tide was going out. They needed a change. The Santa Barbara Bowl was up for sale, together with its pool hall and café. There was a perfect place to set Ray up in a job in which he could be part owner, and have some pride in what he did. She hadn't told him about it yet, but now she thought she would. They had to move away. They would move up there as soon after the baby was born as possible. Just as soon as the baby was old enough to travel.

Who was she? Stella thought. This woman who looked so much like her, but years younger? Dorothy had pulled poor eyesight out of a hat, the distance at which she had seen them. If her eyesight was good enough to see that the man was Ray, it couldn't have failed to cast doubt on the identity of the woman. For a moment she felt helpless to protect the innocent child in her womb from what was happening. Helpless to protect herself from the blindness to what could be the beginning of the end, and she would go on like the baby, living in darkness, not knowing what the light would bring. Only in that darkness could a different truth exist than the one that had created a nameless woman who, but for her age, looked exactly like her. Take away the baby, she thought, and she might be attractive again. But that would happen one day, when the baby finally came. Going on and having it was worth the risk. Love child. His child, that he would hold, and rock to sleep, and she felt that other little heart beating Ray's love back into her own. A child with his name, his name in lights: Ray Strawn, Owner: The Santa Barbara Bowl. She had to get to work on that, cement the deal. Prepare to move away as soon as the baby was old enough to travel.

25

The rain had begun to let up some by the time Lou reached the house. He saw Strawn's car in the driveway, parked just ahead of Dom de Serpa's Ford, but not his mother's Cadillac. He glanced at the for-sale sign, dripping water from along the bottom rim. The stake was deeper in the ground than yesterday, and Lou could see, by the wood split away from the flattened top, that Strawn had used a hammer to pound it back in this time.

He looked through the drizzle at the kitchen window, praying they weren't there behind it, watching. They must have seen the note he'd left for his mother, telling her that he'd be back in time to straighten up his room, and take the garbage out. He didn't add why, for the first time, he was so eager to be the one to dump the garbage. *That* he would have to keep to himself, for now.

He stepped into the muddy patch where the sign stood facing the street under the dripping Sycamore. He waggled it to see how fast it held to the ground. There wasn't much give, but he grabbed the stake down low, anyway, and was about to heave when, leaning backwards, he got the feeling it would snap, like getting the weed but not the root. He'd leave it alone this time; but it felt like another defeat on a day when defeat seemed to lurk around every corner.

Instead of cutting straight across the lawn to the patio he walked all the way around outside the shrubs to the driveway, then up from there to the door off the patio to his room.

His soaking Pea Coat weighed a ton as he got out of it. He hung it from the hook in the closet, letting it drip onto the heap of dirty clothes on the floor.

He could hear them talking in the kitchen – Strawn and de Serpa. Strawn was saying, "I've been there but I never stopped." He imagined de Serpa's dark brown wooly head. They'd met on a troop ship coming back from the war. Now they worked together at the Armour-Star plant. In a laughing voice de Serpa said, "You lucky stiff. Why don't you take me with you?"

"Hop in, pal," Strawn said.

Lou couldn't hear them too distinctly. They sounded like they'd had a few beers. A glass or a bottle clunked on the table. What they were saying now drew him into the hallway. As weight fell onto his first step, the parquetry creaked and he stopped dead still. They kept on talking in the same casual tones. He waited a moment, then took flatfooted, gingerly steps down toward the telephone nook, stopped just behind the entrance. De Serpa said:

"Sounds like some sweet deal, Ray, but what do you know about running a bowling alley?"

"What do I *have* to know? Stella tells me all I've gotta do is rent the shoes and ring up sales. For that I get to be the boss."

"Straw boss," de Serpa said.

"Part, whole – my name's on the business. You should tag along. I'll talk to Stella. You could run the pool hall, easy."

"Yeah, but Maggie wouldn't go for it. She likes where she is at the studio. She'd never pull up stakes."

"Are you the man here, or the puss?"

"It takes a puss to know one, pal."

They both laughed. More clunking on the table.

"I can't wait." Strawn said. "My own business. I'll put these lazy kids to work. They'll set pins till their tails drop off. They'll know what real work is after that."

"You better count your blessings first, pal, then settle scores with the kids."

"What scores?"

"I seen how they act around you. Not so much the little guy, but the other one. The way he clams up and walks around you like you got the plague."

"What a royal pain that kid is. He hates me, and what've I ever done to him? I'm gonna work his butt off. He won't have time to hate nobody."

"Does it bother you, his hating you?"

"Who says he really does?"

"Was it you, or Charlie McCarthy over there?"

"I never done nothing to him," Strawn said sullenly.

"Did you ever think he might be jealous?"

"What of, Einstein?"

"What you're taking from his mother."

"What am I supposed to do, not take it?"

"I know, I know. I'll tell you one thing. She's one fine lookin' woman for her age."

"Don't I know it. She never goes nowhere without those boobs."

Lou was not quick enough to turn that blow aside like all the other things about Strawn that tried to change his mother into somebody else. He tried to contain the pestilence that crept around his heart like bugs on something dead, and held his breath, trying to starve Strawn out, and blunt the old heart that no longer served him but to drag her bound and gagged and stolen from his love that made him feel helpless. A foot knocked against hollow wood. Were they getting up? Lou tensed, taking a step backwards. De Serpa said:

"So what're you gonna do about Jeannie?"

A glass or a bottle struck the table again, followed by a windy sigh.

"Yeah," Strawn said. "That's one I'm gonna have to think about."

"Especially if she wants to follow you."

"She won't if I tell her not to."

"I never saw nothing like it – how much she looks like Stella. They'd be twins if Stella didn't have twenty years on her. You must have a thing for busty babes with freckles. If only Jeannie would've come along a few months earlier. Of course she hasn't got a dime one. But look at the mess she would've saved you."

"What mess?"

"You should ask? What're you gonna do about this baby Stella's carrying? You musta been nuts to let that happen?"

"It wasn't supposed to. She kept sayin' it'd be all right, and I kept thinking she's too old."

"You know what I'd think if I wasn't brought up in a monastery? I'd think even if something did happen to Stella, like – you know, she didn't pull through - you'd still be sittin' pretty. Now wouldn't you?"

"Let's get one thing straight, pal. She was the one that wanted this kid, not me."

"So if things go wrong – let's say she doesn't happen to make it - that's the breaks."

"Like I said, if having a kid makes her happy, c'est la vie."

Behind Lou suddenly there was the clash of a door shutting too hard. The sketch of fear in his mind stopped inching toward his mother's death. There was no use, any more, holding his ear to the words that, in a nightmare, described a murder as an accident. Joe came blundering out into the hallway.

"Lou! Guess what! You'll never guess what I found!"

Lou hustled Joe back into their room. Joe angrily pulled away from him, rubbing his arm.

"What's the matter with you?"

Suddenly Strawn was there, in the doorway. De Derpa stood behind him, a tall, swarthy man with washboard wavy hair.

"What're you kids up to, anyway?" Strawn said.

"Nothing," Lou said.

Strawn squinted at Lou.

"You're all wet."

"I left a note for Mom," Lou said.

"I seen it. How long you been home?"

"Just a few minutes," Lou pleaded.

Strawn's mouth pulled aside, dragging a grimace from his grin.

"Time enough to dick around with that sign again, huh? Like nobody'd think you'd do it in the rain."

"What sign?"

"It wouldn't come up, would it? I made sure it wouldn't."

"I don't know what you're talking about."

Strawn sleepily raised his eyebrows, turning toward de Serpa.

"Will you listen to that, Dom? And I thought good kids never lied." He looked at Lou again. "I'll tell you what. You and me'll take a little walk outside. We'll bring a hammer, just in case the boogyman messed with that sign again. In fact from now on, you can be my watchdog. You be in charge of that sign. Report to me every day if anything goes wrong with it. Deal? I'll add a quarter to your allowance."

Lou didn't know what to say. Anything but okay. He stared, turning red, at Strawn's one-sided smile. De Serpa said:

"I'm gonna take off, Ray. Walk me out to the car?"

Strawn stared at him, eyes leaving behind his rictus of a grin like a placard of his face that badly misrepresented him.

"In this rain?"

"What're pals for?"

They walked together back into the kitchen where de Serpa got his jacket. As soon as they were down the hill beside de Serpa's Ford, Joe said excitedly, "Lou! I found it! I found your big gun!"

"What? Where?"

"Right here in the closet. It was way up on the shelf."

"I looked up there before."

"Well, that's where I found it. Aren't you glad?"

"Yeah, but Joe – listen. I've gotta tell you something." Lou stopped himself, looking at Joe's wide-eyed, expectant face. People who thought Joe got into trouble all the time, because he would fight anybody, didn't know anything about his practical mind that could straighten out any crazy, snarled thing. That was the face that waited now, wide open with the same trust in which they'd never kept a secret from each other.

"What is it?" Joe said.

"You know that letter we wrote to Dad the other day?"

"Yeah."

"Well, this morning when I took the trash out to the incinerator, I found it in there, mostly burnt up. Mom wouldn't do that."

"Who would?" Joe said.

"Ray. I know it was him."

Lou saw through the French doors that the rain outside had stopped. Shadows and sunbursts alternated like somebody was playing with the houselights in a theatre.

"We can drop another letter into that box down near the bakery," he said. "Take it with us to school."

"We'll have to write it all over again," Joe said. "That makes me mad. Did the pictures get burnt up, too?"

"Yeah. I was gonna save the pieces, but they were too far gone. I'm gonna try to be the one to take the trash out from now on."

Joe gritted his teeth, clenched his fists.

"Maybe it was Ray who put your big gun back on the shelf, Lou. Maybe when he took it to the hock shop, they wouldn't give him enough money."

Now that it was Joe's idea, for some reason Lou didn't feel like wholeheartedly agreeing. He said:

"Yeah, maybe. Let's write another letter. Take it to school and mail it down there when we go for a chocolate éclair."

"I'm mad enough to tell Mom, Lou. First he steals it, then he burns it. God! What if we told her? Whatta you think she'd do?"

"She'd get mad at us," Lou said. And that was it, he suddenly realized. Joe stared at him. It was a stare of accusation: *I thought you hated him. Here's your chance.*

"I'll tell you one thing," Joe said, scowling, "I'm not gonna be so nice to him any more. And if he doesn't like it, that's tough."

Lou was thinking. Seeing how Strawn would think he'd swayed Joe onto his side. Strawn couldn't hate him any worse for that. Was he supposed to get away with burning up a letter? Was now the time to tell Joe what he'd overheard? She'd only take Strawn's side. She'd only be unhappy, trying to save her baby from the truth.

"Don't say anything about it, Joe. Not yet, okay?"

"I wasn't going to. I'm not gonna laugh at his jokes anymore, though. You can darn well bet on that!"

26

"Tank," Marla said, "did you really want to come up here? Or are you just trying to keep a promise?"

"Why?"

"You don't act like you're having any fun."

"The fish aren't cooperating. I haven't caught a damn one, yet."

"You can take credit for the one I caught."

"Nope. I'll help you eat it, though."

Marla kicked her bare foot at Tank, and some of the bilge at the bottom of the rowboat sloshed from side to side. They had been swimming. There was that smell of the dank lake water baking on their skin. Marla's legs were getting red. She had a floppy straw hat on that the stiff breeze kept trying to blow off. They had driven up through Mojave, Big Pine and Bishop to the lake. They'd stopped at Bishop long enough to buy a couple loaves of Sheepherder's bread. They had the cabin in the pines across the road for one more day.

"Aren't you happy?" Marla pursued.

"Sure I am. This is God's country."

"You looked like you were someplace else."

"That sunburn's gonna really hurt tonight. I'd better row us in."

"Before we catch a fish? Not on your life, buster. Anyway, I like the way you look with your shirt off. That scar hardly even shows, you know."

She was lying, Tank knew, to make him feel good. He guessed what she really meant was, in her eyes, the scar was not ugly because it was a part of him. He'd got the diamond for her just as he had promised. Its glitter on her finger made it look almost as big as the one he couldn't afford. He knew it wouldn't have mattered to her if he'd got her one of those Indian turquoise rings, even. She knew how much he loved her. Yet he felt strange, now, about the littleness that seemed to keep him at his end of the boat. He'd been holding something back, without which his love felt somehow sold for less than it was worth. He had to tell her.

"I didn't deserve it," he said.

"Deserve what? To get shot?"

"No. The Purple Heart they gave me."

"Why not? Every soldier who got wounded deserved one. What makes you so different from the rest of them?"

Her eyes were serious, partly squinting against the sun, while she smiled. She looked so pretty there with the sun on her shoulders, the new freckles coming out on her legs. He knew he couldn't go on being in love with her, and not tell her.

"I was a cook," Tank said. "Food service. I was in a rear-area command post when I got wounded. Me and a pickup platoon of other cooks, clerk typists and staff officers. They said afterwards, we halted the most devastating banzai attack of the war. When the mop-up was all finished, and the pictures taken, 4,311 Japanese bodies were counted on the beaches at Tanapag. I saw some of the photographs on the boat we took out of there. The Japs all had their eyes closed. Somebody must have gone around and done that for the photographers. The guy who showed the pictures to me said there were so many dead Japs, it made you think the Army could afford to let you have one for a souvenir."

She leaned forward and took his hand.

"You'd better know one thing. You never needed any Japanese to sacrifice his life to make you look more like a man."

It was one thing to love her, but to be loved . . .

Tank knew, then, what he would have to do, the next time he saw the boys - even if it cost him his reputation. Even if it cut him off from them forever.

27

Lou gave up on his peanut butter sandwich and took the back steps down to the basement. A wooden wedge under the door held it open. Dust drifted out into the sunlight. De Serpa's voice inside said, "This one, too, Ray? You don't want to keep it for yourself?"

"Naw. I've got enough sides of beef down at the plant to keep me in shape."

Lou went in, turned the corner into the space that, yesterday, had still been his dad's workout studio. They had taken almost everything apart. Incline benches folded up and lying flat, weights stacked in pyramids, half the canvas mat rolled back exposing the raw concrete. Strawn stood there, hands clinging to a large, heavy disc. He stared at Lou as if his sudden presence was keeping him from dropping it.

"What is it, kid? Too much racket for you?"

"I was just wondering what you were doing," Lou said.

The weight left Strawn's hands, clanked loudly on the growing pile.

"What you see is what you get, kid."

De Serpa had his sleeves rolled up. Sweat was running down his forehead from his wooly head. He gave the medicine ball a kick, it rolled toward the mirror, up against its image. Lou said:

"How come you're – I mean –"

"Organizing all this stuff?" Strawn said. "We got no more use for it."

"This all belongs to my dad," Lou said desperately.

"Now, how do you figure? I don't suppose he'll be coming back for it. Do you?"

"I don't know. At least he – what are you gonna do with it?"

"Not sure, yet. Dom could use some space for storage before he moves into his new place. Instead of barkin' at the moon, there, why don't you pitch in and give us a hand? We'll be finished before you even know you've strained a gut." Strawn shared a grin with de Serpa.

Lou wondered how he could ask a thing like that. Help them tear down the workout studio his dad built up, and paid for. He knew what Strawn expected him to say, and he said it.

"I'm sorry but I can't."

"Huh! Did you hear that, Dom? A big husky kid like him *can't*? What's the world comin' to?"

"How's about we pay you a quarter an hour, Lou?" de Serpa said in the sleek tone of a salesman giving him a deal. "Will that persuade you?"

The two men exchanged glances. Lou knew for sure, now: Strawn had taken his gun. Maybe it was Mom who'd found out, and made him put it back.

"No, I don't need the money that bad," Lou said.

"That bad!" Strawn's voice rose against the insult with which this kid dared to throw his friend's generous offer in his face. "Well, we'll just have to see about that, after I subtract what you might've earned from your allowance. How does that sound?"

Lou didn't say anything. He turned around and walked out, hearing nothing behind him. He wanted to see Tank. Wanted to go up there right now, but he wouldn't be home, yet. He'd gone up north with Marla for a few days.

He climbed the steps to the back door slowly, dragging his legs like they weighed a ton apiece. What, now? He heard some movement up the hallway in his mother's room.

She came into the living room wearing a pale yellow maternity dress. She must have just got home.

"Oh, hi, honey. I was wondering where you were. Just get back from school?"

"A little while ago," Lou said.

"Is everything okay? You look kind of – tired."

"No, I'm fine."

Stella hesitated, then said, "Well, I'm glad of that." She looked down the length of her dress to her feet in white pumps.

"What do you think of my new dress?"

Lou looked at her beaming face before he gave the rest of her the once-over. How quickly she dismissed his hangdog look for his opinion of her dress.

"Oh, it's beautiful," he said.

"Think so? What about me? Do I look a little younger today, maybe?"

"Gee, Mom, you really don't – you never do look old." Lou felt the slump in his heart, and he went over to the nearest easy chair and fell into it. He wanted to get away from something. Away from the way he felt every time she was so near and warm that he could smell her, and marvel at how young she looked; so healthy, too. It could vanish any moment. He had no control. What good was there in trying to keep her safe by never stepping on a line or a crack out on the sidewalk?

Stella's eyes became alert, worried. She came over to him.

"You look so tired, honey. I guess it's that paper route. A lot to do after a whole day at school."

"Yeah, I guess so."

"Is there something else?"

"No."

"Honey, whatever it is, you can tell me. I want to know."

"I know, Mom."

"Ray tells me you've been doing things he's asked you not to do. He wanted me to talk to you about it."

"You mean about the grass?" Lou said.

"That's one thing, yes. But there's the for-sale sign out front. I can't say this is true, but Ray says you've been pulling it out."

"What makes him think it's me? He's never seen me do it."

"If you are, honey, you should stop. We have to sell the house, no matter what."

Lou clammed up. He didn't want to talk any more. His mother said:

"Something's eating you, honey. I can feel it. What is it?"

"Nothing."

Stella got onto her knees on the rug in front of Lou.

"Is it that brooch you got me? Did you hear Ray – did you overhear him talking about it?"

"No. Anyway, whatever he said about it, I don't care."

"You know how much I love it, don't you?"

"Yes."

"Well, then –" Stella laid her hands on Lou's knees. Her eyes glistened with tears. "I don't want to think you won't tell me, anymore, if something's bothering you. What is it, honey? We'll work it out."

He heard the anguish in her voice. He tried to think of something he could feed her.

"D'you think I'm fat, Mom?"

"What? No! What makes you ask?"

"Well, it's Cheryl Jones. She keeps calling me Butterball, Crisco in a can."

She pursed her lips and swallowed back the laugh he got ready to resist.

"Honey, why she'd say a thing like that is beyond me."

"Joe says girls are really flirting when they call you names."

"Oh, does he? Maybe so. At any rate, don't let that make you think you're fat. You're husky, like your dad."

Lou sank back to where he'd been, and Stella said:

"Something else is bothering you, honey. I can tell. What is it?"

"Nothing, Mom." And Lou clung to not telling her as tight as he clung to his hatred of Ray Strawn. If he told her, he might have to give up on that hatred. And that was all he had to fight him with.

Stella leaned forward and drew his head down onto her cheek, and let her tears fall between them. A lump came into Lou's throat. He thought of Tank, just a few doors up the street. Dad was too far away. He felt tears hotly in his own eyes. They ran down his cheeks like her life rushing away from him and he couldn't stop it.

"When are you going into the hospital, Mom?"

She pulled back and looked at him, and he could see her trying not to be afraid, or make him think she was afraid. All at once she smiled and patted his knee briskly.

"You know just after you were born we took you out for the first time. It was January and so cold out, we got you all bundled up, and we were going down to the skating rink to show you off to some friends. Well, you can't heat an ice rink, and it felt like we'd stepped into a meat locker. As soon as Betty saw us she skated over and thought you were so adorable, she had to hold you and skate around a little with you on the ice. Jackie Coogan, her husband then, he called your dad over and they got to talking about one thing and another, and I was a little apprehensive about turning you over to somebody on ice skates, but Betty was so good on them. She'd been practicing for the movie she was making. She took you out there and was so careful, gliding around and looking at you to be sure you wouldn't start to fuss or cry."

"Mom, I –"

"She only took you once around the rink. That was all she thought you could stand in that cold. Jackie and your dad got up and came over there to where I stood watching. Betty came back around and said she wished she didn't have to give you up. I was just taking you back and she said, Stella, he's what I want when I have one. She said you're just the way a baby ought to look. Did I ever tell you that story, honey?"

Lou nodded.

"Dad told me one time. Mom, how long d'you think before you go into the hospital?"

"Oh, pretty soon, the doctor tells me. Could be a couple weeks. Maybe less. I'm gonna stay with Franny Kopnik for a while – you know, a week or so before the doctor thinks I'm due. You remember Franny? Since Ray's working and she's not, she can drive me to the hospital when the time comes. She's closer, there in Thousand Oaks. She was a nurse during the war, while Vince was away with the Fleet."

Lou almost brought up Vince's pea coat, that he had worn in the rain the other day. But he caught himself. In that sodden coat, still not completely dry in the closet, his secret seemed to be doing the same thing, trying to dry, but it wouldn't.

"You're gonna be okay, aren't you, Mom?"

"Why, sure I am. Why wouldn't I?"

"I don't know."

"You stop worrying, now. The doctor says I'm in perfect shape. Otherwise we'd have to call it off. He tells me I'm as healthy as a woman ten years younger. Pretty soon you'll have a baby sister – or a brother. How'll that be?"

"Would you rather have a girl, Mom?" Lou said.

"I have to admit – a girl would be nice. For you guys, too. Next week I'm having a baby shower. A bunch of ladies are coming over. No men allowed. That means you." She smiled as she brought the point of her forefinger down onto his thigh.

Lou felt a small smile trembling on his lips.

"What happens to a man if he gets caught in the room?"

"Well, first all the ladies scream. Then he gets pinched."

Lou's smile opened up, unearthing a frail laugh that snapped a chain like a dog running away, and they were running away together into a fairyland of everything a bunch of ladies could do to make her happy.

"I'll stay out of the way," he said.

"You'll get some cake and ice cream afterwards," she said, "so don't go wandering off."

"Don't worry," he said, "I won't."

All at once there was a loud clank from below. Stella straightened up abruptly.

"What in the world was that?"

Lou couldn't bring himself to tell her. He would let her find out for herself. Let them explain, take the heat if there was any left. She could make her own mind up, without him in the way, letting them off the hook.

"I don't know," he said.

28

Mr. Crutchley said, "He's up in the workshop. Why don't you go on up there? He'll be delighted to see you."
"Thank you, sir," Lou said.

Lou took the flagstone walk around to the back of the house, threaded his way on the narrow gravel path through the spiny Chollas, the Staghorns, the little Pincusions and the delicate red flowers nestled in the Hedgehogs. He climbed the wooden steps, being careful not to clomp his feet; it felt like he was trespassing, even having Mr. Crutchley's permission.

The door to the workshop stood wide open. There didn't seem to be anybody in there. Nothing but the stillness of the metal lockers, the unlit light bulb swaying faintly at the end of its cord, the lathe and the vice clamped to the workbench. The smell of old motor oil and creosote that Lou remembered was still in the air, plus something else - that tinge of decay, like in a museum, where things once used every day were now merely stored as a memento of bygone usefulness.

All the sawdust had been swept up off the floor. The garden tools weren't scattered around but leaning together against the wall on the far side of the workbench. Four sawhorses were stacked one atop the other at the back of the room. Lou looked for the long toolbox in which the dead Jap soldier, by now, could be pretty far gone. The box wasn't in the same place where it used to be. It wasn't anywhere that he could see. So much time had gone by, maybe it had dried up, turned to dust like Tank had said could happen. Or maybe Mr. Crutchley had got in there for some tools, seen the mummy where some curtain rods should be and slapped himself to be sure he was awake before he tracked Tank down and asked him what the big idea was. Lou called out:

"Tank! Are you in here?"

A flicker of motion mussed the static, dingy sunlight that fell upon the clay pots on the old warped table at the far end of the room. Cobwebs wiped away still left the windowpanes with a bluish, indelible grime, and Tank, rising more as a shadow than himself seemed to have been there all along, as still as a wooden Indian, into which Lou's voice brought life.

"Lou?"

"Hi, Tank. Your dad said you were up here."

Tank started toward him, slipping past the table and then striding along the narrow corridor past the jumble of old floor lamps, plumbing fixtures and furniture.

"Boy, it's been a while, Lou. What've you been up to?"

"Oh, I don't know. School's almost out. We might be going up to Redding to see Dad for the summer. Mom's tryna sell the house."

"Yeah, I saw the sign out front. When's that supposed to happen?"

"Never, I hope."

"How's your mom coming along? I heard she's gonna have that baby any time, now."

"Yeah, any time," Lou said, and then he looked up at Tank and swallowed. "They're having a baby shower at the house right now. I'm not supposed to be there, only the ladies."

"Well, you can stay here with me until it blows over."

"It shouldn't last much longer. They're all supposed to be gone by four."

"Stay here as long as you want. We'll catch up on lost time."

Lou looked around the room as if he'd missed something. On the old warped table under the window the P-38 lay on an oil-stained rag. Tank said:

"Oh, I've been oiling that. I'm gonna tackle the rifle next."

"I don't see that toolbox any more," Lou said. "Did you have to get rid of the mummy?"

"Well, in a way. Yeah, I had to get rid of it."

"Did it fall apart?"

"You could say that. I think I would've had a pretty hard time explaining it to my dad."

"We never told a soul, Tank."

"I made a mistake, Lou, telling you guys. I hope you can forgive me."

"Gee, what for? When a thing like that falls apart, what can you do?"

"Yeah, yeah." Tank nodded, at first ruefully, then after a deep breath he said, "So you're lying low until the ladies leave. Come on down to the house with me. We'll have a Coke."

Lou stood there, looking up at Tank as if his heart was full of a terrible secret that had to be let out but he was afraid to open it up, and he needed Tank to read his mind.

"What's wrong, Lou?" Tank said. "You look like something's eating you."

"Joe and me can't write to our dad any more, Tank. It's no use."

"Why? What's happened to him?"

"Nothing. He's all right. It's our letters. I found one I'd put in the mailbox – the last one – I found it almost burned up in the incinerator."

"What? How the heck d'you think that happened?"

"Mom didn't do it," Lou said. "We know that much."

"So –"

Lou nodded.

"Ray knows I hate his guts. Maybe that's why he did it."

"Have you said anything to your mother?"

"No. She might think I hate him enough to lie about it."

"But you're not lying, are you?"

"No! There's a lot more I could tell her, too, but she's already unhappy enough."

"Unhappy? Why?"

Lou looked down at his shoes, moved them as if he wanted to look at Tank from a different angle.

"It's the way she's been acting. I think maybe she knows."

"Knows what?"

Lou looked up.

"I need your help, Tank. I don't know what to do."

"Well, sure. What's the problem, Lou?"

"Ray's got a girlfriend."

Tank stared at Lou, took in the torment peering out at him as if through prison bars.

"How do you know?"

"You never met Ray's friend from the war, did you? Dom de Serpa."

"I heard about him, but no - we never met."

"He comes over almost every day. They drink beer in the kitchen till Mom ends up asking him to stay for dinner."

"So what's this de Serpa got to do with the girlfriend?"

"They didn't know I was home, Tank. They said some things I wasn't supposed to hear. I can't tell Joe, because - you're the only one I can tell."

Tank chewed on the inside of his lip, looking at Lou.

"Okay, I'm listening."

Lou swallowed. He stepped closer to Tank, measuring down his voice. "I heard them talking about what they were gonna do after we move, and the baby gets born – or doesn't get born."

Tank was nodding faintly, as if trying not to look confused. His face came up sharply as if he'd been tripped up.

"What exactly did they say, Lou?"

"Well, they were talking about what's gonna happen after the house gets sold and we move up to Santa Barbara. That's when –"

"Santa Barbara?"

"Yeah. Mom wants to buy a bowling alley up there. There's a pool hall and a café, too."

"I see. So what then?" Tank said.

"Ray said he'd fix Dom up with a job if he wanted one, but Dom said he didn't want to leave his girlfriend back here, all alone. That's when Dom asked Ray what he was gonna do about *his* girlfriend."

Tank stood perfectly still, barely breathing.

"By girlfriend –"

"They called her Jeannie. She's supposed to look a lot like Mom, except she's younger."

Tank steadied his eyes on Lou, like he was counting seconds between a flash of lightning and the crash of thunder to see how far away the storm was.

"What did Ray say, then?"

"He said he'd have to leave her behind, and then Dom said what if she tries to follow, and Ray said he didn't know. It was a problem. Dom said there wouldn't be any, would there, if Mom wasn't gonna have a baby. Or if, when she did have it . . ."

"What?"

"Something happened."

"Happened?"

"If Mom got into trouble with the baby. Then Ray wouldn't have to leave the girl behind. He'd be – what Dom said - sittin' pretty."

Tank swallowed. In his eyes something trembled that he was trying to keep still.

"What did Ray say then?"

"He said that'd be the breaks. C'est la vie."

Tank looked out at the light in the doorway. It wasn't bright but it seemed to hurt his eyes. He looked down at the gun on the rag. He picked it up, began to fondle it.

"I'm sorry you had to hear all that, Lou."

"I'm not. Now I know Ray never married Mom because he loved her."

"But the thing is, Lou – and I know this is the hardest thing - she wants him to love her."

"What?"

"Your mother. She –"

"Tank, that's the trouble!"

"Your mother's got those feelings, Lou. You can't force a person to feel some way you think they should."

"I know. But don't you think she deserves to know?"

"Yes, but it wouldn't go too good for you if you told her. For her, either."

"What about you? What if you told her?"

"Your mother would only hate me for interfering."

"She might decide not to have the baby."

"But Lou, she can't stop the baby from coming. Not now."

"But if she knew what Ray was doing, she'd divorce him," Lou persisted.

"That might do more harm than good. She doesn't need more grief and worry piled on right now. Not when she's gonna go ahead and have this baby, anyway."

"You mean leave it in God's hands?" Lou said.

Tank's nostrils flared and his lips pressed into a tight, thin arc.

"Lou, we've got to think of your mother's welfare. The baby's too far along. Even if she's got to go into that hospital believing a lie, that could be better than –"

"No, it's not, Tank! I just wish I could tell her myself, but I know it'd be like dad's letter. She'd think I was making it up to get back at Ray."

"How would my telling her be any different?"

"Because you're – I don't know! It just would."

Tank stared at him, and Lou saw the shock on his face, the truth slung at him out of the heart of a boy. Tank was the man. He knew more of life. Why else did the boy look up to him?

"You've heard the expression, Lou – let sleeping dogs lie. I'm telling you - upsetting your mom now, at this late date –"

"But wouldn't *you* like to find out if Ray's girlfriend is real?"

Tank moved his face around uneasily, as if trying to pick up a scent and keeping his eyes averted.

"Sure I'd like to know. I'm just not sure of what I'd do if I found out." Tank's eyes dropped onto the gun on the table, came up like a moth being seared by a light bulb.

"But will you try?"

"I'm not Samson, Lou."

Tears came into Lou's eyes. His voice faltered.

"If you're not, Tank, I don't know who is."

In the middle of the living room, deserted now, Lou stood surrounded by the remains of the party. There were cake crumbs on paper plates on the coffee table, teacups on saucers under the lamps. Little outfits were spread out on the couch, some of them for boys, some for girls. New diapers were stacked on scraps of wrapping paper on an easy chair. Tiny sleepers, like different-colored gingerbread men, were laid out on the davenport. The hood was up on a brand-new stroller. A doll lay inside. A little pair of checkered pants dangled straps over the arm of another chair. There seemed to be more girls' things than boys'. His mother wasn't in the kitchen. He walked down the hallway toward her room. The door was closed. He knocked softly.

"Mom?"

"The door's not locked, honey. Don't turn the light on, please."

Lou turned the knob, pushed and the door swung back.

He couldn't see her very well, sitting there at her vanity in the murky light. He went up and stood beside her. Her face was puffy and a little red. Tears sparkled in the corners of her eyes. Addressing her image in the mirror, he asked, "What's wrong, Mom?"

Stella reached for the gilt-framed photograph that stood behind her bottles of perfume and lotion.

"I didn't get the chance to know your grandmother," she said, "any more than you guys did. I have to talk to this picture when I want to tell her that I love her. Does she look angry?" Lou started to shake his head but then saw that his mother wasn't looking. "I used to think she could hear me. I wanted her to smile. I didn't want her to be mad at me, you know, for being alive."

"She couldn't be mad," Lou said. "You were her baby."

"I mean mad because, when I was born, she died."

"How could that be? She couldn't blame you for being alive. She'd be glad."

Their eyes met in the mirror again, where Stella smiled at him.

"There's loads of leftover cake and ice cream out there, honey. Why don't you guys go and get some?"

"You sure got a lot of nice things for the baby, Mom."

"Didn't I?" She reached out, found Lou's hand and squeezed it. "Go on and get yourself some cake and ice cream, honey. I'll be out in a minute to fix dinner."

"I'll spoil my appetite," Lou said.

"Oh, I doubt that," Stella said, and her smile overtook her tears and seemed to dry them like the sun breaking up a rainy day.

Lou felt a little better, and smiled back at her, as if that same sun shone on him.

"Okay, Mom. If I start poking at my dinner like I can't eat any more, you'll know the reason why."

"I might even forgive you, too," Stella said.

29

Tank sat back behind the wheel and watched the plumes of steam and diesel smoke all bent at the same angle from the smokestacks into the breeze off the ocean. He had a clear view of Strawn's car, empty now. In the other cars nearby there were no heads, no living, seeing things. He was the only one. It shouldn't be long, now.

Four-thirty came around and a few men began to trickle out of the plant, carrying jackets and lunch pails. Some crossed into the lot alone. Others came in groups of three or four, talking and laughing before individuals split off and found their respective cars and piled in. Exhaust spurted from under bumpers, cars backed out of slots. Tank guessed these people must be early morning arrivers, and therefore got to go home early.

A loud steam-whistle blew. Tank looked at his watch. The second hand swept on past five. It took a few more minutes before the workers – about equal numbers of men and women – poured out, and the lot began to swarm like a disturbed anthill. Groups strayed from the crowd, splintered into individuals, and finally became glassed-in faces in the cars.

Then Tank saw him, flopping along splay-footed. The one who didn't lag behind his pace or hurriedly outdistance him was a woman in a tan slack suit and a red and yellow polka-dot bandana. She pulled a pair of dark glasses out of a bag and as she slipped them on she suddenly looked even more like Stella. But this woman, for all her resemblance to Stella in the face, was definitely younger, livelier, more nimble. She didn't have that calm that Stella had. There was a kind of nervous bustle about the way she strode out, arms swinging, hips rolling.

Together they made straight for Strawn's car. He opened the passenger-side door for her, gentleman-like but abruptly, like he wanted to get it over with. He must have given her a lift to work, Tank thought, and probably was not delivering her to any bus stop now. Strawn got in behind the wheel, pulled his door shut. Tank started up the Packard. Just as they got going he pulled out.

This wasn't enough, Tank thought. He wanted to see where they were going. He kept them in sight through Maywood and Huntington Park, then almost lost them where a light they went through on the orange stopped him, and he sat there watching while other cars filled in behind them. As soon as the light turned green, he burned rubber catching up to them where they were slowing to get up onto Arroyo Parkway.

They took Arroyo Parkway clear up to the turnoff onto Colorado. Near the Playhouse, they turned into a side street. Tank eased along behind them under the magnolias and the pepper trees, passing modest houses with their small, brown front lawns and neglected shrubbery. In the middle of the third block Strawn parked along the curb behind a metallic-blue Hudson. The woman got out and hurried up the walk to a small stucco house. Tank drove on slowly. In his rearview mirror he saw Strawn, behind the wheel, lighting up a cigarette.

Tank drove once around the block. As he came back onto the street he saw that the Ford hadn't moved and Strawn was still there behind the wheel, alone. He parked along the curb two houses back and left the motor running. The woman came out. She had a dress on, now, high heels and the bandana and dark glasses were gone. Even to the hair, combed out now, she was Stella all over again. Stella when she was twenty-three or so.

She leaned into the window and said something to Strawn. He blew out a lungful of smoke, started to get out. One shoe dangled over the pavement. The woman said something else and he drew the leg back in, then shut the door, hard. The woman shook her head and laughed, then with a sprightly step came around and got into her side. There was that smile again, off by a slightly different shape that didn't make so many wrinkles, and was without that faintly wistful glow of kindness, slowing it down until it was all eyes.

From a standstill Strawn swung into a U-turn and came back up toward Colorado. Tank leaned over toward the glove compartment, hiding his face behind his outstretched arm. He was sure Strawn didn't know his mother's Packard. He let them pass, then circled back as they had. They were waiting at the light when he pulled up behind them. Strawn's arm was crooked out the window for a right turn. The courtesy hung there, strangely intimate. Strawn was looking right and left, in a hurry to make the turn. He saw the break in traffic, shot into it, then hardly drove two blocks before he braked and swerved into the Blue Onion drive-in lot. Tank went on past and drove around the block. If they were there when he got back, the chances were they wouldn't be aware that he was tailing them.

There was the Ford nosed up to the semicircle where the carhops were busily taking orders and swinging trays toward rolled-down car windows. He parked farther back in the area reserved for people who weren't interested in being served outside. Through the Ford's rear window he could see the woman sitting in the middle of the front seat, close to Strawn. She leaned closer, he turned his face to meet her kiss - a long kiss, too intimate for the street. They kept it up until the beep of a horn nearby startled them apart. Tank felt a wrenching in his throat, as if he was seeing this through Stella's eyes, and how uncanny it was that Stella *was* here, in a way, being kissed by mistake. So I've got it, Tank thought, with a kind of vengeful jubilation before the sight froze as one he could never wish on Stella. 'She's already unhappy enough,' Lou repeated in his mind. 'I think she knows.'

She'll fight back, Tank thought. She'll ask me, who put you up to this? Art? Or is it all you, getting even with a man you hate? He couldn't tell her that he saw the same thing Lou saw, and let Lou take the heat. Playing for keeps, she had once said to him, while she warmed the band-aid on his hand a little too long, and he got this feeling, like there was a sort of tapping at the windows of her eyes, and he was supposed to look up and see a face, just meant for him, that others couldn't see. Now this was how he was returning the kindness.

He'd seen enough. The woman existed. She could go on haunting the dark of Stella's hope or be exposed. He didn't know what would happen. He didn't want to think too much about that. Just to get to her, tell her what he'd seen and let her take it from there. It would almost be easier to plant the rattler in Strawn's car. Tamper with his brakes. No guarantees either way. Grief could drive her on to the maternity ward as well as blind love. Go home, he thought; think on it some more.

He started the car. That was all it took. He couldn't wait. He had to do it now. There'd never be a better time. Strawn was here, occupied with the girl. He'd be a while. It was now or never.

30

Dusk was settling down upon the neighborhood, erasing shadows, tracing the ridgeline with a final streak of sunlight. Stella loved this time of the day, its spell of optimism and romance, and she remembered now a moment long ago in Ireland, before she'd met Art. The lambs out on the hills were gamboling in that same rose-colored hour that now seemed to enchant her boys and hold them to the waning golden light that let them play a little longer.

She had decided on pork chops for dinner tonight. Ray was due home any minute. He'd want to have a beer, maybe a highball. He always tried to get her to join him, but she didn't care for beer; thinking, too, that Stingers couldn't do the baby any good. The boys were still outside, playing. The last time she had looked, Joe had made a turban out of an old sheet, and they were sword fighting with wooden coat hangars. She would give them another half an hour. By that time, Ray should be home.

She didn't hear the shuffling of shoes ascending the porch steps. The voice that suddenly called through the screen door startled her.

"Stella!"

She knew the voice, but said, "Who is it?"

"It's me, Stella. Tank Crutchley."

"Oh, hello, Tank. What brings you over?"

"Would you mind if I came in for a minute? I'd like to talk to you."

She went around the corner in her apron, clinging to a dishtowel. Tank stood out there behind the mask of the screen, the same big, good-looking boy she had liked so much before Ray came along, and still did.

"Oooo, sounds kind of serious."

"Oh, I don't know. I won't keep you long, I promise."

"Don't worry about that. Come on in, Tank. I'm getting dinner. Ray's due home any minute. He's almost always on time – these days."

Tank pulled back the screen door, stepped into the washroom and stood there with one hand on the Bendix.

"Maybe not tonight, Stella. Ray could be a little late tonight."

All the weirdness about Tank that she had once easily forgiven now suddenly took on the form she had dismissed, and she felt strangely afraid.

"What in the world are you taking about, Tank? Has something happened to him?"

"Yes, something has. But not the way you think."

"Stop trying to scare me, Tank. What's this all about?"

"I want you to know that nobody put me up to this. It's all on me, what I've got to say. You may not like what you're going to hear. God knows I've said to myself, over and over, who am I to be the one – ?"

"For God's sake, Tank, stop being so dramatic! What is it?"

"Can you believe that somebody in this world looks almost exactly like you, Stella?"

A pocket of needles burst under Stella's heart, awakening Dorothy's story from the dead. This time it felt like Tank had thrown a cruel punch and knocked all the wind out of her. She swallowed, trying to keep her equilibrium. Trying to keep him from seeing that she could hardly catch her breath. Her voice didn't want to function except in the contralto.

"I suppose so. We all have doubles, so I've heard. What about it?"

"I've seen that woman. The one who looks like you. If she was pregnant, and a little older, she'd be you."

Brittle laughter flew from the agony on Stella's face.

"What's that got to do with me? A case of mistaken identity - so what?"

"No, I didn't mistake this woman for you. I couldn't. She wasn't carrying a baby like you are. I wasn't looking for you, anyway. I was looking for the person who looked like you."

"And did you find her?" Stella said. She held the scrawl of a punishing grin on Tank, as if her jeering could smite him, and he and all he'd said would go up in smoke.

Just then she heard the slap of loafers out on the parquetry in the dining room. Strawn shuffled in, hugging a heavy load in a big paper sack. He was wearing a short-sleeved blue paisley shirt, open three buttons down his hairless chest. It wasn't the shirt she'd sent him off to work in that morning. He hadn't yet caught sight of Tank out by the Bendix when he said:

"Hey, hon! Get a load of this ham I got for us. It's one of our premiums – hickory smoked." He dumped the load on the tiles under the spice cupboard, tore the sack off and said, "This oughta last us a month a' Sundays."

"Where did that shirt come from, honey?"

Strawn stood back, spreading his arms as if in readiness to be frisked.

"This? I got those extras in my locker at the plant, remember? You don't want me to come home smellin' like a stockyard, do you?"

She saw his eyes, then, finding Tank and she said hurriedly, "We've got a visitor. Tank just dropped by."

"Well, whaddaya know? Old friend Tank. What brings you around, chief?"

"I was in the neighborhood," Tank said evenly.

Strawn started with a slow smirk, then shook his finger at Tank and cackled.

"That's a good one. In the neighborhood. I thought maybe you moved away, been keepin' yourself so scarce."

Stella said, "Ray's been working down at Armour-Star in Bell Gardens, Tank. Did you know that?"

"Yes, I did," Tank said.

"The money's not bad, either," Strawn said. "Say, if you're stuck for a job, chief, drop by the plant. They're still hiring."

"Thanks, but I'm not doing too bad," Tank said, "coaching up at Flintridge Prep."

"Is that a fact? Well, in your spare time, then, baby-sit for us and pick up a few coins. You know, honey, like when we want to go out to a movie or somethin'" Strawn had a little private laugh as he moved toward Stella. He reached around her shoulders and pulled her close. "So what brings you around, chief?" he said over his shoulder.

"Old time's sake," Tank said. "Just wanted to say hello to old friends."

"So did you say hello?"

Tank didn't nod. He didn't blink or move a muscle. No hint of apology crossed his face. He stared at Strawn with the look of an animal coming face to face with its arch enemy in a tableau vivant. At last he said, "I'd better be going. Nice to see you again, Stella. I'll be around if you – need a baby-sitter."

"Be careful crossing that war zone out there, chief," Strawn said. "You might get cut to ribbons."

Tank turned and pushed on the screen door and walked out.

"Goodbye, Tank!" Stella called out. She felt her voice going out like a frantic SOS. He hadn't got to tell her everything. It felt as if, when she finally found out, somehow it would be too late.

They waited until his footsteps died away down on the walk. Strawn walked over to the refrigerator, yanked it open and took out a bottle of Blatz.

"You want one, hon?"

"No."

"Okay. You don't mind if I crack one for myself, do you?"

"You didn't have to be so rude to him."

"Who was rude?"

"Who do you think?"

"What did he want here, anyway?"

"He just came by. There was something about a woman he saw that looked like me."

Strawn's face jerked sharply toward her. He blinked and turned away with his beer and went to the drawer for the opener.

"Boy, what a weird one that bird is. Comes over to say he saw some woman that looks like you? Whoop-dee-doo! You could hardly wait, right?"

"He didn't get to explain. I would have dismissed it if Dorothy hadn't told me almost the same thing."

Strawn's hand in the utensil drawer came out, holding nothing.

"Told you what?"

"Oh, that she was shopping out at Bullocks and saw my look-alike. This woman looked so much like me, Dorothy almost went over to say hi. The only thing that stopped her was –"

"Yeah? What stopped her?"

"Well, actually I don't remember. Something."

"Maybe it *was* you. Ever think of that?"

"Ray, I haven't been to Bullocks in over a month."

She watched his face, the shaky stare that seemed to dangle from a broken limb. She wouldn't tell him any of the rest – how Dorothy had seen *him* with the woman. She didn't want to know if it was true. As long as she didn't know, it wasn't.

"Well, if that's all Dorothy saw, I don't see what the big deal is."

"She sure gets around a lot, doesn't she," Stella said, feeling the vindictive shove behind her voice that caught her in the line of fire.

"Who?"

"The woman who looks so much like me."

"You mean, because – the weirdo saw one someplace, too?"

"There's no need to call Tank a weirdo."

"Oh, suddenly you're on his side? So where did he say he saw her?"

"He didn't say."

"Didn't say, didn't say," Strawn mocked. "Like a whole slew of 'em are out there on the loose." Strawn squinted at her, cocked his head a little. "What else?"

"What else what?"

"About the goddamn woman!"

"Nothing else. That's all. Were you expecting something else?"

"Cut out the cat and mouse with me, Stella. You want me to think you're not telling me everything?"

"Why? Would you like to hear some more?"

"You're asking all these questions, but you're pretty goddamn short of answers."

She still couldn't bring herself to tell him. All that was left to say was, Dorothy saw you, too, Ray. Two look-alikes don't usually run around together. What was Tank getting at? Just seeing somebody who looked like her was no reason to come over, make it sound like the end of the world. There was more, and she had to find out. What was she talking herself into, here? This had to stop. She said:

"Honey, I don't have any more answers than what I've told you. This is all so silly. Open me a beer, will you?"

"I thought you said it's bad for the baby."

"I said a cocktail, not one beer. In fact I think a beer could be good for her."

"How do you know it's gonna be a girl?"

"Oh, I've had that feeling for a long time, now, for some reason."

"Okay by me. We'd better get to crackin' and think up some names. For boys, too, just in case."

She went over to him, stepped into his embrace and let him hold her a while. It felt like something had dropped away, and suddenly it was too hard, trying to get it back. The baby didn't know. She felt the little life in her that bulged against him, the little girl he was going to love and dote on, the way fathers did. The way they couldn't help but do. He tried to kiss her, but she turned her head aside.

"Open me that beer now, honey," she said.

"Comin' right up," he said.

There was a crack and half of Joe's wooden coat hangar flew off.

"Now I've got you!" Lou said.

"No, you don't!" Joe threatened him with the sharp remainder of his stick.

"Time out," Tank said, coming up to them on the grass.

Joe and Lou both looked.

"Jeez, Tank," Joe said. "Where did you come from?"

"Mars," Tank said.

"I knew it," Joe said. "I knew that's where you've been all this time. It had to be that far away."

He'd been right to tell the boys he was from Mars. He was. He might as well be. My name is Gorgon. Come with me and you won't be harmed. We only want to conduct a few experiments. Don't be afraid. Force won't be necessary, unless you resist.

"I've gotta get back to my space ship," Tank said. "Otherwise I might be stuck on this planet for the rest of my life."

Joe giggled uncontrollably.

"Shut up," Lou said. "Tank, did you -?"

"Yes. But Ray came waltzing in. I didn't get everything said. But that's all right, she got the picture. Not all of it, but - don't worry, I'll find another way."

When are you coming back, Tank?" Joe said. "We sure have missed you."

"Well, soon – I hope."

"Promise us you won't get on that space ship ever again. Pul-eeeze?"

"I don't know. Martians get homesick too, you know."

"You're not a Martian, Tank. Lou says you're Samson. He's gonna be like you when he grows up."

"Shut up, Joe!" Lou said. "You're making fun of Tank."

"I am not!" Joe said angrily. He thrust his sharp stick up in front of Lou's face.

"Better get yourself a new sword there, Joe," Tank said.

Joe looked at the splintered point of his crippled weapon.

"There's not too many of these left in the closet."

Tank laughed.

"So long, you guys," he said, turning, then he started off across the grass. As he approached the mailbox, he saw the for-sale sign out at the edge of the shrubs – that symbol of escape like V-J Day splashed on the headlines, and he was going home with a Purple Heart. He half turned without breaking his stride.

"Hey, you guys! Something's wrong with that sign! It says For Sale!"

But the boys weren't there any more. As if they never had been. Maybe that trip to Mars wasn't such a bad idea. He stepped off the curb into the street and made for home.

31

Though he wanted to go along, Joe had a bad cough and a fever, and Strawn said he'd better not. He should rest, but over and above that, there was the danger that his mother could catch his cold. Joe understood. It didn't hurt any that he'd get out of a day of school, either.

Strawn called up Roberta Cahill and told her he would pay her $10 to sit with Joe for the four or five hours they expected to be gone. Lou didn't envy Joe one bit, but then Joe had always been able to put up with Roberta, since she had never tried to get him into any bear hugs. Lou couldn't stand Roberta's loud mouth, how she loved to wag her finger at him, saying, 'Come here,' and get him in a bear hug and lift him off the ground like she was some kind of a lady wrestler. What was it about older girls who had to cut boys down to size?

Franny Kopnik lived up in Thousand Oaks, about halfway to Ventura, where Stella had told Strawn she'd meet them at the amusement park, Playland on the Beach. Lou had long known that Franny was his mother's best friend, but he had only seen her once, right after the war, when Franny and Vince, his dad's fullback on his championship team of 1933, lived in a trailer down in San Diego and Vince was about to ship out with the tuna fleet. The drive from Thousand Oaks to the Cedars of Lebanon Hospital where Stella would deliver the baby was longer than it would have been from Altadena, but Stella wanted to be with somebody she trusted to get her up there at the drop of a hat. Strawn couldn't take off work for any length of time without risking being laid off. If Stella's water broke, or there was any other sign that she was going into labor, Franny was to rush her to the hospital, and nobody, Stella had insisted, was truer blue than Franny Kopnik.

On the phone Stella had asked Lou to bring her that cashmere sweater she liked so much – the one she often wore to the Playhouse when it was cold out. Lou almost forgot to get the sweater when Strawn said he would be waiting for him in the car, so he rushed into his mother's room, and there was Roberta sitting at the vanity with one drawer open, just dragging out a string of pearls.

"What're you doing, Roberta?"

Roberta jumped and let the pearls slide back into the drawer and pushed it shut.

"Just admiring some of your mom's jewelry," she said with a swift, haughty smile. "What's wrong with that?"

"It better be all there when I get back."

"Oh! What're you, the house detective?"

"You better take good care of Joe. Make him some chicken soup."

"He didn't ask for any soup."

"He's sick. He likes chicken noodle. Crackers with it, too."

"I'll try to remember all that, Doctor Ryan."

Lou glared at her. He had her dead to rights, and he didn't need a fist at all to hit her back. Outside, down in the driveway, Strawn leaned on the horn. Lou turned and left her there, knowing without really trusting her that his mother's things should now be safe.

In the car, sitting beside Strawn, Lou had nothing to say. He meant to keep it up the whole way, if he could. They were about three blocks from the school when Lou saw Cheryl Jones striding out along the sidewalk with – was that Charlie Druce? Lou gave his window a crank downward, Cheryl looked right at him but didn't wave. He rolled the inch back up. She didn't know him. The car was strange to her. Charlie didn't turn his head at all. His weak bloated eyes behind thick horn rims aimed like he was on train tracks. Now as they reeled past

Lou wondered whether Cheryl had got interested in little Charlie, whose britches seemed about to split, the way he had to take two steps for every one of hers. At any rate he thanked his lucky stars he hadn't got the window down. That would have given Strawn a chance to say, 'Who's that?' And flush him out of where there was no call to talk.

They rode in silence clear out to where 101 began its long stretch along the ocean. There Strawn heaved a sigh and said, "Well, it's been a week now since you've seen your mom. It'll be nice to see her again, won't it?" Lou answered tersely, "Yes." That was all.

They were just coming out of the slow zone through Oxnard. Strawn seemed anxious to speed up past the city limit sign. In fact he tromped on the gas, leaning forward with his jaw set as if, Lou thought, this was one way of getting a rise out of him.

Way out at sea a fog bank loomed, white in the misty sunshine. Shreds of fog sailed in across the road, causing Strawn to turn the wipers on. The silence between them had gone on and on like a contest: which one of them would break first? Finally Strawn reached over and turned on the radio. He played with the dial until he got a station he liked: Rosemary Clooney was singing *Come on'a my House*. One time out on the playground Charlie Druce had said secretively, 'Y'know, that song is dirty.' When Lou asked him why, Charlie just threw up his hands helplessly, eyes floating like jellyfish behind his thick glasses. What did Cheryl see in him, Lou wondered.

Up ahead on the left Lou saw the long breakwater that led out to the lonely Coast Guard post. Strawn began to slow down, sticking out his hand for a left turn. Lou felt afraid and said, "Where are you going?"

Strawn swung viciously into the turn.

"I want to talk to you."

Lou thought of those movies in which some doomed squealer in the back seat knew full well that he was being taken for a one-way ride. The gravel under the tires crackled. There was nothing ahead but a desolate locked gate, behind it a flagpole flying the American flag outside a shack with a corrugated tin roof. Strawn drove all the way up to the gate, where a large rusty padlock hung from the two ends of a chain as thick as an anchor chain. He pulled right up to it, turned off the radio, then the motor. Lou was afraid to look at him, as if so small a thing as the movement of his head would stir some violent outburst. Then way down inside him courage seemed to take the shape of Strawn's face caught right in the middle of his eyes, and when he turned, Strawn was already looking at him, not savagely as he expected. There was instead a kind of haggard pleading in his eyes. He opened his mouth, the words aborted and he blinked out at the fog. His mouth came open again and he said, "Why? Why do you hate me so much, kid?"

Lou felt like he'd been hit in his throat. He wondered why all of a sudden it mattered to Strawn, and if they weren't trapped here in the car together, it wouldn't. Heat stung the back of his eyes. He couldn't speak.

"What've I ever done to you?" Strawn pressed. "I married your mother. Is that why you hate me?"

Lou dug in. It was supposed to be *his* fault, as if he'd just picked hatred out of the blue, and could be talked out of it. The trap was supposed to make him see the light. Sit here until an end came to the unbearable sitting next to this sullen kid, the mile upon mile of seething silence between him. That way to throw his mother off a little longer: just look how hard he's trying to bring Lou around? Anger now came into Strawn's voice:

"Are you gonna sit there for the rest of your life not saying a god-damn word? Is that it? Like somebody cut your tongue out?"

Lou clenched his fists between his legs. Strawn's hand came off his lap, faltered in the air between them before it fell onto the seat. "Listen, we've got a baby coming. She'll be your little sister – or brother. I'll be that baby's father. You won't hate the baby, will you, just because it's part mine?"

The trick reached into his heart, played around with it as if he wouldn't have one if he answered, 'No.' Strawn watched him. Lou felt him watching; God only knew what was going on behind those snake eyes. Lou had to remember, everything about Strawn was a snake. A snake had ways of looking harmless. But you never wanted to let your guard down near one. Strawn reached over and started the car, sat back sighing, letting it idle.

"Okay, if that's the way you want it. I'll tell you one thing – this ain't gonna make things easier on your mother, that's for damn sure."

'As if *you're* easy,' Lou said in his mind.

Strawn glared at him as if he'd heard, and Lou braced himself for a sudden vicious blow. It didn't come. Instead Strawn clunked the gearshift into reverse, pulled back far enough to turn around, and started back toward the highway.

They were driving along the placid sea again, slicked in the grey light and the swaying kelp out to where the fog tore off into the wind, coming their way. A few miles on a Ferris wheel came into view against the grey sky.

"Well, there it is," Strawn said. "Too bad the sun's not out. You'll get to see your mother, anyway."

She was waiting by her car, leaning back against the door with her hands behind her, wearing a nice two-tone dress with a bow in front that fell to her waist. She had her hair done up in that way she liked, with the curls in front and tied with a big yellow bow in back. Lou thought she looked beautiful, there in the misty chill that swept in off the sea, now even more as she began to wave and her face lit up with a big smile. Strawn parked next to her Cadillac and got out, saying, "You drove down here by yourself, honey?"

"Yes, I felt like it. I'm feeling great!"

Strawn went over and they kissed while Lou got into the back seat and pulled out the cashmere sweater. He ran with it up to his mother.

"You look like you need this, Mom."

"Oh, I do!" Stella hugged herself and shivered.

Lou stepped to the side of her, letting the sweater drape from her shoulders as she turned to slip her arms into it.

"Thank you, honey! Come here, now." She took him in her arms and he smelled her *Tabu* and the damp wool of the sweater and a scent of lemon in her hair, and he wanted to squeeze clear through to what he'd missed and worried about until it was all gone, but he held off, stretching across the bulge in her belly, afraid to hurt the baby. "Well, did you guys have a nice drive up?" She was holding him by the shoulders, now, looking down at him. Before he could say anything Strawn said:

"We made it in record time – watching out for cops, of course."

"We listened to some music on the radio," Lou said.

Stella looked at Lou a moment, then glanced at Strawn, who was struggling with a smile.

"You did, did you? I tried to get some on mine, but there was too much static." Stella began to button her sweater down toward two buttons from the bottom.

"What does the doctor say, honey?" Strawn said. "When's that baby coming out?"

"Well, he told me yesterday I'm doing real good. My blood pressure was a little high last week, but now it's down and stable. Nothing really out of whack. I'm good to go, he says – his words. He can't pin down a day – could be tomorrow, could be early next week. But he's pretty sure I'll have a very normal labor, no need to go in prematurely." She pressed her hand against Lou's cheek. "If this baby's anything like you, honey, she'll take her time coming out."

"She won't be much like me if it's a girl, Mom," Lou said.

"Won't you be happy with a little sister, honey?"

"Oh, sure!" Lou said.

"Ray's kind of hoping for a girl, too, aren't you, hon? Or have you changed your mind?"

"No, no. A girl sounds pretty darn sweet to me."

"What would you call her?" Lou said, looking at his mother. Before she could answer Strawn said:

"Well, we've been kinda thinking about Louisa, after her grandmother. Right, hon? There's a couple others, so I guess it's still up for grabs."

Stella came away from the car and took Lou's hand.

"Honey, what about you and me going on a ride? I've got to stay away from the ferris wheel and those other ones that make me dizzy. There's the merry-go-round, and the – well, the house of horrors. They tell me you ride through it on a rail car, pretty fast, so none of the spooks and zombies can get you."

"Is that what you want to go on, Mom?"

"Sure, let's give it a whirl. Would you like to come, Ray?"

Ray shook his head.

"Count me out on that one, hon. I'll stay here and have a smoke. There's plenty of scares still left out there on Highway 101." In his voice you could tell he thought he wasn't really wanted.

Stella gave Strawn a peck and took Lou's hand again. She looked happy.

"Okay, it's over there, honey," she said, pointing. "You lead the way?"

On the way over to the House of Horrors they stopped at the kiosk near the concession stand and Stella bought a string of tickets. They walked over to where a few people were waiting for the next ride. They all seemed to be part of the same group, and were talking in a foreign language, he couldn't tell what. He thought the chance to ask her might not come around again.

"Mom, how long are you gonna have to stay in the hospital after the baby's born?"

"Not real long, honey. A couple days. Three or four at the most."

"And then Franny's gonna bring you home?"

"No, Ray will come and get me."

"Mom, you know me and Joe can take care of ourselves after school. You don't need to hire Roberta."

"Oh? I thought you liked Roberta?"

"She's not doing us much good. She just sits there and watches Tom Mix and stuff on the television. She's only a couple years older than I am."

"Honey, to tell you the truth I feel better if you guys aren't there alone. Roberta seems responsible enough to me. She's always been in the past."

Lou wasn't going to tell her that he had seen Roberta rooting around in her jewelry box. She hadn't stolen anything, yet, as far as he knew.

"I'm old enough to do anything she does, Mom."

"Oh, sure, I know you are. It's me, I guess. I just feel better if you guys've got an older person with you."

Lou reached for the reins to the runaway pounding of his heart.

"What about Tank? He'd be ten times better than Roberta."

Stella looked down at him, something came into her eyes that he was not prepared for. She said wistfully, "You think so?"

"Yeah. I mean, he sure beats Roberta - by a long shot."

"Well, we'll have to ask Ray what he thinks about that. He's in charge while I'm gone."

"I could ask him," Lou said, and he saw how she fought to ignore the speck of surprise that lit like a fly on her face.

"We'll see, honey."

They heard the rumbling of the iron wheels on the rails and the cars burst through the swinging doors, carrying people wide-eyed, fresh with excitement. They climbed out, some a little unsteady on their feet, little kids shaking their fright off into the sudden light of day. The attendant came along the queue, taking tickets. A tall man from among the group of foreigners gallantly motioned Stella and Lou ahead of them, and she led Lou over to the third car in the row and they got in. As soon as the others got settled into the first and second cars, and the attendant made sure the iron handles were down and locked for people to grip onto, Stella took Lou's hand and said, "Here we go, honey!" The cars jerked and started to move off, slowly. Lou looked out at Strawn standing there with his cigarette. Strawn waved and then they entered the tunnel that bored into the jagged plaster mountainside, gaining speed into the darkness that smelled like musty canvas, then there was the hoot of an owl that warned them of the things that lurked deep in the scary, spiny forest.

The hamburger didn't sit too well on Lou's stomach. It had tasted good, along with the fries and the chocolate shake that he had lit into, causing his mother to say, 'Did you eat any breakfast, honey?' She hadn't felt like eating anything, but shared his milk shake with him. Lou hoped now it wasn't the shake that made him feel sick, or else the same thing might affect his mother. The fries had tasted funny – like the oil they'd been fried in was old.

She was on her way back to Franny's house – must have arrived by now. Strawn had eaten a cheeseburger himself, but hadn't complained of any stomach problems. He had the radio on again, Bing Crosby was singing *Would you like to Swing on a Star*, but you couldn't hear it too well for the wind whistling through Strawn's wind wing, sucking out the smoke that curled off his cigarette.

They hadn't gone on any other rides after the House of Horrors. Strawn had bought a pail of baseballs for a dime and threw them at the ever-moving metal ducks and knocked so many over, he won a teddy bear for Stella. At first Lou didn't want to take Strawn up on his offer to buy him a pail, too. But finally he gave in and threw so wildly, he hardly hit a single duck. Strawn offered to buy him another pail, but he said no, not wanting to add insult to injury. Strawn didn't keep after him about it. He said well, we're all out of tickets, anyway.

Lou thought he could hold out the whole way back, saying nothing, the same as he had coming out, but he wasn't so scared of talking any more. Being with his mother on those rides and stuff had made him feel different. They were nearing Glendale on the freeway when he said, "Ray?"

Strawn finished blowing out a lungful of smoke before he said, "Yeah?"

"I told Mom I wanted to ask you something on our way home. She said it was okay."

"Oh, yeah? Well then I guess it must be. What's on your mind?"

"Would you mind if Tank took care of us while Mom's in the hospital, not Roberta?"

"Absolutely not! We made the decision on Roberta, so she's it."

"Both Joe and me like Tank a lot better, Ray."

"D'you think that means diddly to me? Like or dislike? My ma used to tell me to sit up straight for Auntie Forbush. So she could drink herself silly playin' cards with the men in the next room."

Lou wasn't sure what Strawn was driving at, but he said, "Tank would never drink with us around."

"Did I say he would?"

"I know Mom wouldn't mind it if —"

"She left it up to me, right? And I say no. Roberta stays."

Lou let the silence fall like a gush of water down a drainpipe. Strawn took a long drag on his cigarette. Not a thoughtful drag, but one that seemed to forego thought so it could be blown way off into space. The disk jockey on the radio introduced Frank Sinatra, who broke into *Time after Time*.

"And I don't want any arguments?" Strawn added suddenly. "You got me?"

"Yes, but there's something I think you should know."

Strawn groaned.

"Aw, Jeez! What, now?"

"Well, just before we left this afternoon, I caught Roberta in Mom's jewelry drawer."

Strawn flung his head toward him, his cigarette dropped out of his mouth and he spanked at the stub on his lap like a bug that wouldn't die, spewing sparks and ashes. The car swerved briefly toward the shoulder, Strawn swung it back onto the lane.

"Did you see her stash anything away?"

"No. She claimed she was just admiring Mom's pearl necklace. But she sure put it back quick. Like if I wasn't there, she might not've."

"How come you never told me right away? She could've stole us blind by now."

"No, not since I caught her. We'd know it was her if anything was missing."

Strawn pursed his lips, his eyes went funny, like he'd bit down on a lemon.

"Of course. And there was nobody else, was there, since we were in a hurry."

"No, sir."

Strawn looked over at him warily. Lou gave him a manly look back, defending the bounds of respect.

"Well, now we got a problem. God damn it! This should happen now. I've got a million things on my mind. I guess –" Strawn reached over, stubbed out the ragged remains of his cigarette in the ashtray, then flicked it out the window. "Okay, leave the dirty work to me. I'll get rid of her."

"Does that mean -?"

"I don't know! I'm thinkin' about it."

They were near home, now. Strawn turned into the driveway, stopped and sat there a while before he shut off the ignition. He made no move to get out. As soon as Lou's hand fell upon the door handle Strawn said:

"Just a minute."

Lou brought his hand back onto his lap.

"I'll let you have Crutchley for these few days or whatever it takes. But there's conditions. One - no playin' with real guns out in the yard. You got that?"

"Yes."

"Second, you cut out diggin' up the grass with your cleats. That stops."

"I understand, Ray."

Strawn searched his face suspiciously, as if despite being told there were no feathers in his soup, there were.

"Third, you stop dickin' with the for-sale sign. You leave it alone."

Lou didn't want to admit he'd had anything to do with that. He watched the leer on Strawn's face, knowing he was trapped. He didn't say anything.

"Was that a yes I heard?" Strawn said.

Lou blinked at him, hoping that would be enough. Apparently it was.

"We don't know if Crutchley can do this, but I'll inform him, not you."

"Okay," Lou said.

"I'm not gonna make a big to-do about dismissing Roberta. She'll go peacefully, considering."

"Oh, yeah," Lou said, "I believe she will."

"All right, get in there and see how your brother's doing. I'll handle the girl."

Lou plunged down the door handle, started to get out. Strawn raised his voice.

"Don't forget, now. No funny business with that sign no more. No more diggin' up the grass."

"I won't forget," Lou said. He shut the door and started toward the house.

32

A light came on, dimly. Silence hovered in the night sky. Stars twinkled at Tank, lying there on the chaise longue. The aspens rattled and a few leaves fluttered into the fish pond. He heard the phone ringing in the house, then it stopped; there was the indecipherable voice of a boy, then that stopped, too. Tank started to get up but just then Lou came out of the living room.

"That was Franny Kopnik on the line, Tank. She asked if Ray was home. I told her no, but you're here."

Tank rubbed his eyes and sat up. He looked at his watch, seeing that he'd slept for almost half an hour. He said:

"Does she want to talk to me?"

"No, she just said for us to tell Ray, as soon as he gets home, she's driving Mom to the hospital. Her water broke and she's beginning to get cramps."

"Did Franny try to get hold of Ray out at the plant?"

"She didn't say." Lou came out onto the patio, fiddling with his fingers. "That's nothing bad, is it? Cramps and the water breaking?"

"Oh, no! Perfectly normal when a woman's about to have a baby."

Lou nodded. He looked out toward the driveway.

"I wonder where Ray is."

"I guess he'll be along," Tank said. "Remember now, your mom's in real good hands with Franny. And where she's going – the Cedars of Lebanon Hospital – that's one of the finest hospitals in the country, bar none."

Lou came over and sat down beside Tank on the chaise longue. Tank felt his love for the boy traveling up and down his arms, backing up into his throat.

"I'll bet I know why Ray's not home, yet," Lou said.

Tank looked at him.

"Why?"

"He's with *her*, that woman."

"We don't know, Lou. He might have had a flat tire, got delayed in traffic. You know how choked the freeways get at going-home time."

Lou looked down at his hands between his knees. For a while he sat there that way, silently. He looked out at the night through the aspens over the wall. Suddenly Lou threw his arms around Tank and hugged him, then drew back quickly.

"Besides Joe, you're my best friend, Tank."

"Well, the feeling's mutual," Tank said.

A gust rushed through the aspens, the leaves whispered like polite applause. In the pond there was the plop of a goldfish gulping at the surface. On the phonograph inside Joe was listening to *Tubby the Tuba*, narrated by Victor Jory. Lou looked up at the stars.

"You think Mom's gonna be okay, don't you, Tank?"

"Why, sure. There's no reason to think otherwise."

"I sure hope she gets to come home tomorrow," Lou said.

"She might have to stay a couple days or so, to rest up and make sure the baby's in good shape."

"Jeez, a sister. Mom says she wants to call her Louisa, if it's a girl."

"That's a real pretty name."

A car drove by on Morslay, heading down toward Mendecino. The silence afterwards reached around the mystery of where Strawn was; when, if ever, they would hear the sound of his car, see his headlights flash off in the driveway. Strawn hurrying, or just taking his time on the way up the walk.

By the time Tank got the boys into bed, it was going on ten o'clock. Coy scratched on the back door, he let her in and she trotted down the hall and hopped right up onto Joe's bed. Tank read a chapter out of *Gulliver's Travels* until he could see the sound of his voice was making them both sleepy. As soon as he turned out the light, Lou rolled over on his belly and started to hum *Praise the Lord and Pass the Ammunition*, bouncing his head on the pillow to keep time. Joe pulled the covers up to his chin. Tank stood by the doorway in the dark for a minute. He was about to go when Lou stopped. His voice sounded small and forlorn, like he was afraid of being left alone with a comforting routine that no longer worked.

"Could we say a prayer for Mom, Tank?"

Tank came back into the room and sat beside Lou on the bed. Joe's eyes were open. In the milky light from a slice of moon outside Tank saw him press his hands together. Tank lowered his head, both boys shut their eyes.

"Dear God, be with the mother of these boys. Be with her not only through this night but all the days and nights of her life to come. Keep her safe and well and help her, God, to deliver a healthy baby. We ask this in the name of our Lord, Jesus Christ. Amen."

Lou sat up, leaning on one elbow.

"When Joe and me play catch, and I pitch to him, I pray for strikes. I get one every time."

"You never told me that," Joe said indignantly.

"Well, I'm telling you now."

"If God does that," Joe said, "He'll take care of Mom. Won't He, Tank?"

"Of course He will. He'd never answer the little prayers and send the big ones back."

"That's right." Lou snuggled under his covers, turning on his side.

Tank told the boys, then, that it was time to get some sleep. They said goodnight to him, he walked into the living room and stretched out on the davenport. He lay awake there for a while, listening to Lou bouncing his head on the pillow and humming

My Adobe Hacienda. These were the 'lullabies,' Joe had said once, he couldn't go to sleep without. In about five minutes Lou wound down, Coy made a sound of contentment getting settled on Joe's bed, then all was quiet.

Sometime during the silence that wrapped around the dark in the house Tank dozed off. The jangling of the phone woke him. He hurried to get it before it woke the boys. It was Dr. Hap at the Cedars of Lebanon hospital, asking for Mr. Strawn. Tank told him Strawn wasn't here.

"May I ask to whom I'm speaking?" Dr. Hap said.

"I'm Vincent Crutchley, a friend. I'm looking after Mrs. Strawn's two boys."

"I see. Well, she asked us to call - to see if we could locate Mr. Strawn."

"Oh, is everything all right?"

"Well, yes. The main thing is Mrs. Strawn is asking for Mr. Strawn. She'd like to have him here, during the delivery."

"I see. Other than that, no complications?"

The doctor didn't answer that directly. Finally he said:

"Once we get the child out, we think it'll be smooth sailing. Mrs. Strawn was expecting her husband to be here. It's been rather upsetting to her – worrying about him. Would you have any means of getting a message through to him? Possibly a telephone number?"

"Well, he might have been kept over at work, but the plant shuts down at five, so my guess is he's been held up in traffic. As soon as he gets home I'll send him straight out to the hospital."

There was a silence on the line, then:

"Yes, we'd appreciate that. You might impress on Mr. Strawn that – well, so far, so good. But we don't like to see Mrs. Strawn in any distress that can be avoided at a time like this. In a couple of hours, hopefully, we'll have a very proud mom and a beautiful, healthy baby in her arms."

Tank tried to shut out any alternatives to that as he stared at the murky corners of the room, the glow from the streetlights streaked along the closed Venetian blinds, the shapes of baby things still on the window seat.

"I'll see what I can do to locate him," Tank said.

"Thank you, Mr. Crutchley. Tell Mr. Strawn to call our nurse's station here at the maternity ward. We'll be available all night."

"Yes, I will," Tank said.

"Goodbye, sir," the doctor said.

As Tank hung up Lou's words raced through his mind, 'He's with *her*, that woman.' Raced like Tank's own car across town to that little stucco house to see if it was true. And if it was . . .

He picked up the pencil beside the phone, wrote on the notepad, *Had to go out. Nothing to worry about. Hold down the fort. Be back before 1AM. Tank.*

He left the note under the lamp and stole out the front door, locking it behind him. He walked up to the Packard, parked along the curb by the mailbox, got in and started her up. It felt like he was driving off into a dream. Like seeing a banzai charge in front of him, getting louder, and he'd been told to fire into it. He pulled on the headlights, rammed the gearshift into first and started off.

33

The drive to the little house off Colorado took hardly any time at all. Tank wasn't prepared for what he saw. Somehow he hadn't expected to see Strawn's car, but there it was, parked right behind hers in the driveway. He drove slowly past, seeing the dim light in her windows, then went around the block and came back to that same sight, unchanged. This time a voice seemed to whisper in the empty seat beside him, 'What are you waiting for? You can't run away, now.'

He parked across the street, pulled on the brake and as he got out his heart began to thump hard in his chest. He had that, nothing more, to pave his way across to her doorstep - the cadence of a parole officer riding herd on a man he'd rather gun down in some swift backstairs skirmish. He was about to climb the two steps to the darkened porch when a woman's laughter wailed behind the shaded window in which the sash was raised halfway.

"That's better, baby!" A man's voice prompted. Strains of music swelled from a phonograph.

The voice was Strawn's. He sounded drunk. Drunk with a woman on the night his wife was going into labor. Tank felt like the bellboy carrying that message on a tray. He raised his fist and slammed it repeatedly against the door.

"Hey, who'd that be?" the woman said poutily.

The door swung back and Strawn stood there in sharkskin trousers sagging off his hips and a dingy white T-shirt. He reeled a little, getting Tank into focus. His mouth worked itself into a lop-sided smile. He jabbed his finger at Tank shrewdly.

"Now wait a minute. I know you from someplace. I know-oo you!" He said it like the time had come to call out, 'Ready or not, here I come!' And the smile grew with a kind of priggish affability as he looked around at a freckled young woman with lush auburn hair who could be Stella in her second year of college. She stood beside a phonograph in bare feet, pulling a red satin dressing gown around her shoulders. On the phonograph Rudy Vallee was crooning 'Tiptoe through the Tulips.' "Look who's here, hon. You didn't invite him, did you?"

"Me?" She took it seriously, then caught on and grinned. "Stop it! But I would have. How come all your friends are so good-looking?"

Strawn flung his palms out helplessly.

"Birds of a feather, I guess. Well, shit oh dear. How did you find me, Chief?"

"What matters is, I did," Tank said.

Strawn looked at him, surrender coming to a stop in his eyes.

"Yeah. Hey, sorry for the informal attire. We was havin' a private party."

"It's my birthday," the woman preened. "Too private, if you ask me. We should be out somewheres like Ciro's – y'know, slumming." She cackled and looked around for where she'd left her drink.

Tank could see she wasn't exactly a floozie. She was no lady, either. She wouldn't have grown up to be Stella.

"Well, when are you gonna introduce me?" she whined.

"You can't be starved for company that bad, sugar," Strawn said. "Wait here while I get out my bullhorn and invite the whole block."

"Gee, nice talk," the girl said.

Tank noticed the bourbon bottle on the coffee table; the two glasses at opposite ends. It was funny, seeing Strawn this drunk. For as big a jerk as he was, he always seemed to play things close to the vest. But not tonight.

"You didn't even get me a cake," the woman pouted. "So how private is that?"

"The flowers don't count?" Strawn blinked at the bouquet of carnations in the glass vase at the other side of the couch.

"Why, sure they do. I thought that was sweet. I couldn't of blown out all the candles, anyway."

"Right," Strawn said, "all twenty-four of 'em." He walked over and gave her a squeeze. "You better save your breath for me."

Tank wondered what they were up to, talking so loosely in front of him, as if the jig was up and Strawn no longer cared to keep this girl a secret. What made him think that, at a time like this, he could afford to take the night off?

"Would you like a drink, Mr. – ?" the woman began.

"No thanks," Tank said, "I can't stay."

"Call 'im Tank," Strawn said. "Believe it or not, that's what he goes by. Hey! A couple vets of Hellzapoppin' Ridge like us? How come we never got to be buds?"

The woman hooked a finger on her lower lip.

"Tank," she mused. "Gee, that's a pretty crazy name. I bet people're always askin' stuff like did you drive a tank in the war. Or is it just because you look like one? Must drive you nuts, huh? Well shoot, come on in out of the draft, why don't you."

Tank stepped in, she padded over behind him and drew the door shut. She went to the coffee table and picked up a glass, shook the ice at the bottom.

"I know I never seen you around the plant. I would of remembered if I did. I keep a close eye out for – new people." She gave her head a naughty toss and sipped from her glass.

Tank looked at her and couldn't reconcile her face with what she was saying, her flippant tone with the woman she looked like suffering far away in a hospital bed. He wanted to hit Strawn, but he had harder words to deliver than a blow.

"Stella's gone into the hospital, Ray. She should be going into labor right about now, and she's been asking for you."

The drink slipped out of the woman's hand and splashed onto the rug without breaking. She backed away from the wet spot and the ice cubes.

"Ray, for Christ's sake! On my birthday?"

Strawn stared at her, his face ashen.

"How did I know, babe. Don't be so goddamn ungrateful."

"Whatta you mean how did you know? You said it was a few months off. We'd have time to think it out. How you were gonna leave her. Now I see you were just stallin' for time. You want her money more than you want me. And here she's havin' your kid – *your* kid on my birthday. Some day you could be whoopin' it up while I'm in *my* agony! That'll be the day!"

"Baby, we don't *know*, yet. Remember what I told you?"

"Yeah, like I could still be with your sorry ass when I got to be as old as her!" She threw her face into her hands. "God almighty, what've I got myself into? Why did I have to look so much like her?"

Tank saw her, then, crushed too early in her youth, as if she were Stella, with her whole life ahead of her, caught up in the future in which time had run out on the woman she would never be. He wanted to wash his hands of them both. He wasn't here on a mission of mercy. Neither one of them had any.

Strawn nervously polished off the remains of his drink, then reaching for the bottle he tripped on a crimp in the rug and caught himself on the table.

"Aw, shit!" He stomped his foot. "Listen, Tank. I'll never make it to that hospital alone. I can't drive. Take me out there, will you?"

"Sorry, Ray," Tank said savagely, "I don't give a shit if you get there or you don't. If you need a ride, she'll take you." He pointed at the young woman.

"Like hell I will!" she said. "Listen, mister. You came to get him, didn't you? You've got to take him to the hospital. Get him out of here. See if there's one decent bone left in his body. Here, I'll make a pot of coffee. We'll get that into him. Just wait, then you can –"

Tank heard the growl in his throat as he reached for Strawn's shirt, it twisted in his hands and he grabbed the flesh under his arms like it was cloth and lifted him off his feet and held him there, suspended.

"You son of a bitch! I'm gonna kill you!"

Strawn stared at him, his eyes bulging with fear, and Tank knew he could see the trigger in his eyes, and feel all the unbridled hate left in him squeezing. A thousand years ago he could have done it. A thousand years that blinded him, like Samson, but he didn't need sight to bring the Pillars of the Temple down. The Pillars trembled in his hands, and he let go. Smashing his face was too good for him, it wouldn't hurt as much. Strawn crumpled miserably onto his knees and the woman stupidly stared down at him, fingers stepping on her lips like a Tarantula. Tank didn't wait. He'd had enough. He turned and hurried out.

"Wait a minute, Mister!" the woman screamed in the doorway. "He's in no condition! I can't drive him! I don't even know where the goddamn hospital is!"

Her voice shattered the quiet in the street, then died out in the meek secrets of the late hour. God backed away, clearing the night for fate to step in, knowing when He wasn't wanted.

34

Lights streaming overhead cut the corridor in two – bolts of light that joined in a reeling stream while the walls like a train pitched this way and that. Doors banged. One glaring hooded light bore down. She heard herself moaning and it scared her as if she was somebody else she couldn't help. Pain moved up like a sludge dragging blackness in behind it, chasing her toward a tighter and tighter space where there wasn't any air. She saw herself as a child, foreseeing this. Daddy had told her not to ride that horse. But she got on him while he wasn't looking, bareback, and for a while they were one, she and that proud beauty, crashing up one hill and down another. She would never know why he had thrown her. He and Daddy knew, as if she should have listened, and this was what she got. Now the day had come, and she knew how it felt. Here was the hiding place she had prepared for like a bomb shelter but the bombs were tearing down the walls: they had only been built by a child. In the dark she felt Lou's hand in hers, clinging tight as they pitched through the house of horrors. She felt like crying. Her tears were too hot to bear. The darkness kept on filling in behind, pushing them on, and there was a light that slit the doors ahead, a carousel was playing somewhere in the fog that lay like a washcloth on her forehead.

Art wasn't dead, yet, lying there all by himself on the desert floor. He clung to the happier days – just yesterday! and held out his hand.

He wanted to go. He said come with me, darlin', we'll meet in the Golden Room. In there he wasn't scared to die. There wasn't any death in there, only peace and the gold that glittered everywhere. Glittered from the tall chairs, the chandelier and the air that drew him onward; and from his hand in hers once more, the way she'd always known it would be one day. They started toward that golden light, hand in hand. Ray wouldn't mind, he was so far behind. They had to leave him there. A woman stood aside in the mist, too, dressed for a wedding. You could smell her now, the flowers in her hand, the freshness of her skin, and she was smiling. The air smelled of her youth. Art said look at her, darlin', small wonder you're so beautiful, and he beckoned her to come along, but she hung back. She wanted to look for one last time at the smile on her mother's face, and she was still smiling when she disappeared.

35

Tank was dozing on the couch when the telephone startled him awake. The luminous dials of his watch read 3:44 AM. He got to the phone in the midst of its third ring.

"It's me," Strawn said. "I'm at the hospital."

The girl must have pumped him with a lot of coffee. He sounded rough but sober.

"Good," Tank said. "How's Stella? Did you get to see the baby come out?"

"No."

"Then – how is she? Was it a boy or a girl?"

"Girl," Strawn said."

"Well, did you – what did you name her? Louisa?"

"No, there wasn't time for that. There's no use, Tank. The baby's dead."

Tank felt his breath catching in his throat, as if he had to hold it to keep something worse from coming in. The infant's body seemed to drop at his feet, the precious little life now left to be discarded.

"Listen, Tank," Strawn said, "I know what you're gonna say. Go ahead, I've got it coming. I can't tell the kids. They hate my guts. You do it for me, will you?"

"But why should – wouldn't it be better if Stella -?"

"She can't," Strawn said.

A streak of cold moved like a snake along his spine. It wasn't for him to be there, to be the only living thing and save Strawn from his cowardice. He wanted to get back on the magic carpet that he had left for the boys to fall asleep on.

"Why not?" he said stupidly.

Strawn took in a big breath that seemed to flutter in his throat.

"They wouldn't let me see her, Tank. They were working on her. She almost had the baby, but that was when it all went wrong. She got a fever, her blood pressure shot sky high. She was retaining water, then her kidneys – Christ!"

"But she's all right, now, isn't she?" The lump in Tank's throat clung to hope. Keep him talking. Keep the sun from going out.

"No," Strawn said.

"But why not? What do they have to do, now? How long before she'll be out of danger?"

Strawn's breath fluttered in his throat again.

"She won't," he said.

"What are you talking about? What is it, Ray? What happened?"

Strawn seemed to empty all the air he had into the phone. The first sobs came from far away, air pumping uncontrollably from a broken windpipe.

"She fell into a coma. She had a brain hemorrhage. The doctor called it eclampsia. She's gone."

For a moment Tank felt paralyzed. Then it all broke up and he screamed "No!" He slammed his hand down on the counter, making the telephone jump and faintly jingle. He shut his eyes, feeling tears like a water level rising, but they stopped somewhere down in the dark into which his heart had fallen and was trapped. He scratched and clawed what he couldn't say on the dank walls, 'Why couldn't I have stopped it? Why didn't I try?'

"Put the doctor on!" he yelled. "God damn it, she's in the best hospital in the United States!"

"He won't tell you any different," Strawn said. "I'm her husband, Tank, whatever you think of me."

Tank was a boy again, being told by his father that his mother was dead. It was not what a small boy was supposed to grasp. Dead was the kind of news that God should show up personally to bring, with tricks to make you know it wasn't really the end. The dead fell off a shelf, like a doll, and went to get mended in another world.

Strawn seemed to feel the need to tie some weight to the silence before it fled without him.

"While they were trying to save the baby," he said, "that's when she had the hemorrhage. The baby came out dead. It was a girl."

Tank heard in Strawn's voice the fight to hold blame and grief at bay, and the result was a strange discordant indifference. For all the times he'd seen it, Tank guessed he still didn't know what death really was. It could escape from the toolbox in his father's shop, but not from that sunlit corner where his mother used to grow things in clay pots. Strawn said in a husky voice:

"I can't tell the boys, Tank. I just . . . you've got to do it for me. I can't."

"Who's that?" Lou said. He was standing sleepily in his pajamas near the entryway to the hall.

Tank wheeled to face him, feeling a horrible, uncanny resentment.

"What are you doing up, Lou?"

"I heard you talking." Lou rubbed his eyes. "Who's on the phone?"

"It's Ray," Tank said.

"Oh, how's Mom?" Lou said. "Did the baby get born, yet?"

Tank brought the phone back up to his ear.

"We'll see you when you get home, Ray."

"You'll take care of it for me, won't you?" Strawn said frantically.

"Yeah. I'll take care of it."

"I may not be home tonight. You understand."

"All right. Lou's here. We'll talk later." Tank didn't wait for a response. He lowered the phone into the cradle. He saw that Lou was staring at him and said, "Lou, come over here."

Lou obeyed, shuffling and yet coming with a purpose, as if he was crossing a bridge that any second could drop into a gorge. Tank pulled him gently into his arms, then took him over and sat down with him and Lou leaned back against his chest, saying, "That was about Mom, wasn't it? How's she doing?"

The voice came to him from boot camp, the recital of a lie that might as well be true as if that was a skill you had to learn to stay alive.

"She ran into some trouble, Lou. They had trouble delivering the baby. Things didn't go quite the way they'd hoped."

"You mean the baby came out dead?" Lou spoke in a rush, as if he wanted to hear that the baby was dead, then they wouldn't speak of death anymore.

"Yes," Tank said, "it was born dead."

"Well, when's Mom coming home, then?"

Tank took a breath, and felt his heartbeat dropping down into a sickening void.

"There was some bleeding in your mother's brain. The doctors had a lot of trouble stopping it."

Lou looked at Tank starkly. The panic in his eyes accused him of betrayal.

"We prayed to God, remember? God wouldn't let her die." The tears were coming in his voice, now, and Tank held him, remembering the prayer. How they had tapped and talked to God on His side of the prison wall. Some day, when the time was right, they might break out together.

"I didn't say –"

"Yes, you did! Don't lie to me, Tank! Don't lie to me!"

Tank's heart swelled up and took in this boy's grief to be his own, and he pulled Lou around into his arms and held him tight. Lou's nails dug into his back. His body began to shake. He cried out in a voice all tightened up, like rope around his broken heart.

"Oh, God, oh God! What are we gonna do? What are we gonna do, Tank? What are we gonna do?"

36

The date for Stella's burial was set for the morning of May 3rd, almost to the day of her birth in 1906. Vultures in various forms descended on the house, most of them Bradleys of one stripe or another. Aunt Ellen's eldest daughter took charge of going through Stella's clothes, her jewelry, mementos from abroad, anything that Strawn hadn't nailed down. Strawn didn't seem to be interested in keeping any of the living room furniture, so this woman arranged to get that, too, claiming that a lot of the pieces were Bradley heirlooms.

Until the day of the funeral, Strawn made himself scarce. Either he was out talking to lawyers, or stealing a few crazy moments in the arms of Jeannie, with whom the picture might have changed, now that Stella was gone. Tank thought he was the only one, besides Lou and Joe, who knew about the girl until one afternoon, as the clothes hawk was on her way out the front door with an armload of fur coats, she sidled over to him and whispered, "We've got to get these out of the house before *he* starts giving them away to that . . . Oh, God . . . to think she actually *looks* like Stella when she graduated from Mills!" The woman made mournful eyes at Tank, like the thief who says he's here to wash your windows. Tank wanted to tell her and the rest of them how sorry he was that they were in any way related to Stella.

On the day of the funeral Strawn asked Tank if he wanted to ride with him and the boys in the car behind the hearse. Tank said he did, if it would be all right for Marla to come along, and they all gathered in the living room to wait for the cars of the cortege to arrive. Aunt Ellen sat with everybody else, although she and Stanley were going separately in her limo. Nobody, including the Bradley people, said a word about Harry MacPherson's absence, as if he would show up at the last minute at the cemetery, hopefully keeping his distance. It had been left to them to inform Harry, but it wouldn't be their fault if he failed to show up. The general feeling was that Art wasn't welcome, either. Only Aunt Ellen dared to break ranks to say amidst a roomful of stony faces, "Has anybody thought to inform Arthur?" Tank remembered the name of the doctor that Art had gone up north to work for, and called the office to ask them to pass along the news of Stella's death. There'd been no reply, so far. The boys weren't up to writing their dad: they knew a letter wouldn't reach him, anyway, until the funeral was over.

Strawn, wearing a dark green double-breasted suit, sat beside Aunt Ellen on the davenport. Her head behind her veil trembled as she fingered a handkerchief with her gloved hands.

Lou sat in a chair across the room from Strawn. The two of them began to eye each other furtively. Strawn turned his face away from what he must have thought was hate in Lou's eyes. Hate that saw the wrong person still alive. Strawn looked trapped there in his corner of the couch. He glanced around from time to time like a chameleon that wasn't sure what color he should turn. Once Tank thought Strawn was going to cry. He looked at Lou. Lou's face was full of weariness, now. It wasn't quite forgiveness, but it was not hate, either.

They rode to the Episcopal Church in silence. The Nave was filled to overflowing. Tank spotted Morrie Ankrum, Victor Jory, Keenan Wynn and Van Johnson. But this was not a funeral that Louella Parsons would be covering.

Tank sat between the boys as the pastor read the eulogy. It wasn't overly long. He made reference to Stella's kindness, the many people who had loved her, the bond that God would not allow the death of flesh to break between her and her children. Joe began to whimper. Tank heard a sob catch in Lou's throat. The pastor closed his bible and invited mourners to pay their last respects.

The catafalque was smothered with stocks and gladiolus, mums and roses, snapdragons, carnations and camellias. A man stepped forward, opened the half-lid on Stella's casket. People were getting up, shoes knocked against the kneeling boards. A line began to inch along toward the casket. Tank looked around for Art. For a moment the shape of a head made his heart race, but then the man's profile turned him into somebody who didn't look at all like Art. Tank whispered to the boys, "Let's go up and say good-bye to your mother."

Joe took Tank's hand. Lou shook his head firmly, saying, "I don't want to."

Marla said, "I'll take you, honey, if you'd like."

Lou adamantly shook his head.

"No, I'll stay here."

Behind them Strawn whispered, "This is your last chance to see your mother, Lou. You oughta pay your respects."

"No," Lou said obstinately. "I don't want to look."

Strawn sighed, letting his hands flop back onto his trousers. Tank said:

"Why don't you go on outside, Lou? Wait for us out there."

"I'll go with you, honey," Marla said, and started to get up.

"No, it's okay," Lou said. In the aisle he turned the other way against the movement of people shuffling toward the casket. Tank took Joe's hand, Marla followed and they got into the crowd, and as they drew nearer, Joe squeezed Tank's hand and looked up at him. He nodded, indicating the view of the two bodies in the casket.

One was the upper half of Stella, the other was the infant in her arms. Tank kept expecting Stella to make some move, as sometimes people do in their sleep. They had smoothed off all the freckles on her face with makeup. The baby girl had wispy auburn hair. Her lips were a delicate, bruised red. They hadn't erased the freckles from

Stella's arms. The baby rested in their false strength, a stricken pose of motherly protection. Tank glanced down at Joe, whose hand clutched the edge of the casket as if he wanted to touch the little girl who would have been his sister. God had switched bodies from the world of make-believe to this peacefully hideous, velvet-lined fact. Joe looked up at Tank. He seemed to be asking if that was enough. Tank nodded and they moved on.

Tank and Marla found Lou outside the side entrance where the hearse and the two black limos were parked. Smog smeared the sky with a milky brightness. Joe said, inexplicably, he wanted to sit there a minute if they didn't mind. They left him sitting on the steps and walked down toward the cars where Lou was pacing back and forth.

"We'll be going to the cemetery in a minute, Lou," Tank said.

"I know. I wonder where my dad is."

"I don't know. He might still be coming."

"I hope so. He's our dad."

Tank didn't want to get his hopes up, so he just nodded. Lou pulled on the back door of the limo, but it was locked. They had to wait until the church began to empty, when the driver hurried down toward the car and let them in. Strawn came out into the sunlight, squinting. He slipped on dark glasses, saw Joe sitting there and took his hand and they came down together to the car. Tank couldn't be sure, but it looked to him like Strawn had been crying.

The drive to the cemetery took about twenty minutes. The cars turned onto a quiet, shady road that wound up a hill studded with dusty old oak trees. They came out at the top into something like a city for the dead with its neo-gothic vaults, statuary, sarcophagi and headstones. A few people were already parked around the grave site. The hearse drove ahead and parked behind a pickup truck loaded with flowers from the chapel.

Three rows of metal folding chairs surrounded the open grave. From the hearse the pallbearers brought the casket over to the grave and let it carefully down onto the suspension straps. The sun shone brighter, it seemed, because of the smog. It seemed impossible to Tank that Stella, locked up in her casket, no longer needed air, or couldn't fear the darkness. He took the boys around to the front row and they sat down. Strawn sat beside Joe. The casket resting on the straps looked very heavy. The sun leaned like more weight on the green metal. Another funeral came to Tank: his father sat beside him, holding his hand. He couldn't fathom the good of lowering his mother into the ground, leaving him alone. He hadn't seen her dead, either. He wouldn't go, like Lou. Too many years without her pulled her down into that impossible eternity. He looked to his right at the side of Lou's face. Lou had told him something yesterday, a great regret he hoped his mother would forgive him for. It was his hatred of Strawn. One time she came to him, he said, when he was pouting in the living room. She got on her knees on the rug and begged him to tell her what the matter was, but he wouldn't, even though he knew it hurt her.

Stella would not be going home again. She would never eat another meal, never prepare another batch of her knockout spaghetti sauce. Never see Lou's face again, or Joe's. That blindness that imprisoned her, whatever better face God's point of view might put on death, hit like the blow of a sledge hammer on the dam that had been holding back Tank's tears. He wept and felt the boys' concern on either side of him, their leaning toward him, his name on their anxious voices. He was aware of the swishing of the pastor's robes, his words taken up by the breeze and distributed among the photographs and souvenirs of Stella's short life.

Strawn gave Lou and Joe each a camellia to drop down onto the casket. He stood over the grave and let one fall himself, then walked away alone. There was a plot reserved for him to lie beside her. Tank wondered if he ever would. She had loved him that much.

The crowd broke up, people scattered for their cars. One of the laborers, a Mexican who was helping to pull the tarp off the mound of earth to be shoveled into the grave, passed a tender smile to Lou, and Lou smiled back, weakly. Some other laborers began to carry flowers over from the pickup. Tank and Marla walked the boys past rows of headstones on the spongy grass. Something made Tank look up.

In the shade of a cypress that towered over a tomb, about thirty yards away, the figure of a man stood facing them. He raised a cigarette to his lips. Smoke vanished into the air in front of his face. Art raised his hand to wave. Tank stopped and stood there, trying to be sure it was him. By now the boys were looking too.

"That's Dad!" Joe cried, but he didn't move.

Art dropped the cigarette, mashed it into the grass and started hobbling toward them. But just then Strawn, loitering back around the limos and the hearse, caught sight of Art, and started marching at a clip he knew would get him to the boys first, and Art stopped dead in his tracks. Taking Marla's hand, Tank said, "Wait here, you guys. Wait for your dad."

They did, although Art wasn't moving, yet. Strawn came up behind them, saying, "Sorry, but he's not invited. You boys come on with me, now. The cars are ready to take us back home."

Marla suddenly detached herself from Tank and said angrily, "You have no right to talk to them that way, Mr. Strawn. That man's their father."

"I know who he is, and I'm saying he doesn't belong here."

"I think you'd better ask his boys about that," she said in a voice burning with fury.

Lou looked up at her; she laid her hand on his shoulder.

Tank saw now that Art was coming down toward them again. He came slowly, the only way he could, and Tank stood behind Joe, hands draped across his shoulders, calming him. Marla stood close to Lou, holding his hand.

Art stopped a moment to light another cigarette. Then he came down to within about a yard from Strawn, blew smoke through his nose. The boys both lurched toward him, Tank and Marla let them go. Joe hugged his father's good leg and Lou threw his arms around his waist and shut his eyes. Tank saw tears filling Art's eyes.

Strawn's voice broke in stridently:

"Don't get any ideas, Art. These boys aren't going anywhere."

"I'd like to talk to them alone, if you don't mind," Art said.

Strawn hesitated, as if he didn't like that idea. Then he flung out one hand.

"All right, as long as you know how things stand. They're staying with me."

"We'll let them decide that."

"I'm afraid not. I'm still their legal guardian until the court says otherwise."

Art took a drag on his cigarette, squinted at Strawn through the smoke.

"The court will uphold the law that says they're old enough to decide who they want to live with."

Strawn gritted his teeth and began to tremble a little.

"Don't try anything funny, Art. It'll be kidnapping. I wouldn't advise that."

Tank thought he saw something pass between them, then, like two men who had once done business – a nasty business that both would just as soon forget. Each one knew who he was, and what he'd got. Art hadn't meant for it to come out this way, but this was what he would have to live with from now on: his bride frozen forever in his heart like a girl imprisoned by the Phantom of the Opera. And the assassin wasn't through collecting, yet.

"Make it fast," Strawn said. "The limo's waiting." He wheeled and marched back up toward the waiting cars.

Art pulled a small card out of his shirt pocket. He huddled with the boys and spoke in quick, low tones.

"Here's where I'm staying, pals - the Hacienda Motel on south Colorado. Now listen. Let one day go by – just *one*. That's time enough for him to think I'm gone. But the *next* day – very early in the morning - I'll come for you. Let's make it four o'clock. I'll park out behind the guava tree. Hang onto this card and call me at this number if anything goes wrong. Call anyway, tomorrow night, to let me know if the coast is clear. Don't pack early, and if you have to, call from Tank's or Dorothy's house. That okay with you, Tank?"

"Yes," Tank said, "definitely."

Art pressed the card into Lou's hand.

"Tuck this away, pal. Remember, do your packing at the last minute, but don't bother with a suitcase. Use paper sacks."

"What shall we bring?" Joe said.

"The bare essentials, pals. You make up your minds."

"Okay, Dad," Lou said while Joe nodded.

Art turned to Tank, took his hand in both of his.

"Take care of yourself now, pal. I appreciate all you've done for these guys. You'll never know. I mean that sincerely."

Tank supposed he did, but in another minute or two, it would all slide blindly into the deep of the past. He squeezed the offered hand before Art got the jump on him. They looked into each other's eyes. Art was a man Tank thought he would have liked to play football for, back in high school.

Lou stood waiting with his shy smile. Tank made a move and Lou flew into his arms. Joe came over, too, more warily. He grabbed Tank around his waist and pressed his head against his ribs. Tank said keep your chin up, now, you guys, and we'll be seeing each other, that's a promise. He turned to Art.

"So long, Art. Take good care of these two major leaguers."

"We'll be seeing you around, pal."

But that was the last time Tank would ever see Art Ryan. That is, in person. He couldn't count the times he would remember him, or he would come to him in a dream. He always came alone, like he was delivering ransom money, but the woman he wanted to buy back was already dead.

37

Strawn got his younger sister on the first plane out of Buffalo after the funeral. As soon as he came home with her from the airport, he said, 'This here is my sister, Dorrie. She'll be taking care of you guys while I'm at work." Dorrie was young, and she wouldn't be very pretty at all if she didn't have big boobs, Lou thought. She got the guest room to stay in, and when she reminded the boys that she would be just down the hall if they needed anything, it sounded like she wouldn't know what to do if they did.

Lou couldn't get to sleep that night. He saw his mother once, her smile, like his mind was the life raft she had clung to, but he was on the ship going down. The sea was all around him now, like the God he'd prayed to for so many strikes pulling him under. His mother's desperate last breath settled on his heart and he cried out, "Oh, Mom! Mom!" and he brought the pillow over onto his face, afraid of waking Joe, and sobbed while a voice somewhere, that was once God's, kept whispering, 'Run along, now, little boy.'

Dorrie must have heard him, for it wasn't long before she was there beside him on the bed, stroking his forehead, telling him that it was okay, go on and cry. I'm here. She was so young, and a stranger, but there was nothing rushed or shallow about her being there. She sat there with him a long time. In the morning, when he couldn't remember how or when he'd gone to sleep, it came to him that he would never get to know Dorrie any better. One more day, then they would have to betray her kindness. They had to get ready. They had to figure out what they were going to take. All they had to leave behind.

At first Joe refused to go to school. He didn't want to go through the motions of looking like his usual self in order to avoid the explanation that would surely make kids wonder why he hadn't stayed home in the first place. Finally Dorrie talked him into getting dressed and having a bowl of shredded wheat before she packed them a nice lunch - liverwurst sandwiches, an apple each and some fig newtons. Lou could see that Dorrie was not just mechanically playing the part to relieve Strawn of the chores he was no good at. He could see it by the way she talked to them; how in a respectful voice she persuaded Joe that it was better for him to go on to school, until Joe believed it, and said on their way across the golf course, ten minutes before the bell was due to ring, "She's not so bad, is she?"

That afternoon, during lunch recess, Lou went into the lavatory and saw that he still looked like he'd been crying. He splashed cold water on his face and dried it with a paper towel, but the chlorine in the water made his eyes look even redder. Outside he saw Cheryl Jones eating by herself at a table under the shelter. It seemed like such a long time since they'd walked home together. He wondered if she still liked him.

He started to walk past her, not wanting her to see his eyes. But her face came up so brightly, so expectantly, he hesitated, and she said:

"Hey, Butterball! What're you doin'?"

"Oh, hi, Cheryl. I didn't see you."

"Yes, you did. What's the matter? Mad at me or something."

"No, I really didn't –"

"Cut it out, Lou. I know you. You don't not notice *anything*."

Lou turned back toward her, feeling strange about talking to her once again the way they used to, not knowing whether she wanted him to sit with her, or it was all the same to her if he moved on.

"Waiting for somebody?" he said.

"Well, come to think of it, yeah. If you don't mind sitting with somebody who doesn't exist."

Lou's lunch pail banged the top of the table as he slid in onto the bench across from her.

"You look as real as ever, Cheryl," he said, feeling bold somehow.

"Well, don't worry. I gave up wondering why we never walked home together any more. It had to be because you couldn't get over Vivien."

"There was nothing to get over."

"Ha! Tell me another one. But anyway – you know what?"

"What?"

"I saw you in the rain the other day. You were pretty far away and you looked like you were in a hurry. I saw you were soaking in some big old coat, and I had my umbrella and I thought we could've shared it. Oh, well. Next time it rains."

Lou looked across at her, how pretty she looked with the freckles sprinkled under her bright eyes, how much she'd filled out, too. He kicked himself for all the times he had neglected her. Her pretty face spread out like an old map of the future, on which they were supposed to go on to junior high together, then high school. Lou snapped open his lunch pail.

"You like fig newtons, Cheryl?"

"*Do* I! But don't cheat yourself to give me any."

"I've got so many, I can't eat 'em all."

"Well, okay. I'll trade you for a couple of my Oreos." Cheryl dug into her sack, came out with the cookies wrapped in waxed paper. "My Mom's tryna fatten me up, but I just won't fatten."

"You don't have to fatten up to look good, Cheryl."

She let out a breath of laughter as she poised a newton near her open mouth, looking older than she was. He saw her like a falling star that streaks back into darkness and goes on without you, then, forever. "You know, Lou," she said, "I never meant to call you Butterball. I don't know why I did. I didn't mean it."

"Oh, that's okay – I am a little overweight," Lou said.

"Sure you are! Like I'm a beanpole, huh?"
"You're not a beanpole," Lou said.
"Yes, I am. But I don't care."
Lou took his apple out, then put it back.
"Cheryl?"
"Yeah?"
"My brother and I have to go away, soon."
Cheryl stopped chewing.
"What do you mean, go away? You mean this summer, when school lets out?"
"No, sooner than that. We have to go up north, to where our dad lives."
"Oh, gosh! Your mom and dad got a divorce?"
Lou looked into the lunch pail at the sandwich Dorrie had carefully wrapped. At the apple, mottled red and yellow. She'd poured some grape juice into his thermos.
"Yes, they did," he said, "but that's not the reason."
"Oh? What is it?"
"My mom died," Lou said.
Cheryl's face froze except for the twitch of a smile that gambled on its being some terrible April Fool's joke. He looked across at her, hating himself. The wounded look on her face strained to hold back the tears that slicked her eyes.
"God, what happened, Lou?"
"She had a baby that died." He tried to go on, but couldn't. Tears suddenly flooded Cheryl's eyes, ran down her cheeks. He felt the warmth of her hand tightening around his.
"Oh, Lou, I'm so sorry! I'm so sorry."
He swallowed hard as tears came into his eyes, too. He didn't want to choke on the feelings set loose by her hand in his.
"Don't tell anybody else, Cheryl – don't tell Miss Fowler. We're leaving tomorrow morning with our dad."
"Tomorrow morning?" Cheryl swiped at her tears. She put one hand up over her eyes, then took it away. "This isn't fair, Lou. I don't

care what you say. Some day you're coming back. I'll see you again – you'll see, if it takes a million years." She clutched his hand as if that was the short cut to a million years.

Lou wondered why he couldn't have fallen for her long ago, at the start of school. There was no time, now.

"I'll walk you home tonight, Cheryl. We'll take the long way."

"Oh yes, Lou! The long way. I always wanted to do that. It might take hours and hours, but who cares? We'll get there some day, won't we?"

38

At a quarter of four, Joe woke up. They had their big paper bags packed and hidden in the closet. The house was quiet. All they had to do was steal out.

Coy stayed on Joe's bed, ears pointing, watching their every move. But as soon as they were out on the patio she jumped off and began to bark frantically. Each bark struck Lou's heart with fright.

"Come on, Joe! We've gotta run!"

Their mother's bedroom window blazed with light. Behind them from the patio Dorrie's voice cried, "No, no! What are you doing! You can't go! For God's sake, don't go!"

The big Cadillac parked out behind the shrubs roared to life, headlights flashed on. Lou could see his dad behind the windshield, gripping the wheel. Beside him sat a woman wearing swallowtail glasses. Art rolled his window down. Behind them trapped in the house Coy was still barking desperately, and as Lou ran from her he saw her being comforted by Dorothy and Ricky, taking her back. Then he couldn't believe that. Too many people were running around in a murky loneliness they kept insisting was absurd.

"In back, pals! Hurry it up!"

Lou tossed his bag into the back seat and piled in after it. Joe did the same on the other side. Art spurted off, the car's momentum swung the door shut just as Joe was reaching for the handle. They were down on Mendecino, swerving onto Allen when the lady sitting beside Art turned a smile back over the top of the seat.

"Hello, boys. I'm Phyllis. I'm a real good friend of your dad's."

Lou looked at her and didn't exactly like her smile. They passed under the streetlight on the corner and a shaft of light swept across the woman's face. Lou saw the kind of prettiness that somehow didn't seem to be his dad's type. Ruffles of blued gray hair lined her forehead. Her teeth glistened artificially behind thin lips.

"Phyllis is my fiancée, pals," Art said. "She lives on a farm. What do you think of that?"

Why was it, Lou thought, that the people you loved had to change so much? Why did they have to give up the best, and come down so many pegs to settle for somebody else?

"Where are we going, Dad?" Joe said.

"Up to that farm. It's gonna be a new life, pals. You're gonna love it – chickens to feed, a cow to milk. There's a creek nearby where you can swim. Phyllis has got a honey of a little dog - a Boston Bull. His name's Pug. You talk about personality! And get this. He can jump four feet straight up from a standstill."

"Wow!" Joe said, but Lou could hear the exhaustion in his voice. "D'you think they'll send the police after us, Dad?"

"Nah. They know it won't do them any good. They haven't got a leg to stand on. You've seen the last of them, pals. There's nothing but the future, now. Future farmers of America!"

Lou heard something funny in his dad's laughter. It wasn't him. Or like he didn't mean it. Phyllis was smirking at him tolerantly, as much as to say life on a farm wasn't all roses, was it?

The lights swept by, one after another. Headlights on one side, streetlights on the other. And then, way up there, the faintly struggling stars. It seemed to Lou that she was not really dead, but there was some terrible mistake and she was waiting in a dream for him to come and wake her. Or he was the one asleep. He could almost feel her hand in his, and something came to him, a swirling in the darkness, the rush of iron wheels on rails. His mother had his hand in hers and she was screaming, not in real fright but with excitement, joy. The next turn brought them face to face with rattling bones, a witch raised a knife and cackled. The sharp turns jolted them from side to side. He clutched onto her hand and she was laughing as the car banged through the double doors and they saw the Ferris wheel turning in the bright, foggy sunlight.